7/06

THE LIMEHOUSE TEXT

TEXT

A Novel

Will Thomas

A Touchstone Book
Published by Simon & Schuster
New York   London   Toronto   Sydney

TOUCHSTONE
Rockefeller Center
1230 Avenue of the Americas
New York, NY 10020

Touchstone and colophon are registered trademarks of Simon & Schuster, Inc.

For information regarding special discounts for bulk purchases, please contact Simon & Schuster Special Sales at 1-800-456-6798 or business@simonandschuster.com.

Designed by Melissa Isriprashad

Manufactured in the United States of America

10 9 8 7 6 5 4 3 2 1

Library of Congress Cataloging-in-Publication Data

Thomas, Will.
  The Limehouse Text / Will Thomas.
    p. cm.
  "A Touchstone book."
  1. Barker, Cyrus (Fictitious character)—Fiction, 2. Private investigators—England—London—Fiction. 3. Great Britain—History—Victoria, 1837–1901—Fiction.
  4. London (England)—Fiction. I. Title.
PS3620.H644L56 2006
813'.6—dc22   2005046613

ISBN-13: 978-0-7432-7334-3
ISBN-10:   0-7432-7334-6

To Caitlin and Heather,
who have always shared my love of all things Oriental

East is East, and West is West,
and never the twain shall meet.

—Rudyard Kipling

THE LIMEHOUSE
TEXT

Prologue

I WAS THE LONE OCCIDENTAL IN A ROOM FULL OF
Chinamen, and all of them were talking at once. On either
side of me, they were arguing with one another, chanting in
unison, or beating the wooden floor with their rope-soled
shoes. There was a good deal of wagering going on, with
both English pounds and Chinese taels changing hands
quickly. Despite the heat of such activity, there was a chill in
the room as the smoky breath from all of us condensed
overhead in a fog amid the old gray timbers of the quayside
warehouse. I pulled my coat closer about me and wished I
were at home in my room with my feet on the fender in
front of a good fire, where any sane person would be on a
dreary February evening, while the chant continued to
boom in my ears.

"*Shi Shi Ji! Shi Shi Ji! Shi Shi Ji!*"

As luck would have it, they were chanting one of the
few Mandarin phrases I recognized: the name my employer,
Cyrus Barker, was known by among the Chinese. Where he
was at the moment I couldn't say, but he would be coming
along shortly, of that I was certain. A hundred or more Chi-

namen were massed impatiently around this sunken ring I'm sure Scotland Yard would be very interested to know about, and there was to be a fight soon. I seriously doubted whether anyone besides myself here had ever heard of the Marquis of Queensberry rules.

There was movement in the ring, and I leaned forward with a sudden sick feeling in my stomach, but it was only a troupe of Chinese acrobats. A girl of fourteen balanced her twin sister upright, head to head, with but a fold of cloth between them, and a fellow flopped about the ring on his stomach like a seal, but their efforts were jeered at by the audience. I might have been entertained by their performance myself under other circumstances, but I had not come here to be entertained. Shortly, my employer would be coming into that ring to fight for his life or, rather, both our lives.

I brushed aside Asians attempting to sell me treats of dried squid and unidentifiable meat on wooden skewers, trying to concentrate on the matter at hand. I looked about the room at the faces of the three men I knew. Old Quong, father of my employer's late assistant, had his hands on the rail in front of the pit and was watching the acrobats anxiously. Jimmy Woo, an interpreter for the Asiatic Aid Society, was absently chewing on his knuckle through his glove, in danger of gnawing a hole in the silk. Ho, one of Barker's closest friends, had his hands in the sleeves of his quilted jacket and a sour look upon his face. All of them looked down into the ring as solemnly as if they were watching Barker's coffin pass by.

The acrobats gave up their poor efforts to entertain the

crowd and fled. Cyrus Barker stepped out of the shadow into the nimbus shed by torches set into the arena's structure. He wore a pair of black, baggy trousers gathered at the waist and ankles in the Chinese manner, and his forearms were encased in leather gauntlets covered with metal studs. Despite the cold, he wore a sleeveless shirt with a mandarin collar, and from fifteen feet away I could see the burns, marks, and tattoos on his brawny arms, souvenirs of his initiations into many secret societies. I remarked to myself how, with his broad nose, black hair, and swarthy skin, he had successfully passed himself off as an Oriental for many years prior to returning to the West. In place of his usual black-lensed spectacles, his eyes were now hidden behind a pair of round, India-rubber goggles I had never seen before.

At the sight of him, everyone began chanting his name even louder, and more wagers changed hands; but Barker ignored them and began warming up, loosening his joints and stretching. My tension eased a little. The Guv seemed confident, and why shouldn't he? He was six feet two inches tall, after all, and weighed over fifteen stone, dwarfing most of us in the room. Given the short notice before the fight, what sort of fellow could they have found to face a man as formidable as he?

As if in answer to my thoughts, another man stepped into the ring, and I felt my stomach fall away. If the crowd was excited before, it went into a frenzy now. The wagers redoubled now that the combatants could be compared.

Ho shot me a cold glance after we had both surveyed the opponent, and his eyes were reduced to mere slits in his face. I knew what he was thinking. It was the same thing I had been thinking myself since we'd been brought here: this was all my fault, mine alone. Barker was down there about to begin the fight of his life because of my mistakes. If I hadn't followed the girl, if I hadn't fought the Chinese, if I hadn't lost the dog, then perhaps . . .

Well, perhaps I should start at the beginning.

1

———◦———

"FOUND SUMMAT," INSPECTOR NEVIL BAINBRIDGE said, betraying his Yorkshire roots as he fished among the pockets of his tunic. It was a Wednesday morning, the fourth of February, 1885. I didn't know the man from Adam and was assessing him primarily because it was one of my duties but also because I was curious. I'd only met one Scotland Yard inspector before, Terence Poole, who always wore civilian dress, whereas this fellow wore a long jacket with frog fasteners and a peaked cap. I had no way of knowing whether or not his uniform was standard issue, but the truncheon inserted into the inspector's wide belt certainly was not. It was as thick as my arm, hung to his knee, and displayed scratches and dents I'd wager it didn't get from being drummed along fence posts. "Here it is."

He handed over a small wafer of faded and water stained pasteboard to my employer, private enquiry agent Cyrus Barker, who regarded it solemnly. It appeared to be a simple pawn ticket. Since I'd entered Barker's employ almost a year earlier in March 1884, I had never once heard the name of Inspector Bainbridge. How long had the Guv known this fellow?

"Where did you find this?" Barker demanded in his deep rumble. His black brows slipped behind the round lenses of dark glass he always wore. He was frowning. Both men were, in fact. Whatever matter of business had brought them together was being taken very seriously.

"It were in the sleeve, tucked under like, and slipped into a small rip," the inspector answered. "I could see why we missed it. I was about to send the effects on to his family. I allus go over old cases after first o' year, hoping to nail some down, and this cold spell has been keeping me in station more than reg'lar."

"How remarkable that it survived," Barker said. "Did you attempt to exchange it?"

"Course I did," the inspector answered, stroking his long beard. "Pawnbroker wouldn't let me see it, would he? Said I wasn't the next o' kin, and the law says he didn't have to let me see whatever it was until I produced one. Bloody Dutchmen. They have no business opening respectable shops in London, not that it were 'zactly respectable, mind. It's in Limehouse. A more draggle-tailed aspect you'd have to work bloody hard to find."

Barker stared intently at the card, as if willing it to give up its secrets. Finally, he put both hands on his desk blotter and pushed himself out of his chair.

"This is a mystery," he said, "and I cannot abide mysteries. Quong had no reason to pawn anything. I always saw that his needs were adequately met. Come, Thomas."

"Yes, sir," I said, reaching to the stand by my desk where our hats and coats hung. Quong had been my employer's first assistant. He'd been found dead a year before, floating in Limehouse Reach, shot with a single bullet between the eyes. Barker had been unsuccessful in finding his murderer and, being the Scotsman he was, had brooded over it often. This break in the case was important to him, I knew.

"Jenkins, we shall be out for the rest of the day," Barker said as we passed the desk in the outer office. Our clerk was buried behind an issue of *The Illustrated London News,* which was in danger of catching fire from his cigarette. He muttered a reply and returned to his reading. Jenkins didn't exactly shine in the mornings, if indeed he ever shone at all.

I was bundled into a cold hansom cab, squeezed between Barker's brawny left shoulder and Bainbridge's equally brawny right one. The two men were of a size—and a large one, at that. I felt like a kernel of wheat in a mill.

A half hour's cab ride later, we alighted in East India Dock Road in front of a building that would have been nondescript were it not for the three gold-painted balls over the door. The street, along with others nearby such as Orient and Canton, had been named after the first successes of the East India Company in Asia, but if I was expecting an Asian fantasy I was mistaken. Ming Street looked about as Oriental as Camden Town.

A notice on the door informed us that the Hurtz Pawnshop had closed its doors permanently and that anyone with a ticket had better claim the property soon. Bainbridge agreed to remain outside while we went in and attempted to retrieve whatever had brought us out on our errand. The door was unlocked despite the notice. Moving between racks of musty clothing, oil lamps, and old violins, we found the counter vacant, but there was some evidence of movement in the back room. Someone was using a broom vigorously. Barker pounded twice on the floor with the metal tip of his walking stick.

After a moment, a head popped through the baize curtain and a body eventually came with it. They belonged to a fastidious-looking Dutchman with a pair of sandy sidewhiskers, like two chops glued to a face, and a handkerchief on his head, knotted at each corner. As he came forward, he plucked off the kerchief and used it to wipe the dust from his shoulders.

"Gentlemen, we are closed," he said, biting off each syllable as if it were a herring. "Unless, of course, you have come to retrieve something in pawn."

"We have, sir, if you still possess it," Barker said, pulling the ticket from his pocket and presenting it to the proprietor. "Why are you closing shop, if I may ask? Has business fallen away?"

"No. My brother has unfortunately passed on. This was his shop."

"We are sorry to hear that. Was it an illness of some duration?"

"It was no illness. He fell down the stairs in the back and died. I came here from Rotterdam to settle his affairs."

The shopkeeper opened his ledger and compared the ticket number to the entry in the book. Only then did he stop and put up his hand.

"Hold a minute, gentlemen, if you please. I recall this item. A fellow claiming to be a police official came here just this morning attempting to retrieve it. I shall tell you the

THE LIMEHOUSE TEXT   —   9

same thing that I told him. If the claimant is dead, it must be picked up by his next of kin."

"I am his next of kin."

The Dutchman crossed his arms and stared at Barker skeptically. "I find that difficult to believe, since the name on the ticket is Chinese."

"If you will check your book, I'm certain you shall find that the name given is Quong and the address 127 Three Colt Street, Limehouse. He was my assistant. The building is mine."

Three Colt Street, I thought to myself. The name was new to me. Quong had lived in the room I presently occupied in Barker's home in Newington, but Barker had just given a second address. Did he really own a building in the area, or was he spinning a yarn to get past the Dutchman?

Mr. Hurtz checked his ledger and read the writing there. "And you are?"

"Cyrus Barker, sir. Here is my card."

"Private enquiry agent," he said, studying the card skeptically. "You understand, one must be cautious in this day and age. My brother was never cautious. If he had been, he would have known there were seventeen steps on that staircase, not sixteen. Very well. I suppose you detectives shall continue to pester me otherwise. I shall keep your card, and if someone else comes along claiming to be this Mr. Quong, I shall refer him to you. Do you have any objections?"

"None whatever. On what date was the item taken in pawn?"

"The first of the year, according to the ledger."

"He was found dead the next morning."

"Forgive me if I have been curt. My brother was always a trifle disorganized. He kept poor books and threw the items he took in into any convenient mouse hole. It has taken me weeks to rearrange everything systematically, and do you know what happened when I finished? The shop was broken into."

"How terrible!" Barker said.

"Yes. I will never be so glad as when I board the ferry to Amsterdam and can say good-bye to this wretched business."

"Was much taken?" my employer continued.

"A few trinkets and some gold pieces. Obviously, Jan did not do business in a large way, not in this district, certainly. But the thief overturned everything, you see. I had to rearrange the stock all over again."

"You say your brother fell down the stairs in this very building. Were they steep?"

"Steep enough, sir, though Jan was uncommonly clumsy. He lived above the shop, you see, and was found dead at the foot of the stairs with his neck broken. Unfortunately, he lived alone and nobody reported that his shop remained closed for over a week. Poor Jan. Always unlucky in his affairs."

"When did he pass away?"

"A month ago. I had to rearrange my affairs to come here."

"You have our sympathy, sir, for your loss," Barker said, bowing his head in respect. "Is it possible the item my assistant had in pawn was taken in the burglary?"

"No, sir. I am sure I still have it, if you will give me just a moment."

When the Dutchman disappeared behind a curtain, I tried to dispel the image of Hurtz lying dead in his house for a week by asking Barker a question. "Why do you suppose Mr. Quong was in a pawnshop, sir?"

"Quong had a fascination for small, out-of-the-way shops selling old curiosities. He said they gave him a better understanding of Western culture. I've never known him to put an item in pawn, however."

Hurtz returned from the back room. "Here you are, sir," he said, setting down a small parcel done up in brown paper. Without ceremony, Barker seized it and tore open the packet. Inside was a small, disreputable-looking book with a faded yellow-brown cover of raw silk. There was a label affixed to it with Chinese lettering aligned vertically, and instead of a hard spine, the binding strings hung down in knotted strands, like tassels.

My employer gave it little more than a perfunctory glance, opening and perusing a page or two before sliding it inside the pocket of his jacket. "Yes, that's it. All appears to be in order," he said. "How much do I owe you?"

"One and sixpence, sir. If I may ask it, what possessed your assistant to place such a small item in pawn? Jan could not have given him more than a shilling for it."

Barker tapped his pocket. "I scarce can say. Whim, perhaps. Thank you, sir. Thomas, pay the man."

I fished in my pocket until I came up with the required amount. Barker never carried silver, just the sharp-edged pennies he used as weapons, and he disliked discussing money. The Guv scrutinized the ledger a moment, then dipped the pen and signed on the line provided. Our business concluded, we quit the shop.

"You got it?" Bainbridge asked from a doorway as we passed. He quickly fell into step with us.

"Yes. It is a Chinese book. Are you familiar with Ho's?"

Bainbridge smiled, revealing a horsey set of teeth. "I've been picking up the dross Ho has been tossing out of his establishment for years."

"I'd like him to verify what I believe this to be, if you have no objections."

"None whatever, as long as I don't have to eat any of the swill he serves. It's eels, eyes of newt, and whatever was run over by the Leadenhall meat wagons the night before. They say there are no cats within a mile of the place."

I thought Barker might object to Bainbridge's remarks. Ho's was his base of operations in the East End, and he was on such good terms with the owner that I always thought he might have some hand in the place's affairs. His mind was on the case, however, and he would not be distracted by what might or might not be on Ho's menu. He shot ahead like a dog let off its lead, and the inspector and I followed, dodging along alleys and streets until we eventually came to a narrow lane near the river. A more blighted corner of London you shall not find. We passed beneath bared arches overhead to a wall at the far end and through a ravaged door. Ho's is reached through a long, unlit tunnel under the Thames. Barker took the twenty-one steps down two at a time, no small feat in pitch darkness. With Bainbridge there, however, I thought it more prudent to light one of the naphtha lamps provided, and we followed my employer at a more respectable pace.

We climbed the second set of steps and entered Ho's establishment. I admit to being a bit peckish. Despite the inspector's assertions, Ho is a fine chef, though I don't pretend to be an authority on Chinese cuisine. I was not a little disappointed when Barker skirted the tables and passed into the kitchen without a word.

I'd always wondered what sort of alchemy went on in Ho's kitchen. I imagined it to be like a cookery in some medieval castle, rough servants hacking limbs from freshly killed animals, bubbling cauldrons of bloodred soups full of boar or fish heads, and a complete lack of sanitation. What I found instead was a crew of talkative cooks, much like the men who tended Barker's back garden twice a week. All of them were chattering pleasantly as they cooked over large metal vessels, the antithesis of the waiters outside, whose surliness was legendary.

Barker's progress came to a halt in front of an open doorway. Bainbridge and I came up behind and peered over my employer's thick shoulder into Ho's private office. I had to look twice before my eyes confirmed what I was seeing. A typical European desk was in the center of the room, but its legs had been sawn off, so that the top of it stood but two feet off the ground. Ho was seated on a cushion with crossed legs and he was smoking a metal contraption that looked a cross between a pipe, a lantern, and a small watering can. The reek of Chinese shag filled the air. The only other furniture in the room was a small red altar of wood with an image of a venerable-looking Chinese sage and a small table holding a single Pen-jing tree in a pot. The proprietor looked up at Barker with a frown, then crossed his massive, tattooed arms over his ample stomach. Ho is eighteen stone of ill humor, with weighted earlobes that hang to his shoulders and a queue draping down the front of his dirty apron like a python. He remonstrated in Mandarin, of course—or perhaps it was Cantonese—and Barker responded in kind.

"Here we go," Bainbridge complained in my ear. I could see that he believed speaking to a Chinaman to be a complete waste of time. No doubt he thought Ho the most barbarous of heathens.

Barker pulled the package from his pocket and lay it before Ho, who opened the paper very carefully and lifted out the book. He opened it but a crack and peered inside as Barker had, then set it down on the table at the far end as if it contained a venomous spider.

"*Quen pui,*" he stated. "*Dim mak.*"

"What is a *quen pui*?" I asked, hoping Barker would answer; but for once, Ho spoke directly to me.

"Hidden text of a boxing school. It is very secret. It contains all techniques, history, and genealogies. It is the most important document a school or monastery owns."

"I see," I said. "And a *dim* whatever?"

"*Dim mak,*" Barker answered. "It means 'death touch.' It is the deadliest of techniques, taught only to the most exemplary of advanced students. This book should never have found its way to a London pawnshop or into Europe at all, for that matter. It is the kind of book that is guarded fanatically by the monks who care for it and by the government, as well."

"So," I said, beginning to grasp the import of what they were discussing, "This is a book some people might be willing to kill for. Do you think it has some relation to Quong's death?"

"It might. He was found dead but a few streets from

here. Also, I would question the coincidence of Jan Hurtz falling down the stairs, though it was almost a year later."

"All over a bloody book?" Bainbridge asked.

Barker shrugged his shoulders. "The Holy Bible is a book. The Koran is a book. Right now, in the Sudan, men are killing each other over both of them."

Ho had picked up the book again and was thumbing through it, back to front, since that is how Chinese is read. He'd stopped at the back page and was reading the vertical script.

"It is from the Xi Jiang Monastery in the Jiangsu Province. Do you know it?"

Barker nodded. "It's just outside of Nanking. Nothing has happened there since the Chinese Civil War, twenty years ago. Ho and I both fought in it near Shanghai."

"Shanghai?" Bainbridge asked quickly. "With Gordon?"

"Aye," Barker said. "With Gordon."

I had to hand it to the inspector. In one sentence, he'd uncovered something I'd been wondering about for days. It had been announced in *The Times* the previous week that General Charles "Chinese" Gordon had died in Khartoum, Prime Minister Gladstone's liberal government having dithered too long over policy to rescue him. Barker had said it was a shabby way for a hero to die, but I hadn't made the connection between Gordon's time in China suppressing the Taiping Rebellion and Barker, who must have been in his late teens at the time.

"Now hold on there, Barker," the inspector said. "I'll admit your Chinese lad's death might have been due to this book here, but I read the report on Hurtz's death before I came to see you. He broke his neck on some stairs. It could have been an accident and the boy's killer gone a year ago."

I had followed Ho's example by seating myself on the floor cross-legged and the inspector did the same. Western trousers and boots were not meant for that position and neither were Western limbs, I suspected. I'd retrieved my notebook and begun scribbling down what we had learned so far.

"If the killer is Chinese, he shouldn't be too hard to find," I said. "How many Chinese are in London now?"

In response, Bainbridge shrugged his thick shoulders. "Six or seven hundred, perhaps. Maybe a thousand."

"As many as that?" I asked. "I wouldn't have imagined it."

"They work hard to be inconspicuous," Barker said. "They do not trust the government and some are here illegally. Most are sailors from the Blue Funnel Line on furlough, but a few have set up businesses. London is a sailor town and they are the same everywhere. I was unable to get anywhere in my investigation last year. I wonder if I shall glean any more information now."

"Perhaps it is forbidden," Ho responded with a hint of menace in his voice.

"Forbidden by whom?" I asked.

"Mr. K'ing," Ho said, digging into the bowl of his pipe with a metal skewer. I had heard the name once before. Whoever he was, he had been used as a threat in front of a villainous fellow named O'Muircheartaigh. It had stopped me from getting shot.

Bainbridge snorted. "K'ing! He's barmy if he thinks he can tell me what to do."

"Who exactly is Mr. K'ing?" I made so bold as to ask.

"He is the leader of the Blue Dragon Triad," my employer explained, "unofficial leader of the Chinese here. He is a very powerful man, by all accounts. He runs the opium dens and fan-tan parlors, extorts money from the Asian merchants in the East End, and lives the life of a potentate. I have seen him twice at a distance, but some say that is merely an actor in the employ of local merchants taking advantage of the superstition to line their own pockets."

Ho lifted the shabby book off the table and held it out. "He is real, and he will want to see this."

The Guv took it immediately and thrust it back into his pocket. "That he will definitely not do if I have any say in the matter. That was left to me by Quong. I have promised his father I would find his killer and nothing is going to stop me from doing so."

Ho answered him in Chinese. Barker nodded once and then stood. He rose straight from the floor on the outsides of his ankles like a marionette, as easy as you please, whereas Bainbridge and I had to unknot our limbs and struggle to our feet, with that feeling of pins and needles one gets from sitting in such a position too long. Without a word, we left the kitchen.

"Sir," I said, as we were crossing the dining room, "what was that last thing Ho said to you before we left?"

"He said, 'It is not necessary to dig one's own grave. There are always others willing to dig it for you.' It's an old Cantonese proverb."

I lit the lamp again in the alcove above the stairs while Bainbridge shook his head and Barker was lost in his own thoughts. I suspected Ho and the book had given him much to mull over, and I was playing catch up myself. Apparently, Quong had a father in the area, the "next of kin" to whom

Bainbridge was to return his clothes, though Barker himself had claimed the title.

"I'd take whatever Mr. Ho said about K'ing with a grain o' salt, young man," Bainbridge said in my ear.

"He wouldn't have any reason to lie," I said. Perhaps because Ho was my employer's friend, I felt I had to defend him. It was certainly not due to any personal reason he had given me.

"Tha' knows all these Orientals are natural-born liars. They never say what they really mean, and you never ken what they're thinking. They'd turn a laundry list into a mystery. If there really is a Mr. K'ing—"

It was the last word he ever said. While I was looking at him as he spoke, a black hole suddenly appeared between his eyes. At first I thought it was a cockroach fallen from the ceiling until the gout of blood poured out and the sound of the shot echoed along the corridor. I watched Bainbridge's body sag and drop and instinct told me that if the next bullet were meant for me, it would have to pass through the lamp I was holding in front of my face. I ducked just as the glass shattered, the second report rang out, and Barker and I were plunged into darkness in Ho's tunnel under the Thames.

2

---⦾---

BARKER HAD BEEN TRAINING ME THESE PAST
twelve months, but I was still green enough to stand there
like a total fool, an easy target for the assassin's bullet. It is
not every day one is talking with a fellow and one of you is
shot between the eyes. If I was frozen in shock, my employer was not; I felt his hand grab my collar and swing me
'round until I hit the wall behind him, sliding down to the
hard stone floor.

"What the deuce—"

Barker's thick fingers clamped over my mouth. Bainbridge's murderer did not need light to carry on further assassinations. My employer's hand disappeared and I heard
his boots take two steps before there was a sudden slap of
impact and then another and then a perfect flurry of them.
Barker was engaged in a fight with the killer in total darkness not five feet away from me, and for once he didn't appear to be winning handily. I got up, ready to run or defend
myself, though if the Guv was having trouble I didn't stand
a chance. Barker was suddenly knocked back into me, but I
felt him connect with a left and then a right against our in-

visible foe. A moment later, footsteps echoed quickly down the subterranean tunnel, and Barker pushed himself off the wall. There was a sudden jingle of coins in my employer's pockets and within seconds they were clanging off the walls and rolling everywhere. Barker was quite accurate with his razor-sharp pennies as a rule, but if he actually struck our assassin, the latter wasn't generous enough to cry out. We gave chase, but just then it felt as absurd as running into a burning building.

I heard the creak of rusty hinges and light flooded down momentarily into the tunnel, but all that was illuminated was Barker's stony face as he reached the stairs. My employer continued on gamely, but we both knew what he would find when he reached the top: an empty alleyway.

When I reached the final step I began lighting the naphtha lamps Ho provided there, keenly aware that I'd just done this for Bainbridge a short time before. *Poor fellow,* I thought. *He certainly didn't deserve such an end.* I could imagine him conscientiously attempting to close this case, going over every jot and tittle, and suddenly coming across the wedge of pasteboard in Quong's cotton jacket. Now he was dead, and in the same manner as my late predecessor, a single bullet between the eyes, which only went to prove one thing: this was not merely an unsolved case but an ongoing one in the midst of which one could quite easily be killed. Did the murderer have a grudge against Barker and was attempting to eliminate all his assistants and friends? Had the bullet that knocked out my lamp really been meant for me?

I jumped when the door was suddenly flung open, but it was merely Barker returning. He grunted, took a lit lamp in either hand, and proceeded down the steps again.

On the bottom step at the other side, Ho sat looking as sour as I have ever seen him, his eyes on the corpse. I set the other two lamps at the feet of the late Inspector Bainbridge, which, combined with the ones Barker had set at his head, gave a macabre, ritual-like look to the corridor. Bainbridge lay supine, legs slightly apart, palms up, his mouth gaping open, dead. I realized I believe in the human soul, for there was something there five minutes before that was not there now, something beyond mere animation. That had been a living, breathing being, full of questions about the case and all sorts of plans, from how he was going to catch Quong's killer to what he was going to eat for lunch that day. Now all that was left was inanimate clay, fodder for the grave.

Ho stood abruptly, turned, and climbed the stairs to his restaurant, muttering to himself. Once inside, it turned to bellows, in intermittent Chinese and English.

"*Chut! Hui!* We are closed! Out! Get out now! Watch your step!"

Suddenly, the stone stairway was full of people—diners, waiters, and even cooks—herded unceremoniously out of the restaurant by its volcanic owner. At the foot of the stair, they split into two groups, scuttling along on either side of the corpse like rats in a ship. English, Chinese, Jews, Russians—all were the same now, eyeing, or trying not to eye, the corpse as they hurried along.

"I must send a note to Scotland Yard," Barker stated, reaching into his pocket.

"I'll write it," I said, forestalling him. My employer's handwriting would have been no more legible to them than Chinese calligraphy. I pulled my notebook and pencil from my pocket. "What shall I say?"

"Ask for Inspector Poole. He, at least, has some understanding of this culture. Tell him Bainbridge has been shot dead. Terry has not been here before. Have him meet you outside."

"I could send a telegram instead," I suggested. "It might reach him faster. There's bound to be an office along the docks."

"Good thinking, lad. No telling how long a message would take to reach Scotland Yard from here. Off with you, then."

I was up the stairs and out the door, keen to serve my employer before I remembered about assassins and flying bullets. The alleyway in front of Ho's has no means of entrance or egress and nothing to shelter behind. Should the fellow appear at the far end with his pistol or rifle, he could shoot me at his leisure. Luckily for me, the killer had vanished without a trace.

It took only five minutes to locate a telegraph office, it being a matter of following the wires leading down toward the docks. This was certainly not a picturesque part of London. The salt air of the Thames was doing a fine job of warping the clapboards of the buildings and stripping the paint from the graying wood. There were no gaily painted Chinese signs or dragons or pagodalike structures that proclaimed Limehouse was the Oriental quarter of town. It made a satisfactory attempt at being anonymous.

I waited while the message was transcribed and sent and then returned to the restaurant. It was a cold afternoon in February, and as I walked I noted that the sun produced a good deal of light but almost no heat. I went in to find that nothing was standing guard over the inspector's body but the four lanterns. I continued into the restaurant.

Barker and Ho were seated at one of the tables, drinking tea amid a pile of abandoned dishes. "Help yourself to food, lad. There's plenty going to waste in the kitchen," the Guv said.

"No, thank you, sir," I said. I'd lost my appetite. Instead, I poured myself a cup of lukewarm tea.

"Mr. K'ing must be told," Ho insisted as I set my cup on the last clear foot of table.

"Oh, come now," my employer responded. "Why must I inform him? Am I to take all these rumors seriously? They say he has been here for a hundred years and is responsible for half the evil done in London."

"I believe the last part," Ho maintained. "He has extorted money from me for years. Two cooks were employed by me at his written request, and though they only worked for me a day or so, I have been forced to pay their salaries ever since."

"What?" Barker growled. "You never told me this. I am surprised you didn't snap their necks and hand them back their heads."

I chuckled at this last remark and it even brought a rare smile to Ho's lips, but it was true. Despite his stout stomach, Ho could handle himself well, of that I was sure. Ho gave a shrug.

"So, what was K'ing's group called?" I asked. "This Blue Dragon something or other?"

"Blue Dragon Triad," Barker answered. "Most of the members are present or former employees of the Blue Funnel Line that steams between Liverpool and Shanghai. London is their layover, so the line is responsible for the Chinese being here in the first place. But is the Blue Dragon a part of any real triad in China, or does K'ing exert influence here based upon his own ability to hold power?"

"What exactly is a triad?" I asked.

"They are criminal fraternities that control the opium trade and other interests in China. They began as benevolent organizations whose purpose was to overthrow the Manchu dynasty. They have been corrupted from their original purpose, and their influence is beginning to grow beyond China. There has been evidence of the group's expansion into Formosa, Manila, Sydney, and other port towns. Now K'ing claims his own little branch here. Does he do anything else besides extort money?" he asked Ho.

"I have heard a few people have disappeared without a trace. On the other hand, he has funded some festivals here and given money to the Asiatic Aid Society. I believe he will be sponsor of the New Year's festival in a few days."

"New Year's?" I asked. "It is February."

"Chinese New Year, lad," Barker said. "February fifteenth."

I was at my post in the alley outside Ho's door fifteen minutes later when a four-wheeler clattered to a stop and disgorged Inspector Poole and three constables so alike in size and appearance they might all have been stamped in a press. I raised a hand and he nodded brusquely in my direction. Terence Poole was one of Barker's closest friends and a member of his physical culture classes at Scotland Yard until the bombing last year by the Irish Republican Brotherhood had put an end to them.

"Where is he?" Poole asked in a monotone. Whether he meant Barker or Bainbridge, I did not ask, merely pointing to the door at the end of the alleyway. If I was in any doubt as to the inspector's mind, he made it perfectly clear a moment later. Coming upon a small piece of crumbled brick on the ground, he gave it such a savage kick it spun across the alleyway and shattered when it hit the wall. Though he had never been to Ho's before, he pulled open the door and headed down the unlit steps like a regular.

For a moment the passage was filled with the sounds of our ten shoes. Finally reaching the lamps around the inspector's body, he ignored Barker and Ho, who were now both sitting on the bottom step, and went down on one knee, examining the face of his late colleague.

"Ah, Nevil," he said, as if the man were still alive. "Who's done this to you, old fellow, and however shall I tell the missus?"

Barker stood and came over to us, but all he got for his efforts was a glare from Poole, as if this were all our fault.

"How did he get in this godforsaken tunnel?" the inspector asked.

"We were coming out of Ho's when he was shot from the other end."

"Is it always this dark?"

"Sometimes it is darker. The regulars often come through here in pitch darkness."

Poole gave him a look, as if he had come upon a club of eccentrics. "Who was here when the shots were fired?"

"Llewelyn, Bainbridge, and me, and the killer, of course."

"Did you see anything?"

"No," Barker stated. "The only light was from a single lamp in Thomas's hand, which was shot out by a second bullet from over there."

"So, he was on the stair behind me as you all walked toward him, about twenty-five yards with wavering light. Not a bad shot."

"Very professional," my employer agreed.

Poole looked about at the small, overlapping circles of light created by the lamps. "This glass is crushed. It looks like a herd of elephants has been through here."

"Yes, well, I'm afraid the restaurant was full, and the only way of egress is this tunnel. Ho thought it best to run them through quickly."

"This is a murder site!" Poole barked. It was obvious he was looking for someone to blame. "I do not care how long they had to wait, I do not care if they had to sit up there all day, you shouldn't have let them walk across evidence!"

"These were not the sort of individuals—"

"I don't bloody care!"

There was an awkward silence for a moment. I thought Poole was being unfair. Actually, it was Ho who had sent the patrons off, and the circumstances were perfectly understandable. Also, as Barker tried to say, the clientele was not the easiest to marshal or contain. Some were criminals, some political revolutionaries, and others lived in the shadowy world of exiles, spies, and secret societies. It was amazing that Ho had gotten them all to obey him.

"I take it this is the owner," Poole finally said, jerking a thumb in Ho's direction. "Does he speak English?"

"When it suits him."

"Here, you!" Poole called, which was not a safe way to address the Chinaman. Ho had upper arms the size of a good roast joint and I'd seen him throw a meat cleaver with some accuracy. "Did anyone come in after Inspector Bainbridge and these two entered the tunnel? I was wondering if he might have secreted himself among the crowd and left with them."

"No one came in," Ho stated. Seated on the bottom step, his arms folded across his thick stomach, he looked like a dyspeptic Buddha.

"Blast. Why was Nevil here?" he asked, addressing us. "Were you helping him with a case?"

"He was getting back to me with the results of an investigation regarding my late assistant's death last year."

Poole looked at him shrewdly. "Ah, yes, that's right. Your man was shot between the eyes like Nevil, wasn't he? You think it's the same man?"

Barker shrugged.

"Had you come across new evidence?"

"He merely came to inform me that the case was closed. Apparently, we were wrong."

Poole shook his head and toyed with the hanging ends of his long side-whiskers in frustration. Finally, he sighed.

"You'll be at home or at your chambers?" he asked.

"Yes," Barker answered. "I am setting aside all our other cases temporarily. I believe we can go forward with the supposition that the same man killed both my late assistant, Quong, and Inspector Bainbridge."

"Limehouse," Poole muttered. "It would have to happen in Limehouse. By gor, I hate the place. I don't know what Nevil saw in it, I really don't. You ask for directions or the time of day here and everyone suddenly forgets English and shuts up like an oyster. There is going to be a lot of pressure from upstairs to solve this one quickly. Nevil was a bit unorthodox, but he was an inspector, after all, and Commissioner Henderson does not take kindly to the death of a constable, let alone an inspector. If I do not clear this up quickly, he might put me in charge here permanently, blast the fellow."

Barker's stony face showed no expression at the outburst.

"You there," Poole said, indicating the first constable. "Go fetch a cart to transport the body to K Division." He turned to another. "You take a lantern and walk along the tunnel and look for clues." He pointed to a third. "And you come with me and take notes. Shall we go into Mr. Ho's restaurant, then, and talk, gentlemen?"

Poole questioned us, requestioned us, and then separated us and cross-questioned us. He asked the same questions in so many different ways, I began to get mixed up in the minor details. When he finally let us go two hours later, I'd told him everything. Everything, that is, that my employer wished me to say, for I noted that the one thing Cyrus Barker had been very careful to omit was the existence of the book we had just discovered, the cause of our present misery and of a good deal more to come.

3

———◆———

When we arrived at Barker's home in New-ington, he shot up the stairs while I was still removing my coat. I was certain the little package had been burning a hole in his breast pocket the entire day. I went outside to the bathhouse for a good soak, and afterward I ate a solitary dinner. Apparently, Barker was too caught up puzzling over his new treasure to even inform his butler he was not coming down. I ate my *terrine des lapins* while our butler, Jacob Maccabee, hovered about, venting sighs like a bellows. By the time I had reached coffee and cheese, he could stand no more and marched upstairs to speak with his master. A few minutes later, Mac was coming down again, shaking his head and muttering to himself in Yiddish.

Later that night I was stretching out in bed when my feet came in contact with Barker's Pekingese, Harm, who nipped my toe to inform me he was there. He had a habit of curling up right where I wanted to put my feet or getting tangled up in my limbs, and once or twice he'd even tried to sleep on top of me. I set him right this time and moved him to the side, despite his growling protests. Then I stretched out, all five foot four inches of me, and lay there, listening to the night sounds from the window Barker had permanently screwed open a crack. Another sound came to my ears, enough to make me open my eyes and listen closer.

It was a thrumming sound and it made the house vibrate slightly. It was like the sound a heavy branch makes when a child swings on it from a rope. I knew instantly it must be the heavy bag hanging in the basement. Perhaps my employer was trying out some moves from his little manual. I turned up the gas lamp over my head and consulted my bedside clock, noting that it was almost three-thirty. I admired the man, but sometimes he can be a trifle eccentric. I considered joining him for a moment but instead rolled over and went back to sleep.

Barker was not his usual self at breakfast. I do not believe he had slept at all. He came down with his silk dressing gown tied loosely over his nightshirt and a pair of carpet slippers on his feet. His hair hung down in spikes over his smoky spectacles as if he had worked himself into a lather on the heavy bag.

"I'm not going to the office just now, lad," he muttered. "I'll be along in an hour or so."

"Yes, sir," I answered. For once, I was the more nattily dressed of the two of us. I wore one of my best suits, a dark cutaway coat and trousers, a gray waistcoat, and a striped tie. I'd polished my boots and beaten back my hair and was now ready to present myself to the world. I bade my adieus, put on my coat and hat, and hailed a cab outside.

It was a novel experience being alone in the cab. Both

working and living with my employer, I was at his beck and call through the week, with a half day off on Saturday. I attended worship services with him at the Baptist Metropolitan Tabernacle on Sundays, and at any time, Barker might wish to discuss some part of the case we were working on or to give me instructions for the next day, and there went another hour. I was supposed to go to the office, but just then the thought occurred to me that I might use the time to investigate the building Barker owned. I tapped the trap of the cab overhead with my stick.

"Take me to the docks. Limehouse."

"Dunno 'bout that, sir," the driver said through the heavy scarf he wore over his mouth. Cabmen were reluctant to go to that part of London. They often couldn't get a return fare, their wheels got dirty in the ill-swept streets, and the children of the East End were experts at shying rocks.

"I'll double your fare, driver. I'm looking for a place called Three Colt Street."

In ten minutes we were crossing London Bridge, and I was revisiting the scene of our first case in Aldgate. I couldn't resist a shudder when we passed the Minories and I saw the stable where I had very nearly ended my life. But all things must pass, as my father often said, and here I was, hail of limb, investigating another case. The building had been let to a blacksmith who had assembled a forge in the old trackside building.

I passed through districts and slivers of districts: Spitalfields, Whitechapel, Wapping, Bethnel Green. It was not until we were almost there that the cabman hazarded another remark.

"What was that?" I asked.

"I said, 'Looks like we ain't the only ones a'goin' dockside.' "

I leaned forward, looking over the leather doors and the head of the cab horse. A dark brougham was ahead of us, wending its way down Commercial Road. The vehicle looked vaguely familiar. Then I realized why. It was the one owned by Harm's keeper, a heavily veiled woman who came twice a week to bathe and brush him. The dog had been injured during our first case and she had picked him up in that very brougham. She was another of Barker's interminable secrets. Who was she? Why the veil? I thought it possible that she might be the widow that my employer occasionally kept company with. The appearance here of our two vehicles together was too much for coincidence.

"I say, follow that brougham!"

Barker's late assistant had lived at 127 Three Colt Street, and now the veiled woman was going there as well. I could add two and two, and another two, come to think of it. I was in charge of the accounts in our office, and there was a regular amount paid monthly to a Miss Winter at the Bank of England in Threadneedle Street. Were I a betting man, I would say the veiled woman and Miss Winter were one and the same.

When the brougham stopped in front of a two-story building near the waterfront, I had the cabby stop at the end of the street. I peered through the small cab window in time to see the woman's familiar black-clad figure, with the even more familiar black Pekingese in her arms. I was puzzling over a dozen questions in my mind. Was Barker actually keeping a woman here, and if so, to what end? I paid the cabby and slowly sauntered past.

The house was well kept for the area, without being os-tentatious. It was clapboard, but none of the boards was in disrepair and the building had been recently painted. As I watched, a Chinese maid opened a window on the first floor. It didn't require an enquiry agent to discern that the woman's room must be there. My vigilance was rewarded when I heard Harm bark in the upper room. But was the home a private residence or let rooms? The question was important, since I couldn't go into one but might pass freely into the other. Idly crossing the street, I dared press an eye against the window beside the door. I saw a corridor full of doors, no sitting room or hall. Excellent. I opened the door and stepped inside.

I stood a moment on the threshold and closed the door slowly, acclimating myself to the sounds around me. I tensed when a door opened and an elderly Chinese man came out, but he shuffled by without comment or interest and left the building.

I could leave, I told myself, *or I could go upstairs and intro-duce myself.* Perhaps I could say that I was in the area and thought I would check on the dog, or that we were investi-gating Quong's death and I wished to see the residence whose address he had written in the pawnshop register. No, none of those would wash. I should leave.

I should have, but I didn't. In his novels, the writer Thomas Hardy often speaks of the Fates as if we are all fig-ures in some universal Greek tragedy, always getting into trouble because of inner weaknesses we cannot control. I though it rather an un-Christian viewpoint, but I went up the stairs just the same.

The upper floor was much like the lower, save that it

had a few feminine touches. The maid had just come from serving her mistress and had taken a moment to idly look out of a window in the back of the house that butted against the docks. She turned when she heard me reach the top of the stairs.

"I wonder if I might have a word with your mistress," I said.

She did nothing save regard me coolly. It occurred to me that she did not speak English.

"Your mistress," I repeated, a trifle louder, as if it would help. "Miss Winter. I wish to speak with her. I believe she has my employer's dog."

I'm convinced that Harm, for all the five years or so he had lived upon this earth, knows only about three words, but one of them is "dog." From the flat to the right, he began his clarion cry, a sound that conjures up images of his being roasted on a spit alive. The maid still did not move. I took three steps before her arm went out, braced against the wall, barring me from the door. Apparently, she thought herself a bodyguard as well as a maid, which was laughable. She was a pretty little thing, in her pigtail and silk pajama suit, and her China doll face was difficult to take seriously.

"Look here, if you'll just move," I said, putting my hand on her shoulder.

The next thing I knew I was sliding across the floor on my back. My shoulder hit the railing so hard I careened off it and slid down a short flight of steps to the first landing. Where had this slip of a girl learned to kick like a mule? Had I been alone, I would have nursed my wounds, but the girl who had been so unladylike as to kick me was still watching, so I shook it off. I'd had worse, or at least as bad. I stood up and tried again. I was not going to be stopped from speaking with Barker's dog keeper by a chit like her.

The girl actually dared raise her arms up in a fighting stance, left hand out, weight on the back foot, front foot up on its toes—what Barker called a cat stance. I was not going to get by her, if she could help it. *Very well,* I thought, *I shall go through you then, if it must be.*

I moved forward again and when I was within her reach, she tried another kick, but I was too smart for her. I blocked it handily and the two punches that came after it. It left her vulnerable for a punch of my own and my hand shot out involuntarily before I stopped myself. I had never struck a girl before, and I'd like to believe it was not in my character to do so. Apparently, she had no such scruples. She clouted me on the chin with her small hand rather like the knock from a wooden cane, then kicked at me. I had no choice but to retreat, which brought a small smile to the girl's face.

I had no idea what to do. I knew six or seven good kicks myself, but I wouldn't use them on her, she-tiger though she was, and the dozen or more hand strikes, eye gouges, claws, punches, chops, and others were all forbidden as well. This was an absurd situation. I had been taught all my life that women should be treated with kindness and respect by a gentleman, and though she was Chinese, she was still very much a girl. Kicking and striking were out, which only left one alternative and a very intimate one at that: the Japanese wrestling holds that Barker had been teaching me, which he had formerly taught at Scotland Yard.

She clipped me with another left to the chin, but it was a glancing blow, for I was already moving to my right, catching her around the waist with my left arm and coming 'round behind her. Before she had a chance to react, I snaked my other hand around and clasped it over my first as solid as if they had been locked together. I was suddenly very aware that Chinese girls do not wear corsets, if in fact they wear anything at all under those silk pajama suits. I felt a blush rising from under my collar, but it stopped suddenly as a pair of thumbs went into my eyes.

I would like to think in the past eleven months of constant practice and tutelage under Cyrus Barker that I had grown more lean and muscular. Nothing can be done, however, to train a pair of eyes to withstand a woman's thumbs, save to pull back one's head, duck away from her, and put one's head down out of harm's way. As I pulled away, she hopped on my toes and kicked my shins. Female or not, I was going to have to do something. But what? Bearing down with my forehead as hard as I could, I succeeded in reaching my arms down far enough to get my hands around her lower limbs and I scooped her up off the floor as if she were a basket of laundry. She began spitting words at me in Chinese, no doubt casting aspersions upon my ancestors, kicking her feet madly in the air and clutching for whatever projecting hair or ears I might have about my person. The worst part was, now that I had her I had no idea what to do with her. For the first time, it dawned on me that coming here had not been one of my brighter ideas.

I spied a window off to the side, the very one she had been looking out as I came up the stairs. My ear caught the call of a gull as it swooped by and my nose could not miss the smell of the Thames. It was a matter of a moment to lift her out the window and to drop her out of my arms and I hoped, out of my life for good. As it turned out, the tide was not yet fully in, and the young maid, pigtail flying, pink pajamas rippling, landed in a deep mudbank below.

Western literature makes much of the almond eyes of the Oriental, but hers were as round at that moment as the sun overhead, as she sat covered in mud from her slippers to her plaited hair. It could have been worse, I told myself. At least I hadn't dropped her on a wooden boardwalk or a stone pier. When she finally caught her breath she began bellowing and I left her to it. I pulled in my head, crossed the hall, and opened the door. Harm surged out, tail wagging, barking his protests that he had missed all the fun.

The chamber of Miss Winter, for it could only be hers, was empty, but a window in the back was open and the curtain billowed outward. Sticking my head out, I saw steps leading down to the ground floor. The woman had decamped while her devious maid had distracted me. Taking a brief glance about the room—a frilly, girlish place with fans on the wall and low, silk-covered chairs—I tucked Harm under my arm and together we set off in pursuit of the elusive Miss Winter.

Going down the stairs I had a feeling I was being watched. Remembering the death of Inspector Bainbridge, I suddenly felt very exposed and unprotected. Looking over my shoulders, I noted that every window along the docks was filled with Chinamen and every one of them was pointing my way and shouting. It seemed that being shot might be the least of my troubles and that it would be prudent to make my way as far from Limehouse as possible.

There was an alley at the foot of the stair leading back to Three Colt Street and I shot through it, right into the first group of Chinese youths who had been rallied by the girl's cries. They were not expecting me and I bowled them over like skittles. There was, unfortunately, another group forming behind them, and a smarter and better group they were, too. They met my rush well. I was pulled up off the ground, a man at each limb. I don't know if Harm had decided at that moment that he'd had enough and jumped or whether he was pulled from my hands. All I knew was I heard a sharp yelp and the dog, Cyrus Barker's dog, was gone.

Losing the Guv's prize dog was catastrophic, but there were more pressing matters, such as the fellow pulling on my arm as if it were a drumstick from a Christmas goose. I heard a sickening pop and felt the shudder of the bone leaving the socket.

I realized that if I didn't get out of there soon, what was left of me was going to end up fluttering from one of the balconies overhead. Luckily, Barker had been training me for just such an emergency. I kicked two of the fellows; threw a good, clean punch at another's jaw with my good arm; and landed a blow with the side of my hand to the neck of a fourth. I was the number one student of the best fighter in London, after all.

Momentarily, there was a break in the crowd, and like a flash, I was through it, running for my life. The next thing I knew I was passing down the very middle of Limehouse Causeway pursued by a perfect wall of angry Chinamen.

4

———◆———

I KNEW BETTER THAN TO LOOK OVER MY SHOULder. I could tell they were still behind me, because I heard their footsteps and angry cries. Then suddenly, I did not. I ran on a few hundred yards before daring to risk looking back. I was alone, save for the few shopkeepers and patrons coming out into the street to see what the fuss was about. I stopped and caught my breath, a little self-conscious but ready to run should the mob appear again. However, they were gone. A young ruffian in bell-bottom trousers and copper-toed boots brushed past me in the opposite direction, giving me a curious once-over, and I saw a few others appear beside him. Apparently, the Chinese had reached the end of Triad territory.

I continued limping west, hoping to find a cab, and as I did, I took stock. I had lost my hat and stick, both lapels of my coat were ripped, and my shirt could be seen through the seams at each shoulder. My shoulder was throbbing, and, oh yes, there was the small matter of losing my employer's dog.

Barker doted on that dog. The apple of his eye was running about the Asian quarter, being pursued by who knows what.

It occurred to me that they eat dogs in China. Surely the populace here must know an imperial dog from the more mundane variety. I began running again, this time to get Barker. I cared about the little creature myself. He could be a confounded nuisance sometimes—getting underfoot, sleeping on the bedcovers so I couldn't move at night, wanting in and out, up and down—but we shared rooms and meals. He had accepted me as a member of Barker's household. Now I'd lost him among the quays and back alleys of Limehouse.

An old hackney came into Commercial Street and I ran forward, securing it with a handful of coins. The cabman inspected my clothes unfavorably, but he could not fault the currency. I hopped aboard and sat back, my mind back on the mathematics again. Was the danger I was leaving greater or less than the danger I was heading into? I would have paid all the money I had saved in the Bank of England at that moment to have someone else inform Barker that his prized dog was missing.

He was in his office when I arrived, in his chair like any other day, regarding me stonily through those black lenses of his. Laid out in the chair in front of his desk were a fresh tie, collar, and jacket from a storeroom he kept for emergencies. He knew. Somehow, the Guv knew.

"Get changed, lad, and hurry," he ordered. It was the telephone. Miss Winter had emerged from whatever place of safety she had hidden herself and had placed a telephone call from somewhere. Drat all these modern contrivances that complicate society. I tugged off the remains of my jacket, ignoring as best I could the fresh bloom of pain from my shoulder, and changed quickly. Outside, I joined my employer, who had already secured a cab.

"What happened?" he asked, once we were inside the hansom.

"I'm sorry, sir," I told him, and it all tumbled out. I'd made a hash of things, I realized. I had invaded the Guv's private life, chased off his mysterious dog keeper, thrown her maid into a mudbank, and angered the entire population of an area we were investigating, setting the case back who knew how far. I had lost his dog, injured my shoulder, not to mention destroying a suit he had paid for. My ruin was complete.

"Pray tell me you are not actively involved in bringing this agency to its knees!" he remonstrated.

"No, sir," I muttered. "I mean, yes, sir, I am not."

"It is not your intent, then, to pry into my private life, alienate my acquaintances, and bring me to ruin?"

"No, sir," I murmured in utter misery.

"The fight," he said, after a moment's stony silence. "Tell me about the fight in the street."

I related as well as I could remember what had happened. I thought he would be happy that I had successfully defended myself, using the methods he had taught me. Instead, Barker slid a finger up under his spectacles, pinching himself on the bridge of the nose. He gave one of his long, shuddering sighs.

That was the end of it, my entire dressing-down. It had taken less than a minute, but I knew better than to think it was all over. In Oriental terms—and when working with Barker, one must always think that way—I had lost face and very badly. It was a silent ride to Limehouse.

We eventually found ourselves in East India Dock Road, one of London's meaner streets, but a prosperous one. Open-fronted markets displayed fish fresh from the Channel, and wagons brought in clothing and tablecloths from the West End to be laundered. Many of the shops were general shops, which meant they sold a melange of goods and could easily be fronts for fencing stolen items or houses of assignation. For once, Barker was not there to arrest malefactors. He was merely looking for a lost dog.

He began bellowing in Chinese before the cab even stopped. Standing there in the middle of the busy street, he attracted a lot of attention. Soon there was a circle of Chinamen around him, many of them casting unkind glances my way. Eventually they began talking back and the discussion became quite heated.

Our cabman, despite our request that he remain, pulled back his gelding and, before I could stop him, trotted off to safer climes. I stood pensively on the outskirts of the crowd, ready to either run again or jump into the melee as the situation required, while Barker stood in the very center. I could not make out what they were saying from their expressions, but Barker appeared to be trying to convince them of his bona fides. He went so far as to remove his cufflinks and pull back his sleeves, revealing the burns and tattoos on his forearms. Apparently, that settled the matter. Several merchants began nodding. Barker made a gesture with his arms, waving with the back of his hands as if to say "search" or "look for the dog." There was another chorus of grins and nods and the crowd dispersed. Barker stepped back.

"That should yield some results," he said, threading the

cufflinks back into his cuffs. "Where did you last see Harm?"

"He was in Three Colt Street, heading south, I believe. I didn't drop him, sir. My arms were pulled apart."

"That is not more than two blocks from here. Come along."

I am convinced Barker has as exact a knowledge of the city as a cabman or constable. Two turns later, we were staring at the residence of Miss Winter, the sight of my recent disgrace.

"Which way?"

"There, sir. Down that alley."

Barker stopped a Chinaman, no doubt to ask after the dog. The old codger broke into a wide grin and began nodding, but quickly turned to shaking his head. No dog. We walked down Three Colt Street, looking into alleyways and calling Harm's name. The trail seemed cold. I was definitely worried now. Regardless of what footing this put me on with my employer, I could not imagine being at home without Harm's scratching to go in or out or dozing in the garden. I am not the kind who dotes on animals, but I had to admit the little fellow had made a place for himself in my life.

There was another matter bothering me, but I hesitated to bring it up. My arm was going numb, and moving my hand was proving less and less easy. I tucked my elbow against my side and went on looking into alleyways.

I let the lid of a dustbin fall as an Oriental youth came running around the corner of the alley we stood in, calling out. He spoke for a moment with Barker, then ran back the way he had come. The Guv crossed his arms and stood for a moment expectantly.

"What's *'Shi Shi Ji'*?" I asked in Barker's ear, remembering what the youth had been calling.

"I am," he said. "It is the name I went by in China."

"What does it mean?" I asked. "Names generally mean something in China, don't they?"

There was a commotion in the street ahead of us.

"It means 'stone lion,'" Barker said, looking over my shoulder.

A crowd of Orientals surged around the corner and parted, and a man stepped forward, his arms full of black fur and a wagging plume tale.

"I say, chaps, might this little fellow belong to you?" the man asked.

Harm barked at us as if he had done something clever and weren't we the fools to be taken in by his little ruse. He jumped out of the man's arms, landed as lightly as if he were a cat, and scampered down the alleyway toward us as fast as his short, crooked legs would allow. Barker reached down and scooped him up, and the dog lay in his arms, as snug as if he were in Abraham's bosom, with his ridiculously long tongue hanging out of his mouth, licking at Barker's spectacles. Unlike myself, he seemed completely unscathed by his adventure in Limehouse. If anything, he looked refreshed.

Barker had his arms full and was paying attention to the dog, but I was free to concentrate on Harm's rescuer. The fellow doffed his top hat and gave a formal bow. As my eyes took him in, I began to wonder if I had somehow followed Alice down the hole after the White Rabbit. For strangeness, the fellow rivaled the mad Hatter or the Cheshire-Cat, but he gave no impression that he knew how bizarre he looked. He merely placed the hat upon his head again and favored me with a big smile.

"Pleased to meet you, old sport. Woo's the name. James Woo, but everyone calls me Jimmy."

Jimmy Woo stood about five foot six and wore a spotless charcoal gray coat with striped trousers. His tie was lavender silk, as were his gloves and handkerchief. He wore a monocle and his pumps were polished to a high gloss that even our butler, Jacob Maccabee, would respect, and all this topped by a face as Chinese as fried rice. He wore no queue and his hair was combed back in one long wave to his neck, brilliantined to a shine that rivaled his shoes. I admit I gawked and am certain my jaw was hanging open, but he did not seem to notice. By now, he must have been used to it.

"Er . . . Thomas Llewelyn," I finally got out. "Where did you find him?"

"Gorging himself on a dead haddock on the docks. The dog and I have been taking the air of the quarter. He's a corking little fellow."

He had no trace of an Oriental accent, but his manner was like a music hall version of an English lord. What series of circumstances had come together to create such a person as this? It was too much to take in.

The Guv came forward and shook Woo's hand, as if he were any other Englishman. "Mr. Woo, I'm Cyrus Barker. Thank you for taking care of my dog."

"Oh, 'twas nothing, a trifle. Couldn't leave the poor chap to fend for himself, now could I? Frightfully dangerous down in Limehouse come nightfall."

"Upon my soul, Mr. Woo, your English is excellent, if I may say it," Barker said.

I'd have been scratching my head if my arm could have reached it. Barker seemed to like the blighter, but then, he always has a soft spot for eccentrics.

"Read history at Cambridge. Been here for a dog's years. I'm an interpreter. Might you be Cyrus Barker, the detective?"

"Enquiry agent, yes."

"Deuced convenient. I've been looking all over for you, you see. I am working for a chap in the Foreign Office upon a certain private matter and he would very much like to make your acquaintance."

"I am rather busy at the moment," Barker told him.

Being refused brought the Oriental out in him. He smiled and bowed his head to my employer. "Sorry, but I am afraid a meeting is essential. You may speak with him today at his club or he shall hie it over to your chambers tomorrow and cut up ever so rough. What do you say? I did find your dog. It wouldn't hurt to talk to the F.O., eh? Say, one o'clock? I'll arrange it."

Barker absently stroked Harm's forehead, which the dog leaned into with his protruding eyes closed. "Where?"

"That's the spirit. The Oriental Club, near Hanover Square. The chap you want is named Trelawney Campbell-Ffinch. I won't be there, I'm afraid. It would be simply too much for them, having an actual Oriental on the premises. Wouldn't want the old duffers choking on their port. Must dash. I've always got my fire stoked with irons, don'tcha know. Nice meeting you, gents."

He patted the dog on the head with his lavender-gloved hand and then skipped off to his next appointment, whatever it was.

"So, the Foreign Office wants me, does it?" Barker mused. "Why did they not send someone 'round to the office? We are but a few blocks away. Speaking of the office, let us return. Mac shall have to harness the hansom and come retrieve Harm."

I would have paid a week's salary to see Mac's face when he heard. He cannot abide the dog and especially any added bit of pampering the Guv orders. This would send him through the roof.

"Certainly, old sport," I said.

"None of your cheek, now, lad."

We walked three or four blocks north, where we met the tram service that runs longitudinally across the East End. I was wondering if they would allow the dog aboard the old vehicle, though Harm had insinuated himself inside Baker's cavernous coat, with only his goggly eyes peering out. Like a dolt, I reached for the bar to pull myself onto the vehicle with my injured arm and instantly regretted it.

"Ahhh!"

Barker stopped and surveyed me quizzically. "Is your shoulder bothering you? Perhaps you have put it out of joint. Let's get back off the tram, lad. There is only one thing to be done."

"What is that, sir?" I asked, wincing through the pain.

"I must get you to a Chinese bonesetter. It is fortunate you were injured in Limehouse."

Fortunate was not the word I would have used.

5

---◆◆◆---

I SAY, IS THIS REALLY NECESSARY? I'M SURE I'LL be all right in a day or so," I assured Barker. I had no idea exactly what a bonesetter was, but the word conjured up a vision of bloody saws, ropes, and tackle.

"Nonsense. Ignoring an injury may result in permanent disability. You have injured your shoulder twice this last year. It must be looked after."

Barker led me down a few streets and turned in to a shop in Canton Street remarkable only for having a sign with actual Oriental letters on it, almost the only one in the quarter. With misgivings, I followed him. Inside there was a counter, behind which was a wall full of small drawers. Bottles stood on the counter with various unguents and roots steeping in liquids. Overhead, drying herbs in racks on the ceiling gave the room an earthy smell. An elderly man came from a back room through a beaded curtain and raised a hand in greeting to Barker. He looked a typical Limehouse dweller, an old Chinaman with a round face and long queue wearing a shapeless tan jacket with cloth-covered buttons and matching trousers. He and the

Guv conversed in Chinese for a few moments, during which the man eyed me professionally and then waved us into an inner room.

"Take off your coat and shirt, lad, and lie down on that table on your stomach," Barker ordered.

"Really, sir, there's no need to go to all this trouble. I shall be fine. Right as rain by tomorrow, I am sure."

"*Thomas.*"

I sighed and began tugging off my tie. The table was a hard wooden affair. I set my clothes in the corner and gingerly crawled up onto it, hoping it would bear my weight. As soon as I did, the fellow seized my arm and pulled it. I let out a yell of surprise and pain. Ignoring me, he said something to my employer, and they both nodded sagely. The bonesetter pulled a stool up to where I lay and sat on it.

"How does one treat an arm out of socket?" I asked Barker.

"Rather the same way you injured it, I would expect," he said, putting down the dog and taking my good arm in a viselike grip.

Suddenly, one of the bonesetter's rope-soled shoes was on my neck and the other against my side under the arm, and the blighter began tugging and twisting for all he was worth. My vision got all spotty and I came close to passing out. The next I knew I was raising my head off the table and my body had gone clammy and pale.

The bonesetter began kneading my arm around like it was a batch of dough while Barker took a jar from a shelf, opened and sniffed it, and then presented it to me.

"What is it?" I asked suspiciously. Inside, there were small, red, wrinkled-looking pellets, like beads.

"Wolfberries. They are mildly medicinal and taste like sultanas. Try one."

I was still a bit dubious, but I tried one, anyway. It was chewy and mildly sweet. I ate a few more just to please the Guv while the Chinaman continued kneading my arm. It occurred to me that my employer was not the type to offer raisins for one's pleasure, and I barked my chin on the table as I turned my head and looked down at my arm. There were more than a dozen pins sticking out of my flesh.

"Good Lord!" I cried.

"Easy, lad. Easy. Don't tense up your arm. This is merely an old Chinese remedy. The needles will not hurt you. In fact, at the moment, they are dulling the pain."

"Why am I not bleeding?"

"The needles have been inserted carefully along the nerve points, away from the veins and arteries. It is an ancient science but an exact one. You are perfectly safe, I assure you. It has been done for millennia in the East. You must lie there for ten minutes or so."

I had to admit the discomfort was beginning to ebb. Barker was having a conversation with the old man, and it did not appear to be about me. The old man's manner was polite and businesslike, but soon he ran a hand across his shaven forehead in mute concern. Ten minutes later, he pulled the pins from my arm one by one and left the room. I watched and waited for blood to start pumping from the dozens of pinpricks. There was nothing, not a single drop.

"Your arm was worse than I realized, lad," Barker said. "Quong says you shall need a cast on the joint for a couple of weeks until the tissue and ligaments heal properly."

"Quong?"

"Yes, Dr. Quong is the father of your late predecessor. He is also our client."

He made a sudden shake with his arm and a knife was in his hand. I sometimes forget that my employer generally keeps a dagger strapped to his forearm and pistols in his pockets. He bent down and before I could stop him, insinuated the blade into the arm of my shirt and began to cut.

"Sir!"

"Easy, lad. Don't move. This knife is razor sharp. You shall need room for the cast. We can always have more shirts made."

The old man returned with a bowl of water and rolls of gauze. With Barker's help, he wrapped my shoulder and elbow in sheeting and then mixed plaster into the water. Then the messy part began. Twenty minutes later, Barker was easing the ripped shirt over my new cast and if I felt foolish, it was nothing compared to how I looked. My employer knotted my tie and wrapped my elbow in a grosgrain sling. As a final touch, he settled my coat over my shoulders.

"There. Good as new and still in plenty of time for our appointment at the Oriental Club and the inquest this afternoon."

"Inquest?"

"The coroner sent word to our chambers this morning. How are you feeling? I could have Dr. Quong prepare a tisane for you."

I declined the drink, wanting as much distance between myself and the premises as possible.

Old Quong turned to Barker and dared raise an admonishing finger. He spoke English for the first time, or at least a pidgin form of it.

"You still hire," he said. "Find my son killer. Come chop chop tell me."

"I shall summon you the moment he is caught," Barker assured him.

"And you," he said, turning to me with the same extended finger. "No water on arm. Rest. Savee?"

"Yes, sir," I replied. "I savee."

I followed my employer back out into Canton Street, feeling glum. The cast was a nuisance and I looked ridiculous in it. In the back it covered one shoulder blade and extended down to my elbow. I was completely trussed. I wouldn't be able to bathe properly in the bathhouse for a while, which I counted one of the chief pleasures of life; sleeping would be extremely difficult; and I'd be about as useless as an Eastbourne octogenarian were we to get into a scrape.

We made our way back to the tram and successfully boarded it. The draft horse in front began pulling the vehicle along the rails. From Barker's coat, Harm sniffed the cast inquisitively, but I could see my employer's mind was back on the case.

"Quong disappeared New Year's Day, and his body was found in the Reach the next morning. I had to collect his father and take him to Bow Street Mortuary to identify the body. You should have seen the fire in the old fellow's eyes. He wanted me to find his son's murderer and to kill him myself. I refused, of course, though nothing would give me greater satisfaction. I promised I would find the man and turn him over to justice. British justice, that is, not Chinese. Now there are three deaths, if it is the same man."

"You are really convinced, then, that Jan Hurtz's death was not an accident? I mean, he was a clumsy man. Even his brother said so."

"It would be a coincidence if a man coming into possession of this particular manuscript should chance to die, and an even greater one that the shop should be burgled afterward. We owe it to the late Jan Hurtz and his untidy habits that the manuscript came into our possession."

Coming to the end of the line, we transferred to a hansom for the rest of the journey. Climbing in was a distinct challenge with my cast, but I struggled along gamely. Harm's eyes were sparkling and he was panting. He dearly loved cab rides. We wended our way through the City, the Strand, and finally into Whitehall, stopping at our chambers just long enough for the Guv to drop off the dog and read a message he had received. I stayed in the cab, my new cast thumping me in the side. Barker sprang back into the cab, and we were off again. We bowled sedately down Pall Mall and then turned along Regent Street.

"Where is the Oriental, sir?" I asked.

"It is in Hanover Square."

"Shall we have any trouble getting in, do you think?"

"Hardly. I am a member."

I don't think the Guv could have said anything that would have surprised me more. My rough-and-tumble employer a member of a gentlemen's club? I could hardly believe it.

"I am considered an Orientalist, after all," he explained, reading my expression. "I have done some translating for various members, who submitted my name for membership. I do not have much occasion for attendance, but it can be of use."

We pulled up in Hanover Square in front of a vaguely ministerial looking building and alighted. We had not taken two steps into the club when Barker's name was called.

"Mr. Barker, sir," the porter spoke from his small office by the door. "What a pleasure it is to see you again."

"Thank you, Chivers. This is my guest, Thomas Llewelyn. Mr. Campbell-Ffinch is expecting us, I believe."

"Indeed, sir. He is in the library. Shall I show you the way?"

"I know it, thank you."

The inside of the edifice was better than the outside. It had the same grubby collection of chairs as any other club, but the walls were done by the famous architect Adams, and I do not mean merely his school. When we reached the library, I took a glance at the pleasing carvings of oak leaves and moldings before focusing on our host.

I didn't care for Trelawney Campbell-Ffinch on the spot. He seemed to be looking down his patrician nose at me, the way Palmister Clay always had, the blackguard who had sent me to prison. Though he was still in his twenties, the fellow already had the look of an established Old Boy. I thought him the kind that would rise from position to position through dropping the right names and mentioning the right schools until his future was assured. Some people float through life while the rest of us pull the barge.

"Barker, have a seat," he said, not bothering to rise. My employer ignored the slight, or at least seemed to. He stepped back into the hall and summoned a waiter into the room.

"Bring us a bottle of port, Sandeman if you have it, and a large bowl of walnuts. Put it on my account."

Campbell-Ffinch raised an eyebrow. Obviously, he had not thought the Guv would be a member here. Having put the fellow in his place, Barker settled into a chair, where he dug into his tobacco pouch like a horse going to his oats.

"You wanted to see me, then?" he asked, stuffing his pipe. "You have a most colorful associate."

"Oh, that Woo fellow," he answered, lighting a Cuban cigar from the lamp. "He's hardly an associate. He works for the Asiatic Aid Society as an interpreter. The office has used him on several occasions, but he's a bit barmy. Been here too long. Fancies himself an English gentleman. He's more like a trained ape, if you ask me."

I'll admit Woo was a bit eccentric, but Campbell-Ffinch was just the sort of fellow to see anyone beneath him socially as being on a lower evolutionary scale, myself included. Aristocratic privilege is one thing, if one appreciates it, but accepting it as one's due and the rest of the world as mere vermin is quite another.

"So, what can I do for you, sir?" Barker asked.

"There is a book that has made its way to London," the man said. "The Chinese government is keen to have it back."

"You wish to hire me to locate it?"

Campbell-Ffinch puffed on his cigar and blew the smoke out slowly. "Not if you've got it already."

I swallowed. The manuscript was probably still in Barker's pocket, since he wouldn't let it out of his sight.

"I have thousands of books. What makes you think I would be interested in this one?"

"You know the one I mean. We traced it to a pawnshop in Limehouse this afternoon, a pawnshop you just happened to stop into yesterday morning with Inspector Bainbridge.

The same Inspector Bainbridge who had his brains blown out a half hour later."

"They were not blown out," Barker corrected. "He was shot between the eyes with a small caliber bullet. Also, he was an associate, if you do not mind."

"So, Mr. Barker," he said, ignoring the remark, "do you have the book or are we to believe the fellow managed to get it off you in the dark in that blasted tunnel?"

"I am most sorry to disappoint you," my employer said, "but I am not currently in possession of it." He sucked on his pipe as serenely as if he were in his garden. I wondered what was wrong with giving the book over to the Foreign Office and having done with it, other than the obvious one of not giving anything to Trelawney Campbell-Ffinch, Esquire, and helping him further up the social ladder.

"Pity," the Foreign Office man said, stabbing his cigar out in an ashtray as the port and walnuts arrived. "I have been following that book all the way from China. The Dowager Empress very much wants the book safely back in China again."

For a moment we were pouring glasses and cracking nuts. They were, anyway. Cracking nuts was a bit beyond me with only one usable hand.

"How is Hsu Tzi these days?" Barker asked. "I have not spoken to her in five years or more."

"She is well," Campbell-Ffinch answered tightly. "Or so I've heard. You have some interesting friends. In fact, one of them has sent you a message all the way from China." He reached in his pocket and removed a small packet of paper with a seal on it. Barker took the papers into his hands.

"The seal has been broken," he noted.

"We are the Foreign Office, old man. We don't give information from one party to another without inspecting it."

My employer frowned and opened the packet. One sheet, in white, had been wrapped in an outer layer of thick paper the color of saffron. The writing was in Chinese script so perfect it might have been hung on the wall. Barker translated it and read it out loud for my benefit.

> *To Shi Shi Ji,*
> *Greetings to you, my brother, from the Plum Blossom Clinic. Information has reached me here of a most alarming nature. A rare and secret forbidden text has been stolen from the Xi Jiang Temple and two monks murdered to obtain it. The apparent thief, a monk named Chow Li Po, has been traced to a vessel bound for your country. It is imperative that the text be restored. We understand each other.*
>
> *Huang Feihong*

"What is that last bit?" Campbell-Ffinch demanded. "How do you understand each other?"

"He reminds me that I am in his debt. His father was my teacher, which makes him my elder brother. I can deny him nothing. Very well. I shall look into the matter, though the text shall not be as easy to acquire as the first time. Anything may have happened to it now. I shall do what I can to aid the Foreign Office, but my first priority is still finding the killer of my late assistant, Quong."

"Damn it, man, this has international repercussions. The whole of Her Majesty's government's relations with the Imperial Court is at risk. What difference does the death of one Chinaman make—or a dozen, or a hundred, for that matter?"

"It makes a difference to me."

"I heard you were a rough player, Barker. I must say, I am not impressed."

In answer, Barker picked up a handful of walnuts and crushed them between his thumb and forefinger. The fragments rained down on the table between us.

"Come, Llewelyn."

6

---◆---

BARKER HAILED A CAB AND CONSULTED HIS
watch. "We are cutting it fine. We must get to the inquest in
time, as we are to be witnesses."

"Are the law courts in the City?" I asked.

"They are. Normally, inquests are held there, but it is up
to the discretion of the coroner where he holds court. In
rural areas it is often in a public house. In this case, it will be
at Ho's."

"Ho's?" I asked. "You mean he has not opened his tearoom again?"

"He never had the chance. After we left yesterday, the
coroner arrived and ordered Poole to seal the room. I assume that was in order for the jurymen to see the tunnel
and how everything is situated there. The coroner is Dr.
Vandeleur."

Vandeleur had been in our first case together. I could
never forget how he had wanted to cut up a corpse because
the victim had been crucified and he desired to write a piece
about it for *The Lancet*. Now it would be we who were vivi-
sected, if only in the dock as witnesses.

At two o'clock, Dr. Vandeleur was sitting behind a table facing the jury, in a spotless black frock coat, while a chair was reserved on the side of his table for witnesses. We and other interested persons sat in chairs along the sides of the room. I was rather nervous, knowing I must eventually give evidence in front of a crowd, but at the same time it was rather thrilling. Then I remembered why I was there—poor Bainbridge—and I was ashamed of my feelings. His widow, it was reported, had suffered nervous collapse and been sedated with laudanum. She would not be in attendance.

Vandeleur called the inquest to order and gave preliminary instructions to the thirteen men of the jury. Being a medical man rather than a legal one like most coroners, Vandeleur gave them all a brief lecture of what he had discovered during the postmortem. As expected, the cause of death had been due to the one bullet through the brain and Bainbridge had been in perfect health for a man of his age.

Next, the jury was taken back to the tunnel and the pertinent facts were presented. I am certain that the gentlemen were mystified as to how Ho's was run and what its exact purpose was. Vandeleur and Poole were interested in that themselves.

I was called as the first witness and moved to the chair, feeling nervous. Barker had counseled me to keep my usual levity in my pocket for once, and I told the main features of the case as lucidly as possible. Also, on his advice, I left out any mention of the book. Perhaps it was because I went first, but there were comparatively few questions asked me by the coroner and none from the jurymen. Soon Vandeleur dismissed me and I crossed the room to my seat again.

Barker was interviewed next. He had replaced his dark spectacles with a simpler pair, with plain leather strips covering the sides. The attempt was to make him look like any other Londoner; and, as might be expected, it failed. His appearance created a murmur in the court which Vandeleur had to suppress with his gavel. For once, Barker was not as lucky as I. They asked him about the book almost immediately.

"Mr. Barker, would you please give us your history with Inspector Bainbridge?"

"A year ago the inspector was in charge of the investigation of the murder of my assistant Mr. Quong," the Guv said in his Lowland Scots accent. "The case had never been resolved. Inspector Bainbridge came to my offices Wednesday morning, the fourth of February, 1885, having discovered a pawn ticket among the effects of my late assistant. With my assistant, Mr. Llewelyn, we proceeded to the establishment at 21 East India Dock Road and redeemed the ticket for a book on Chinese boxing."

"Do you mean a book in Chinese or in English?"

"In Chinese. The book gave every indication of belonging to a monastery, so we took it to Mr. Ho to look at it, for he is a former monk. We discussed the book but came to no conclusion as to its worth or what we should do with it. Returning through the tunnel, Inspector Bainbridge was fatally shot and Mr. Llewelyn had a lantern shot out of his hand."

A man spoke up from the side of the court. "I have a question, sir, about the book—"

"Might I know who the speaker is?" Vandeleur asked.

"Yes," said a sturdily built man in his late fifties with a thick mustache. "I am Commissioner Henderson of the Criminal Investigation Department. I wish to know what has become of the book."

"I gave it to a Chinaman, sir," Barker replied, turning his head slightly in Ho's direction. "It was a Chinese text, after all, and of no use to me."

"My eye!" the commissioner grumbled, loudly enough for everyone to hear. There was a laugh, which Vandeleur quelled with the tap of his gavel.

The head of the jury, a bucolic man who looked more like he should have been planting wheat than participating in an inquest, spoke up. "How long have you been an enquiry agent, Mr. Barker?"

"Six years, sir."

"And do you often work with Scotland Yard?"

My employer gave a stony smile. "The Yard has little need for my services. They have within their ranks some of the best investigators in all Europe. Occasionally, I will be offered a case first, because the victim wishes to keep the matter private. Other times, I am given a case that Scotland Yard has in its wisdom decided to turn down."

"Which one was this, Mr. Barker?" This elicited more laughter from the court.

"Neither, sir. This I believe to be a continuation of an earlier case, in which my assistant was killed. Both men were murdered in the same manner."

"Do you suspect anyone in particular of being guilty in the inspector's death?" Vandeleur asked.

"No, sir. It remains an open case."

"Very well, Mr. Barker. You may step down."

There was widespread conversation among us all after Barker's interview. Behind me, a reporter from the *Weekly Dispatch* asked me if Barker would be willing to be interviewed by a reporter. Before I could answer we were all hushed again by Vandeleur's gavel. Ho was called to the chair next. His appearance was quite interesting. He was wearing an English suit, including a claw hammer jacket and wing collared shirt. One couldn't get beyond the fact that the top of his forehead was shaved, and his earlobes hung to his shoulders, but his queue was discreetly tucked inside his clothes, and he was surprisingly presentable. The most savage part of him—the thick, tattooed arms—were covered by his jacket and boiled shirt.

Vandeleur began the questions. "Is Ho your surname or given name, sir?"

"It is the only name I have," Ho answered stoutly, causing a ripple of laughter in the court.

The coroner turned to his bailiff. "Is this witness sufficiently able to communicate in English?" After receiving a nod, he continued. "Very well. Mr. Ho, what kind of establishment do you run?"

"It is a restaurant and tearoom."

"And yet there is no sign outside, nothing which shows that you are open for business?"

"We do local business. I do not encourage Westerners, but some find their way into my establishment all the same."

"How long have you known Mr. Barker?"

"I have known him for twenty year, in China and in England."

"According to the police, your restaurant is frequently used for clandestine purposes. Is this true?"

"Who says this?" Ho said, looking around fiercely. "It is a lie. I run a respectable business."

"And yet there have been some disturbances here in the past year. Isn't it true that in this very establishment Inspector Bainbridge apprehended an anarchist who was wanted by Her Majesty's government?"

"Yes," Ho admitted, "but only after I throw him out. I do not ask of politics. He was drunk and disturbing other customers."

"What time did Mr. Barker, Mr. Llewelyn, and the inspector arrive?"

"About eleven o'clock, right after we open."

"Did you at any time accompany them into the tunnel?"

"No. I stay in my office."

Vandeleur leaned back and considered for a moment. "Tell me about this book. Did Mr. Barker show it to you?"

"I saw the book."

"In your opinion, is such a book valuable?"

"Not the book but the knowledge inside."

"Might someone kill to obtain such an item?"

Ho considered the questions for a moment. "I believe someone already has."

Any witness following Ho would be anticlimactic, and that position fell to Inspector Poole. I believe Mr. Gilbert said it best: "A policeman's lot is not a happy one." The inspector took the stand and answered questions.

I personally thought Poole gave a rather antiseptic version of what happened, making himself sound the calm,

logical officer leading the case with a cool head, whereas at
the time, I thought the inspector had been overdramatic,
while Barker alone had remained cool.

"Do you feel your acquaintance with Inspector Bainbridge might have in any way prejudiced your judgment in
the case?" Vandeleur continued.

"No, sir. I was acquainted with the inspector. I was more
concerned that a member of the Metropolitan Police force
had been shot."

"Was the second bullet found?"

"It was, sir. It had knocked a chip out of the second step
and bounced along the tunnel. It was all out of shape, but
by its weight, I could see it was a thirty-eight millimeter
shell."

"Were either of the preceding witnesses armed?"

"Mr. Barker was. He carries two American Colt re-
volvers, both forty-four millimeter. Such a weapon would
have done much more damage."

"Did you search the restaurant for a possible weapon?"

"I did, sir. There were no firearms to be found."

"The restaurant's customers left before you got there,
however, and one could have taken the gun." Vandeleur
turned to the jury. "I am trying to eliminate any blame for
anyone on the premises, you see."

"Yes," Poole stated, "it is possible someone might have
picked up a gun and carried it out."

"Did Mr. Barker, Mr. Llewelyn, or Mr. Ho leave the
premises?"

"Mr. Llewelyn left to telegraph Scotland Yard, sir."

I suddenly felt forty pairs of eyes on me. I had only done
what Barker had told me to do. What were we supposed to

do, sit around and wait for Scotland Yard to deduce that one of their inspectors had been killed?

"Very well," Vandeleur replied. "We shall take your comments into consideration, Inspector. You may step down."

Since the court had no more witnesses, the jury convened into another room, one I had not noticed before, while Barker and I sat and waited. It was no more than twenty minutes before the jurymen filed back into the room and took their seats again.

"Have you reached a verdict?" the coroner asked. The head juryman handed over a slip of paper which the bailiff passed to the coroner. Vandeleur nodded decisively.

"The jury finds Inspector Bainbridge's death to be willful murder by person or persons unknown."

Dr. Vandeleur brought the gavel down a final time and we were dismissed. It was not like a court trial in which there are winners and losers, and so there was not much reason to stand about and discuss the case. The coroner was the first out the door, on the way to another postmortem, most likely. Henderson stood in a corner and talked with Poole, while the rest of the spectators and the jurymen left the building, ready to put the inquest and Limehouse behind them as soon as possible.

In the kitchen, Ho popped the button on his celluloid collar and it sprang open. He pulled out the thick plait of hair he had been hiding. He made some remark to Barker in Chinese, and they both gave a grim laugh.

"He said since none of the waiters or cooks showed up for work this afternoon, he doesn't intend to pay them for today," Barker explained.

Inspector Poole suddenly stepped around me and ignored Barker as if he weren't there.

"Mr. Ho," he said, "you are under arrest."

"On what charge?" Barker demanded.

Poole pointed at a slip of paper on one of the walls. "Expired license to serve victuals, to begin with. Commissioner Henderson wants to know what sort of place this is and what sort of patron it caters to."

"How long?" Ho asked. "One day? Three day?"

"I don't know yet, but the more you cooperate the faster you'll get out again. I am going to have to put these darbies on your wrists."

There was a tense moment and I wondered if Ho would fight. His knives and cleavers were within easy reach. Instead, he shrugged a shoulder and put out his hands. Poole, surprised it had been so easy, clapped steel on them.

"Lock up," Ho said to Barker.

"I shall," came the response. The Guv could not let the matter pass. "I suppose these are Henderson's orders."

"Of course they are," Poole said bitterly. "He wants this man in for questioning. Be glad it isn't you. I have no freedom in this case. Everyone is telling me what to do. If they would just leave me alone, I could get on with it. I didn't buy my way to becoming an inspector, you know."

Barker looked away and nodded.

"This one looks like a trained fighter," Poole warned his constables. "Keep your distance and be ready should he try to escape. Let us go."

Then we were alone. A half hour before, the room had been full of people, but now it had an empty, forlorn aspect.

Barker heaved a sigh. "This is not good," he said. "If I engage my solicitor for Ho, it shall only confirm his guilt in the eyes of Henderson. He shall have to spend a few days in custody. But then, it won't be the first time Ho has been in jail."

We turned off the gas and made our way to the stairs. The Guv lit one of the naphtha lamps. It was not a time to be taking chances.

7

---◆---

BY THE TIME WE GOT BACK TO OUR OFFICES, IT
was five thirty, by the tolling of Big Ben around the corner.

"Are we done, sir?" I asked. A great deal had happened
since my less-than-brilliant decision to follow Miss Winter's
cab this morning. I had been in several public conveyances
and would like nothing better than a good, stationary easy
chair.

"One more place, I think. What would you say to a visit
to the Café Royal?"

"The Café Royal? Are you serious?" Barker was not the
type of person who frequented fashionable restaurants and
evening establishments.

"I am always serious, lad. You know that." He raised a
hand and a moment later, a cab glided to a halt in front of us.

Ten minutes later, we pulled up in Regent Street and
alighted. I had always wanted to stop at the Café Royal but
had never had the money and the time together. The Royal
catered to the arts crowd. The arbiters of next year's tastes
in literature, art, fashion, and thought were here, and one

could rub shoulders, sometimes quite literally, with famous men. Mr. Whistler came here, as did Oscar Wilde. I had to wonder what would bring Barker to such a place.

I looked about the room at the gilt fittings, the pantheon of immortals painted on the ceiling, and the mirrored walls, which gave the room added depth. Almost every table was full. I saw one shaggy-looking fellow arguing volubly with another man. Barker stood in the doorway, inevitably drawing attention to himself, then slowly, he reached up and touched the side of his nose. Recognizing it as a signal, I glanced about, to see if it was returned. It was, but in the most unlikely of places. A group of wags were seated upon the crimson velvet benches staring at the figure that is Cyrus Barker. While his comrades laughed, one reached up and touched the side of his nose. He rose and went toward the back to consult with one of the waiters, who wore long white aprons over black waistcoats and trousers. Then he continued out of the room.

Barker raised his chin and I immediately followed the dandy, the Guv after me. We went into the next room, past the entrance of a Masonic temple, of all things, then down a spiral staircase to an anteroom, occupied by one other person, a large burly man who was leaning back with his head against the wall, sleeping. His lips formed an O under his mustache and he was, in general, an uncouth-looking creature.

"I hope you do not mind," the dandy said. "There is nothing as unaesthetic as an enquiry agent, and I have a reputation for taking my frivolity seriously. I had to tell my friends you were bailiffs, like our friend here."

"As hard as you try," Barker rumbled, "I doubt you could

create a debt your father could not repay. Forbes, this is my assistant, Thomas Llewelyn. Thomas, the Honorable Pollock Forbes. Speaking of paying, Pollock, how do we stand on credit? Do I owe you or do you owe me?"

Forbes ran a finger along his chin as he reflected. He had the longest, thinnest fingers I have ever seen. He was a casual looking fellow, in the latest style from Savile Row, a lounge suit. Despite the name, it looked expensive. "I believe I'm in your debt, old man, and it's not the kind the pater can pay off. What are you working on?"

"I have a case involving a book stolen from a Chinese monastery. The Chinese government and the Foreign Office are hunting for it. The latter is represented by Mr. Trelawney Campbell-Ffinch."

"Campbell-Ffinch. I haven't heard that name in ages," he said, fluttering a hand at a waiter in the hall. "Lonnie was in my house at Cambridge, a few years ahead of me. He's always been a bully and a frightful bore. Chumley, bring us a bottle of the Veuve Clicquot, there's a good chap."

The waiter, who had appeared silently at my elbow, glided off as quietly as he came. Something about Forbes's inflection made me pause, and then it came to me. Like Barker, he was a Scot. Detective work was one of those occupations like engineering that seemed suited to the Scottish temperament.

"You'll like it, I think," he said, referring to the wine. "The Royal has one of the best cellars in the world. To tell the truth, I didn't know Lonnie was in London again. He's like a bad sailor, always being posted farther and farther east. Something big must have occurred to have them dare bring him back. Is any of this in my line?"

"It has international repercussions," Barker said, "but I do not believe any heads shall roll, save for one fellow's, who has been killing people to get the book."

"Where?"

"The East End," the Guv stated. "Limehouse."

"Isn't that where. . . . Oh, yes, I see it now. Your late assistant was mixed up in this, was he not?"

"He was."

The waiter arrived with the Clicquot and opened it with a ceremonial pop. I had never tasted pink champagne before. It was sweet and tickled my nose.

Barker emptied his glass and set it back on the table. "Very nice," he pronounced. I knew for a fact that he did not care for wine of any sort and I doubted he could tell a Dom Pérignon from a third-rate Italian table wine.

Pollock Forbes coughed discreetly behind his hand. "So what exactly would you like me to undertake?" he asked.

"I would like to know when Campbell-Ffinch arrived in London again and if he was summoned. I want to learn how he has been spending his free time and with whom. His knuckles are swollen. I believe he may have been fighting recently."

Forbes extracted a short pencil from his pocket and recorded the questions on his cuff. "Got it. Anything else?"

"Have you ever heard of a Mr. K'ing?"

"The Chinaman? Of course. I hear his name often. 'Lost ten quid to Mr. K'ing at puck-a-poo,' 'Lost fifty poun' at mah-jongg to that blighter K'ing.' I gather between the gambling parlors and the opium dens, he's doing all right for himself."

The snoring fellow in the corner had awakened and even

now, they were setting his meal before him: game hens with *pomme frites*. I had heard the cooking here was as good as any restaurant in Paris. All the French political exiles ate here and why shouldn't they? Even if the food were not superb, there was the authentic decor, as if a slice of Versailles like a three-layered cake had been set down in the middle of London.

"Stay for dinner?" Forbes asked, as if reading my thoughts. Barker pondered it as his fellow Scotsman refilled his glass. The Guv tossed it down again like so much well water and shook his head.

"No, we must be going." He turned to me. "What's wrong, lad?"

"Nothing, sir," I grumbled.

Barker took my remark at face value, but I must have caught Forbes in mid-breath, setting him coughing behind his hand. It was then that my instinct or training took over: the coughing, the sunken skin around his eyes, both signs of illness.

We took our leave, after Forbes promised he would look into the matter. I wondered if he was a plainclothes policeman working sub rosa, as I understood the Royal was a haven for refugees and anarchists. But, no, he was too genuine, too imaginative, too aesthetic, to use his word. We passed out into Regent Street again and stood at the cabstand.

"He is consumptive, isn't he?" I asked.

Barker nodded slowly. "Yes. Very good, Thomas, but then, you are familiar with the symptoms, are you not?" He referred, of course, to my late wife, Jenny, who had wasted away of the disease while I was in prison. A shudder went down my back. The memory had been dredged up too quickly, before I'd had a chance to prepare myself.

"How advanced is his condition?"

"He's had it at least three years. His father is the laird of Aberdeenshire and chief of the Clan Forbes. Pollock is the oldest son and due to inherit, but he shall not survive his father. He'll not be getting his threescore and ten, I ken."

"Is he some sort of . . . enquiry agent?"

"Not as you or I know it," he said. "Forbes once said we would split the city between us. He would take the West End, I the East. To be more precise, he looks after the aristocracy. When they get into a spot of trouble—blackmail, perhaps, or a scandal—they come to him. He takes care of them better than they deserve. He is a walking *Burke's Peerage*. He can tell you line by line the honors and lineage of England's most powerful families. It occupies him, I think. He cultivates a flippant exterior, but behind it lies one of the best brains in London. His father does not understand, poor fellow—keeps trying to order him back—but he will not go, not until the very end. I imagine that seeing what he shall miss must be far too painful."

"It is abominable, sir."

"Yes, well, we can merely play the hand we are given, lad. Cursing the Dealer is a waste of breath."

"So, how do you work together, if one of you moves among the upper class and the other among the lower?"

"Cases are not so simple, lad. They overlap and when they do, we help each other. Do you recall the case I had you dictate on the day you were hired? The one involving William Koehler?"

I thought back to that day almost a year before. "It was a blackmailing case, was it not?"

"Aye. Koehler was a petty blackmailer living beyond his

means in the Albany, where Forbes has chambers. He dealt in letters of a revealing nature and was quite successful. In lieu of payments, sometimes he would demand letters of introduction or invitations to balls and soirées, which in turn led to opportunities to find more letters. Forbes kept an eye on him until his rise was getting too high. He was a good-looking scoundrel and had begun to woo a certain aristocrat's daughter. Forbes decided to act, particularly when Koehler began to threaten an MP. We thought it best that the letter warning him off came from me, and I supplied the services of James Briggs, a retired prizefighter, to act as protection. Briggs is awfully good at frightening people away."

I thought Barker not so bad at it himself. Were I a criminal, I would not like to receive one of those icily polite letters informing me that I had come under the private enquiry agent's scrutiny.

A hansom cab arrived and we climbed into it.

"One final thing, lad," Barker said.

"Yes, sir?"

"Dummolard's restaurant is only a few streets away. There is a rivalry between our chef and the Royal. You know how Etienne gets when he is slighted. You would do well not to mention our little visit here."

8

———◦◦◦———

I AM GOING OUT AFTER DINNER, LAD," BARKER
said to me over the coffee and cheese that evening.

"Are you going to see Miss Winter, sir?" I asked, knowing I was breaking a rule: do not ask Barker where he goes
during his free time.

The Guv cleared his throat in disapproval. "Yes, as a
matter of fact, I am."

"Might I go with you, sir? I'd like to apologize to her for
tossing her maid into Limehouse Reach and for chasing her
away."

My employer considered the request for a moment,
stroking his chin in thought, but then he shook his head decisively. "I had better go alone. She keeps a high temper, and
brooks no assaults on her dignity. It is in your best interest
to let her cool a bit before you speak to her."

Barker slid off in that way of his, and the next I knew,
the front door was shutting behind him. Mac disappeared
into his sanctum factotum, closing his door with equal finality. Harm was sleeping off a bowl of braised chicken livers
he'd eaten, awaiting his master's return while perhaps

dreaming of his recent adventures in Limehouse. That left me alone, bored, and uncomfortable in the cast. I was convinced it was an instrument of torture from the malignant mind of Dr. Quong. A gentleman certainly couldn't go anywhere in it, not to the theater or even the music halls. I looked ridiculous in my cut sleeve and plaster cast. Even going down the street to the Elephant and Castle for a pint, I'd have to endure remarks at my own expense. It was not worth the effort. Perhaps, I thought, there was something in the library I could read.

I went in, circumambulating the chair by the back window that overlooked the miniature pond, and went in search of entertainment. The choices were few, I fear. Barker preferred heavy tomes with impossibly long titles and eschewed the sort of frivolous novels that I came in search of. I sat down and looked about. It was a case of books, books everywhere, and not a thing to read.

The thought occurred to me that in most of our cases, the Guv had provided me with materials to study, but he had neglected to do so in this one. Since he had not, I thought I might collect some of my own. Surely there was not a better place in London for such materials than in the personal library of an Orientalist.

The first book I came across concerned Chinese pottery. Somehow, I didn't think that would play a major part in this investigation. Eventually, I discovered a series of small books privately printed in Shanghai that were translations of the analects of Confucius, the *Tao-te Ching,* and something by a fellow named Mencius. It looked like enough material to keep me occupied until bedtime.

A few pages into the analects, I found something interesting. Barker's personal copy had found its way into the downstairs library, complete with his favorite passages underlined. The publication date was 1877. Had he bought the book in China, or had he purchased it more recently in London? For a moment, I considered whether to read it or to give it to Barker in the morning. Then I decided the library was fair game and sat down again to try to make sense of the book and possibly the man who had read it before me.

The first thing I learned was that Confucius was a Latinized version of the word for "Master." The second was that he was not a sage living in a cave somewhere as I had thought, but an inspector of police in China during the sixth century B.C. who was concerned with bettering society in his district. The third was that he was not interested in creating a religion but in practical solutions to problems for the here and now or, rather, the there and then.

Confucius saw contemporary society in his time as divided into two groups, a gentleman class and a peasant class. He believed that if gentlemen studied rigorously and committed themselves to ruling with compassion and wisdom, society would run more smoothly. I noted that Barker had underlined all the analects that had to do with how a gentleman behaves, such as:

"The gentleman must be slow in speech but quick in action."

"In his dealings with the world the gentleman is neither for or against anything. Rather, he is on the side of what is moral."

"The gentleman is easy of mind, but the small man is always anxious."

What I had before me appeared to be a plan for how

Barker was conducting his life, at least since he came to England. That left me scratching my head. Wasn't Barker a Christian? Was he influenced by both? Even as I was getting closer to the core of the man, I was coming up with more questions than answers.

Having got through most of the analects, for the book is short, I turned to Lao-tzu and got mired right away. The words were translated into English, but the meanings were almost gibberish. With my clouded Western mind, I could not make head or tail of it. How does one make sense of statements like: "Though the uncarved block is small, no one in the world dare claim its allegiance"?

As for Mencius, he was one of Confucius's students. I might have understood him better had I begun with him first. Instead, I found myself reading a phrase once, going on to the next, not making sense of it, and going back to the first. I was tired and my brain could not hold any more Oriental philosophy. Like a man of wisdom, I went to bed.

The next I knew, I was awakened by a loud report from the room below. I opened my eyes and tried to focus. It sounded as though there was a fight going on. I heard a cry and threw back my covers, yanked open my door, ran down the steps not two feet ahead of Barker, who had come down from the upper floor in a nightshirt and dressing gown. When we reached the ground floor, we found the back door wide open and Harm disporting himself in the dark of the garden, running in circles and barking as if to say, "What larks!"

We hurried into the study and found Mac on the floor, clutching his leg and moaning. The smell of gunpowder hung in the air. His trusty shotgun lay beside him, and it took but a moment to deduce what had happened. Barker's butler had interrupted a burglary attempt and had been shot in the leg in the course of it.

Harm came bounding in, all energy and excitement, and went so far as to bark at us as if we were complete strangers. Barker bent and put his hand on Mac's shoulder.

"Do not try to get up. Thomas, bring a towel."

I dashed into the kitchen and seized the first cloth I could find. The Guv used it to make a tourniquet around Mac's leg to stem the flow of blood. When he was done, he said, "Tell me what happened."

Mac lay on the wooden floor, propped up on his elbows. He was pale and grimacing from the pain. "A sound of papers being moved about woke me up, sir. I knew it couldn't be you or Mr. Llewelyn, else I'd have heard you coming down the stairs. I took the shotgun I always keep under my bed, threw open the door, and charged into the study, but he came out of nowhere. It was as though he was invisible. He bent my arm down, forcing the gun to discharge into my leg."

"Did you get a good look at him? Was he Oriental?"

"I really couldn't say, sir. He was crouched and came up under my gun."

Barker let out a grunt in exasperation. I don't suppose anyone had dared storm the citadel of his private home before. It was unthinkable, like Mount Olympus having its silver nicked.

"We must get him into bed and call Dr. Applegate," he told me.

Barker and I attempted to lift Mac up from the floor, but the butler gave such a cry of pain that even I felt sorry for him. For once, the Guv was at a loss as to what to do. He managed to get hold of Dr. Applegate by telephone and the latter agreed to come over, telling us not to move the patient but to make him comfortable. Comfortable, to Barker, meant slapping a pillow under his head and grilling him for the next twenty minutes over and over again on events that took all of about twenty seconds to occur.

I suppose I've been rather hard on Dr. Applegate. I have strong views on the medical profession, due perhaps to the loss of my wife, and nothing that has occurred since then has changed my view—that for all our science, we are merely one step away from bloodletting and witch doctors. Applegate has a chilly bedside manner and a pinched face, as if chronically dyspeptic. For all his skills and his willingness to come the few streets from his own private house to Barker's, he lacks a cheery countenance. One feels that if one passed on under his care, he'd merely nod sagely and move on to his next patient without a second thought.

Dr. Applegate eventually arrived and clucked his tongue over the patient. He then called for bandages and alcohol and began pulling the pellets from Mac's wound. A half hour later, the three of us carried Mac to his bed.

It was my first glimpse into Mac's private sanctuary, an odd combination of cleaning supplies and homey touches. There were antimacassars on the chairs, beaded lampshades, and a photograph of a dour Jewish couple who must have been his parents. I saw a bookcase against one wall and, being something of a bookman, I made my way over to it. There were a few serious Jewish texts, Mrs. Beaton's *Book of Household Management,* and some Jane Austens along with a Brontë or two, but the majority of the titles were of a Gothic turn. The novels of Mrs. Braddon were much in evidence, as was Wilkie Collins, Horace Walpole, the American Poe, and the Baroness Orczy. Jacob Maccabee was a secret romantic, and though this was too good a card to waste, it would be unsporting of me to use it now, when my opponent was down. I helped them try to make him comfortable.

Dr. Applegate gave Mac a walloping dose of morphine that knocked him out as stony cold as a mackerel in Billingsgate. Afterward, the doctor put on his top hat, wrapped his scarf around his neck, told Barker to expect the usual bill, and left.

It was then that I realized I had been wasting the last half hour. I had been studying the room and watching the doctor as he went about his business, when all the time I should have been watching my employer. Had I done so, I would not have been surprised by his next statement.

"We are at war," he said.

"Sir?"

"There has been a killer in this house. He has murdered nearly a half dozen people, by my estimate, and he came here tonight prepared to kill again. Never in the five years that I have lived here has anyone dared to enter my home unbidden. He knows my reputation, I have no doubt, and yet he has found it of little consequence."

Perhaps it was a trick of the light, but the yellow from the gas lamps in the room actually penetrated Barker's black spectacles enough for me to see the glint of his eyes. They looked like small flames, and it gave him a hellish aspect. I wondered if the killer of Quong had seriously underestimated my employer, or whether this unknown person was his equal in dangerous matters. He had killed several people now, after all. What does such power do to a person's soul?

"What shall we do, sir?" I asked.

"We must prepare. This is a siege, lad. He may try again tonight."

"Forgive me, sir, but why didn't you just give the book to Scotland Yard or the Foreign Office and have done with it? We have nothing like their manpower."

Barker gritted his teeth, as resolute as I have ever seen him. "Because Quong left it for me to give it to whom I choose. Here." He picked up the shotgun and broke it open before handing it to me. "The shells are on the table."

I had never used a shotgun, but I didn't want to lower myself in the Guv's eyes. I put two shells in the barrels and closed the gun, wondering what I was to do with it. Barker moved into the library and took out a brace of dueling pistols, loading them with powder and ball as if he had done it a thousand times.

"It is possible," he said, "that the killer has not left the grounds. There are many places where a man can secrete himself in the garden. Let us reconnoiter."

Somehow, reconnoitering had been left out of my education. I followed him out into the garden, hoping I cut a more formidable figure than I felt. It was freezing and I was clad only in my nightshirt. I hadn't even had time to put on my slippers. As for Harm, he took the opportunity to show off, barking at shadows, at the goldfish in the pond, at any sound that carried on the wind.

Barker lit an Oriental lantern with a vesta and we began to look around the garden counterclockwise from the back door, taking in the kitchen garden, the Pen-jing area, and the rockery. We crossed the stone bridge, icy cold under my bare feet, skirting the training area, where I had been tossed down more times than I cared to remember. We bypassed the staggered stone path and invaded the potting shed. The Guv was very thorough, even studying the roof.

We stepped out of the gate, where a cold wind fresh from Spitsbergen was blasting down the alleyway. There was no one about, nor any evidence of anyone, yet I knew the killer had been down here within the hour. Where, I wondered, does a murderer disappear to in residential Newington?

Back inside his half-acre garden, my employer closed the moon gate with a finality and gave it a shake, just to make sure it held. We passed the suspended gong and climbed the two steps to the open pagoda. Barker made a very close inspection of the bathhouse, the largest structure in the garden, looking anywhere a man might hide. We crossed the bridge again and then walked the boardwalk that circled the enclosed pond. The Guv even shone the lantern across the water.

"Surely you don't think he's hiding in the pond. It's nearly freezing," I said.

"There are some men I have known who trained in frigid water," he answered, "and some who use the sheath of a sword as a breathing straw, remaining underwater for several minutes."

"Surely he's gone, sir," I said, "and having a cup of hot tea somewhere. Perhaps we should do the same."

For once I'd talked sense. Cyrus Barker nodded and we went inside.

"Look in the kitchen, lad, and do not neglect the pantry. Harm and I will have a look in the cellar."

"But he went out the back door," I protested.

"We have the evidence only of the open back door. No one saw him leave. If he is still here, he might have moved during our search of the garden. I fear we must search the entire house."

I nodded wearily and walked into the kitchen. The room was deserted, of course, the moonlight bathing Dummolard's copper pots in a blue glow. I wanted to go to bed, but now it appeared we would be spending the rest of the night on a wild-goose chase. I opened the pantry door, and the next thing I knew, Mac's gun was kicked out of my hand, sliding across the counter and over it, out of reach. I blocked a blow to my face with my good arm instinctively, since all I could see was a black shape in the darkness.

"Sir—" I began, but a kick caught me in the chest, knocking the air out of me. I don't know if he then kicked my feet out from under me or whether I just fell to the floor. I was preoccupied with trying to breathe. I rolled over, despite the cast, which I now loathed more than anything in the world, and watched the intruder run out the back door. I wanted to yell, to warn Barker, but I couldn't draw enough breath into my lungs to get anything out.

A half minute later, Barker's head came 'round the corner. I waved vaguely toward the door and he was gone. I lay back and closed my eyes, willing myself to calm down. Slowly, the pain in my chest subsided and I was able to breathe again.

Barker returned a few minutes later. "Up and over the wall," he stated. For some reason, he decided I must need a glass of water. He set about searching for a tumbler. It was the first time I had ever seen him in the kitchen, there being some unwritten rule that this was Dummolard's domain. He found the glassware in one of the cupboards and pumped water into it over the sink.

"Gave as well as got?" he asked, as he handed me the glass.

"Not even close, I'm afraid," I admitted. "If you don't mind, now that our intruder is definitely gone, I would like to go back to bed."

"Sorry, lad. We shall have to go over the grounds again. I believe I shall sleep on the sofa in the library tonight with Mac's shotgun close to hand. This fellow has caught me out once. I am not going to let it happen again."

Barker helped me up and we went outside.

"Why didn't he kill me when he had the chance?" I wondered aloud.

"He would not risk being caught in the kitchen. There are too many weapons at hand for a pair of trained fighters. It would have been a bloodbath. When you flushed him out, he had no other thought but to escape to fight another day."

Our second examination of the garden, like the first, yielded nothing. I went upstairs and crawled into bed. As tired as I was, I had little sleep that night. Every creak had me sitting up in bed.

9

NEVIL BAINBRIDGE'S FUNERAL WAS NOT TO BE forgotten. As if in sympathy, rain wept steadily from an iron-gray heaven, icy raindrops that one could hear break on the waterproofs of the constables in attendance. All of us were in black and in misery, as if being here reminded us all of our own mortality. Even the statues of angels and men, ingrained with soot like sketches in charcoal, looked forlorn and miserable, wishing they could be somewhere else; but there was nowhere to go. The whole of London was blanketed under a leaden sky.

Standing under my umbrella, huddled into my macintosh for warmth, I wondered how long the service would go on. There was a great deal of ceremony to get through. It is rare when an officer is killed, and Scotland Yard seeks for an air of solemn grandeur and profound tragedy. Every now and then I got a glimpse within the waterproofs of the dress uniforms, with their epaulettes and braids, helmets and white gloves, of the constables and inspectors. In a show of toughness on the part of the Yard, none carried umbrellas, and the constables stood at attention, chins dripping and ice crystals lodged in their mustaches. Barker and I had no such restriction and made full use of our umbrellas, the droplets drumming on the waxed cotton and falling in a circle around us, save when a gust of cold wind whipped them over our trousers and shoes. I like rainy mornings in London, even in February, but only when I can spend them in a nice coffeehouse or a Charing Cross bookshop. Only lunatics, or someone heavily entrenched in ritual and duty, would be out on a morning like this.

Bainbridge's widow was not a cheering sight. She was heavy and severe under a pair of beetling brows and a bonnet full of black feathers, as if a raven had wandered onto her hat and died of pure wretchedness. She glared through the commissioner's address, she glared through the brief eulogy the minister gave, and she glared as her late husband's wooden coffin was set to rest at the bottom of the grave. I would have liked to have given her the benefit of the doubt and to have said she had once been beautiful or kind or solicitous of the poor, but I was not feeling generous at that moment. Generosity comes with dry socks, I think.

I was in awe of death then, and now after many years and experiences, still am. I have never grown jaded about it. One minute we are sentient beings and the next, fodder for worms. What was the Good Lord thinking? I wished I had the assurance my employer had. There he stood beside me under his umbrella in his black macintosh, bowler hat coming down almost to the top of his spectacles, solemn, yes, but serene. He did not seem to feel the wet or the cold or the fear of death. I knew without asking that he was not subject to the doubts that were causing my misery and that afterward he would comment upon the sermon or the sublimity of the ceremony. I wondered whether it was merely the stoical training he had undergone in his lifetime, or if it was his character—in which case, I might never attain it.

"I think old Bainy would have approved of his funeral," Barker said, as we walked from the grave after the ceremony had ended. "He was finally given the recognition by his superiors he deserved."

We stopped to give way to a knot of Metropolitan Police dignitaries, including Commissioner Henderson of the Criminal Investigation Department and Munro of the Special Irish Branch. They all shot a cold glare Barker's way, as if to ask, "Who let him in?" In the center was Terence Poole, looking worse even than I felt. The responsibility of finding Bainbridge's killer fell foursquare upon his shoulders. I am sure all had taken him in hand, urging him to find this killer, as if he were a lost dog who simply needed to be rounded up. I would imagine there was a barb or two in the commissioner's speech reserved just for Barker's old friend and physical culture partner.

It was not my original intent to become an enquiry agent's assistant, but I was glad at least that we were private rather than public servants. We answered to no one but our clients. We could stop and have lunch and talk about something else for a while and could go home to a nice meal and a good soak, at least most of the time. We had half Saturdays and full Sundays off. Admittedly, on some cases, we might work 'round the clock, but, again, that was part of the elasticity of our position.

I thought the Scotland Yard officials' opinion of us unfair, saying we "lived by our wits," the same phrase they used for safecrackers and confidence men. Some private agents were men who had been unsuccessful as police constables, I knew, and were not above breaking into residences to acquire evidence or performing other illegal activities. Cyrus Barker, whom I considered the cream of his profession, rarely used such techniques. He might bend a rule, but he rarely broke one. Were they jealous of his success, perhaps, or did they look down their noses at the fact that he placed advertisements in the newspapers for his services? For whatever reason, it was yet another act of which the Guv took no notice. As far as he was concerned, it was just more rain down the back of his waterproof.

My teeth were chattering when we came out of the cemetery, and I knew our chances of finding a cab were almost nonexistent. We were in Whitechapel, a very downtrodden section of town hard by the City. Barker seemed to know where he was going, if I didn't. He took a left at one corner, a right at the next, and passed through an alleyway so narrow we had to close our umbrellas. *How much longer were we going to walk?* I wondered. My trouser legs were soaked through and my boots were becoming sodden.

Barker opened the door to a pub called the Ten Bells and I stepped gratefully inside. Warmth from food and human bodies and a roaring fire at one end flushed my features and fogged Barker's spectacles. We stood at the bar and ordered pints and fell upon the free meal offered: boiled eggs and cheese, pickles and pickled onions, and crusty slices of bread slathered in butter. We took it all in and when our stomachs were full and our pint glasses half empty, we took off our waterproofs and sat down on a bench by the fire. *God bless the Ten Bells and proper publicans everywhere,* I thought.

"Do you know every building in London?" I asked.

"Almost, and you should, too. I have some very good ordnance maps, with my own notes jotted on them, that I made during my first few years here. It is important at times to know where the closest constabulary is or even the closest grog shop. Nice place, this, eh?"

"Better than Whitechapel deserves."

Barker got out his traveling pipe and set it ablaze, and we spent an agreeable half hour baking our feet dry again on the fender, thinking of the constables who had changed out of their dress blacks and were back on their beats until day's end.

"Lad, you're falling asleep."

I sniffed and rubbed my face. "Sorry, sir. I didn't get much rest last night. Do you think our killer might simply give up now that he knows you're after him?"

"He won't give up. He has killed several times and has proven how unrelenting his determination is to get his hands on the manuscript."

"It makes no sense. I mean, Bainbridge was right: it is just a book. Let us say the killer did lay hands on it. What would he do with it? It wouldn't make him rich or powerful."

"I'll admit, lad, I haven't worked that out myself. He may never have told a soul. Whatever it is, I feel it is something big, something very important, at least to him. He must not have it. I shall not be content until I see it back in the monastery it came from."

"Even if we have to take it there ourselves?" I asked.

"Exactly."

"But first, you'll have to get it again, because you gave it to a Chinaman."

"I trust I can lay hands on it when the moment comes."

"Is it in the East End?"

Barker knocked his pipe on the fender. "This is not a parlor game, lad. Come. We have work to do."

"Where to next, sir?" I asked, putting down my empty pint glass. My boots had dried out a little, and I had convinced myself that somewhere in the world at that moment a warm sun was shining down and might even come here someday. If anything, the room suddenly seemed too hot, pungent with hops and tobacco smoke. I wanted to be out again in the cold, crisp air.

"K Division, or at least Bainbridge's constabulary in East India Dock Road. I want to get permission to go through his files. If he had a clue or a possible suspect in the crime, he wouldn't have told us, not right away. He came to us only because he could not legally get the book himself. I am almost surprised he did not simply thump Mr. Hurtz with his truncheon and take it. Bainbridge was known for the direct approach, and he was a steady officer for many years."

We took the tram into Limehouse. Sailor town does not improve in inclement weather, save that the pavement is not crowded by street sellers of dried squid and other "treats." We had the streets to ourselves. Merchants halfheartedly called to us as we passed from the shadows of their shops. They recognized Barker now. It was *Shi Shi Ji* this and *Shi Shi Ji* that. They didn't bother translating for my benefit. Barker stopped to talk once or twice. *This was it,* I told myself. *He's going to talk to all six hundred Chinamen in London, and when he's done with them, he'll start on the Lascars.*

East India Dock Road is a continuation of Commercial Road, but the great thoroughfare dwindles considerably when it reaches the dockyards. Bainbridge's constabulary was a red brick building tucked in among the others in the street like a book on a shelf. Only the blue light suspended out in the street gave warning that this was the sole bastion of law and order in this sailor's haven. Stepping inside, I was expecting the chaos I've seen before in the booking area of A Division at Great Scotland Yard itself. It was not so. There were no more than two or three constables on duty, but they seemed to have everything in hand. A lone fellow in a pair of wrist darbies sat talking with an officer, and two citizens waited patiently to be served. It looked as if Bainbridge had run a tight ship. One could get the impression that this was a sleepy little backwater constabulary where nothing ever happens. One would, however, be wrong. The first thing we discovered when we walked in the door was that the constabulary had just narrowly missed being burned to the ground. Bainbridge's files, the ones we had come to see, had been reduced to ash.

"Burned, you say?" the Guv rasped to the solid-looking police sergeant in charge of the desk. "All of them?"

"Aye, sir. A little after midnight, it was. P. C. Threadgill, he does the overnight duty, you see, he smelled smoke and saw it coming from under the inspector's door. The dustbin had been set in the middle of the floor and some files set alight in it. A regular blaze it was, according to Threadgill, and he was afeared it'd burn down the building. He poured water and sand from the fire bucket on it and then opened windows down the hall to kill the smoke. It was burnt to cinders, all them files Bainy—I mean Detective Inspector Bainbridge—had recorded so metic'lously. A crying shame, I says, and the place all reeking of smoke now. The back windows is open and all of us with our teeth chattering."

"May I see his office?" Barker asked.

The constable hesitated a moment. We were unofficial, after all, but then, anything of interest had already been burned. He finally nodded. "A quick look wouldn't hurt nothing, I 'spect."

"You have no suspects?" my employer asked as we were led back to the office.

"Not a one that we can pin down," the constable admitted. "And before you ask, no, not so much as a scrap of paper could be saved. Between the fire, the sand, and the water, there was nothing but moldering ash."

"Murder," the Guv muttered to me as we walked, "of a police officer and now arson in a London constabulary. This killer would appear to have no fear of Scotland Yard at all."

The constable set his key in the lock and turned it. The smell of smoke was far stronger in here, though nothing had been burned save the files. A gray discoloration marked the center of the ceiling over the spot where the bin stood.

"Was this open last night?" my employer asked, pointing toward the open window.

"Aye, sir, but it's a sheer wall. It would take a monkey to climb it."

Barker grunted and moved to the desk on which was a common blotter of green paper, a map of the city, and pencils standing in a cup. A wooden chair on casters was pulled up to the desk, a chair which had been worn down by the seat of Bainbridge's trousers for years but would be worn down no farther. A few prints of the early days of the station and the Bow Street Runners hung on the wall. *There was not much left behind after so many years on duty,* I thought.

"Took the top blotter sheet, too," the constable noted.

"Why?" Barker queried.

"Old Bainy was a sketcher, sir. It was how he worked out his cases. Helped him think, he said. Wasn't a bad artist, neither. Could have had him a job as an illustrator for the newspapers if he weren't a copper down to his boots."

"Interesting," Barker declared, pouring the pencils from the cup onto the blotter. Taking a pencil in his hand, he started in the upper right-hand corner and began to move the lead back and forth across the blotting paper. What child in Britain had not taken a piece of paper to an old gravestone and rubbed an etching of an old knight or dame?

"We shall look this over, and if it bears fruit, you shall give it to Inspector Poole when he comes in."

It took close to a half hour of rubbing and several pencils before the two of us finished the blotter. As imperfect as the images were, they gave us a very good look into the mind of the late Inspector Nevil Bainbridge. The constable was correct: the inspector had been quite an artist.

"Lad, get out your notebook," the Guv ordered.

I retrieved it from my pocket, set it down on a cabinet, and prepared to write in my best Pitman shorthand, despite not being able to hold the pad with one arm in a cast.

"In the upper left-hand corner we have the letters *H* and *P* enclosed in a diamond. There is nothing along that same latitude until we get to the middle of the paper, where we discover the head and shoulders of a sinister-looking fellow in a wide-brimmed hat and fur collar who I suspect is Mr. K'ing. Close to the upper right-hand corner, there is another face, larger and very wild: fierce teeth, bristling mustache, rolling eyes, a complete caricature of an Asian face. By the corner of the face is a wooden flail, two sticks connected by a rope. In the middle, there is a form bent over a line, loose, like one of those string puppets. What are they called?"

"Marionettes, sir."

"Yes. The line stretches for some distance across the picture, then coils into a loop of rope. By the figure's shoulder is a rough shape, which I believe is a coffin. Near the center of the page is a female form, nicely rendered but without a face. She wears a shawl and straw hat, and her hair is cut straight across her shoulders. I presume it is light colored, for he does not appear to have darkened it. Blond or red. The pose, holding the shawl around her, is demure and yet there is some voluptuousness to the figure. Two men are off to the right, in profile, as if watching the girl. One is taller than the other. They are shaded heavily, but I believe them to be Campbell-Ffinch and his interpreter, Woo.

"On the bottom row, there is a figure slumped on the floor and a group of lines going back and forth away from him, like the teeth of a saw or steps. I adduce it is the image of Jan Hurtz, whom Bainbridge would have seen firsthand. There is a small sketch of a ship, possibly the Blue Funnel ship *Ajax*. We shall see. Here, where the coil of rope ends are three balls and a ticket, the one we gave to Hurtz's brother. There is an almost comically menacing face, with a heavy beard, leering and ready to devour the maiden in the center. And here, at the very lower right-hand corner, is the face of my late assistant, whom Bainbridge had the poor taste to show as we found him on that terrible day, eyes half shut, arms thrown wide, and the bullet hole dead center. That is all."

"That's one, two, five . . . nine figures altogether, and we know but half of them," I pointed out.

"Can you draw, lad?"

"Not this well, sir."

"See if you can copy all these images. Let me go get the constable again."

He returned a few minutes later with the constable, who scratched his chin at our work. "That's good thinking," he admitted. "I would never have thought of it. This is the property of Scotland Yard, however. You won't be able to take it with you."

"We understand that. Do any of these people look familiar to you?"

"This ugly brute here," he said, indicating the fierce face in the upper right-hand corner, is Charlie Han. He's a young tough in Limehouse with a sizable corner of the betel nut market in his pocket. Inspector Bainbridge was always hauling him in on small charges. Now this coffin here and the fellow on the line, I think that's Jonas Coffin's place. A Chinaman died there last year. Funny name. Chow, I believe, Luke Chow. Coffin owns a penny hang in West India Dock Road. And there's no missing who the girl is. We call her the Belle o' Pennyfields. Works at a chandlery since her uncle was killed a year ago."

"Killed, you say?" Barker asked.

"Yes, sir. He was robbed one evening. New Year's Day, it was. Found dead behind the counter of his shop, with his neck broke, from what I hear."

"What is the girl's name?" Barker asked.

"Gypsy name, she has. Petulengro, same as her uncle's. Hettie Petulengro."

The Guv turned to me. "There is your *H P,* lad."

"And what, may I ask, is going on here?" an official voice demanded from the doorway. It was Terence Poole, and he did not look pleased. He dismissed the constable with a glower and then turned on us.

"That is Metropolitan Police property," Poole said, pointing at the blotter.

"We were merely deciphering it," Barker said. "We have identified all but one of the figures here."

"You needn't try to sound all helpful with me," Poole said, reaching into his pocket. "I spoke to the Dutchman who says you took possession of the book in his brother's pawnshop." He tossed a business card on the blotter. It was the very one he had given to Hurtz. "I want that book!"

"I no longer have it," Barker stated, shrugging. "As I said at the inquest, I gave it to a Chinaman."

Poole looked at him skeptically. "You handed it over to the Chinese, just like that? I know better. You can't convince me you didn't recognize it for what it was."

"Believe as you like," Barker said.

"I shall. We can detain you here until you talk. I am the investigating officer. I can put you in with Ho. Did you give the text to any passing Chinaman or to one of them in particular?"

Barker sat silent. This situation was a little different from speaking with Campbell-Ffinch or to Dr. Vandeleur. Terence Poole was a friend as well as a police inspector.

"Cyrus," Poole said, leaning over my employer, "did you have the book in your possession in the tunnel when we were there together earlier?"

Again, the Guv was silent. I saw the skin behind Poole's

sandy side-whiskers grow red with anger. He was one step away from having us detained. If that happened, what would happen to me? Barker may be able to sit like a jade Buddha during an interrogation, but I wasn't certain I could.

Cyrus Barker finally broke his silence. "There is more to this than a Scotland Yard matter, Terry. There are international considerations, and there are moral ones."

Poole stood there, looking down at Barker, with arms akimbo. Both men were so still that I was afraid to move, for fear of breaking the tableau. "Get out!" the inspector finally snapped. "Just get out, blast you. I cannot cover this up for you. This is a serious trial of our friendship, Cyrus, and you can get into a great deal of trouble over this."

Barker shot out the door, leaving me to dance around the inspector with my cast and notebook. I followed him out to the entrance, where we turned up our collars and opened our umbrellas before plunging out into the drizzle once more. The Guv looked over at me and I'm blessed if the fellow didn't have a look of satisfaction upon his face.

"Let's make our way to West India Dock Road, lad," he said. "That went better than expected."

10

⸻◆⸻

THE ESTABLISHMENT OF MR. JONAS COFFIN WAS
in a warehouse that had seen better days seven decades before. There was no sign over the door, but when Barker ac-
costed a passing stranger that was the door he pointed to.
Barker opened the door into a room illumined by a single
candle. Our advent brought a cry from the proprietor within,
who must have eyes like a rat.

"We's closed," he bellowed. "Don't open'll eight-firty
tonight."

Barker asked me for a half sovereign and tossed it
onto the table. The fellow snatched it up as quickly as it
landed.

Coffin was a dried-up skeleton of a man with a hooked
nose that looked as if it had been pasted on as a prank. He
might have been a stage version of Dickens's Scrooge. By
the candlelight, he'd been playing a one-man hand of cards,
but now that there was money to be made, he slid them
into the pocket of the greasy old pea jacket he wore.

"I am a private enquiry agent. My name is Barker."

"Yer, I hearda ya. What can I do for you, guv'nor?"

"Would I be correct that there was a death here a year ago?"

"'At's roight. Feller slipped his cable right here on the lines. Nat'ral causes it was ruled. Not a bad way to go, I reckon. Give me Fiddler's Green over Davy Jones's locker any day."

"Lines?" I asked.

"This is a penny hang, lad. Sailors pay a penny to spend the night hanging on lengths of rope stretched across the room."

"All night?" I asked. "Don't they sleep?"

"Of course they sleep," Coffin explained, "which is more than they'd do in some doss-house at twice the price. A sailor's feet might be on solid ground, but his guts is still a-rollin' with the waves. It's agony on him to lie in a real bed, but you just put him on one of my lines and he'll be right as rain. Sleeps like he's in his mother's arms, he does. And the sailor doesn't have to worry that he'd get his hard-earned wages nicked in his sleep, neither. I've got a belayin' pin handy and I'll nobble any suspicious character I come acrost. You see, gentlemen, Jonas Coffin is the sailor's friend."

Despite the proprietor's assurances, I was still a trifle confused. "How do they keep from falling off?"

"They's sailors, young-fella-me-lad. Every sailor worth his grog knows how to catch a kip leaning over the bow or in the rigging. They come by it natural like. And when one man moves, it sets them all swaying, just like the swell o' the seas. After one night on my lines, the sailing man has his land legs under him and is ready to spend the night with his missus again, if'n you get my meaning, sirs."

Barker had used up his supply of patience. "This fellow who died, was he a regular sailor?"

"Chinaman. Blue Funnel man, I reckon. Scrawny like all them fellas, but he walked in on his own two feet. He might've had a drink or two, but I've seen worse."

"The sailors don't mind sharing a line with a Chinaman?" I asked.

"Not at all. We're what you call cosmopolitan. We get all kinds. When I was a sailor, the only ones we refused to have aboard were women and Finns."

"Why Finns?"

"Bad luck," both he and Barker said at once, as if it was common knowledge. I let the matter drop.

"Was the sailor young or old?" Barker asked.

"Middling, far as I could tell. Thirties, maybe. Hard to say with Chinese, sometimes."

"You tended the lines all night—is that correct?"

"It is. Me and my trusty belaying pin. Sleeping's a waste with me, at my age. I throws a hammock up in the afternoons and get a good three hours kip. 'At'll do for the likes of Jonas Coffin."

"He was dead in the morning, then."

"Dead and stiff, and hanging over the line like he'd been carved that way, and not a scratch on him. He weren't shot nor stabbed nor coshed that anyone could see, not even Inspector Bainbridge, what investigated the case hisself. Natural causes, the coroner ruled. I got to speak at the inquest."

"I take it you had never seen the Chinaman before that night."

"Correct, Mr. Barker, and I don't forget faces."

"You've more than earned your half sovereign, Mr. Coffin."

The old sailor flashed a set of horrid teeth. "Well, you and I, we're men o' the world. Care for a tot?" He raised a stoneware jug which could only contain rum.

"I thank you," the Guv said, "but save the ration for your own health. Good day to you."

Outside again, Barker spoke. "I believe we shall find that the sailor slain in this building was the monk who escaped from the Xi Jiang Monastery with the book. His killer must have got here ahead of him, but before he was killed, the monk somehow got rid of the book. That brings the number of deaths in this case to at least six."

Our next stop was the chandler's shop in Pennyfields. The window was full of large coils of rope, ship's lamps, and a headless dummy wearing a sealskin jacket. When we stepped inside, Barker inhaled as if we were stepping into some fine restaurant. I sniffed the air myself. Hemp and creosote, salt and mustiness was all I could smell, but then I was a landsman. Seeing my employer, a former ship's captain, as he stroked a length of rope, made me wonder how much he missed the sea.

"Can I help you?" a woman's voice came from somewhere. It took me a moment to spot her. She had come through a curtain and was leaning against the counter. Were it not for the contralto voice, I'd have taken her for a child. She had a button nose, kohl-smeared eyes, and an air of impudence. Her hair was henna colored and looked as if it had been hacked off all around at the jaw. She wore a paisley shawl over a white blouse and large, hoop earrings. I recognized her as the girl in Bainbridge's drawing.

"We wish to speak to the proprietor," Barker said, removing his bowler hat. I followed suit.

"You're lookin' at her, ain't ya?" she said offhandedly.

For once, my employer was nonplussed.

"Isn't it rather unusual for a Romany woman to own a chandlery?" he asked.

"If it's any of your business, which it ain't, we don't exactly get together for tea, so I wouldn't know. It ain't usual to see two toffs in Pennyfields, neither, but you don't see me complaining."

I saw the Guv suppress a smile. This girl was sharp as a knife.

"I am an enquiry agent, miss, and I—"

"Public or private?"

"We are private enquiry agents."

"Hop it, then," the girl said suddenly. "I don't have to answer no questions. Leave, if you ain't buying."

This girl had brass, I'll give her that. She wasn't bad to look at, either.

Barker seemed to summon himself a moment, meditating or strategizing or communing with his Maker. After a moment he spoke again. "And if we were buying?"

She came down the counter closer to us. "That's different. You buy one item per question and I'll talk me head off."

"Very well." Barker looked through a selection of jack-knives on the counter and set one before her. "Tell me about your uncle's murder."

"Someone broke his neck for him a year ago on New Year's Day, around closing time. Police didn't do nothing, ruddy useless peelers. Said it was a burglary. Burglary, my bonnet. Nothing was taken."

Barker looked both ways, then moved over to a row of books and scooped them up. They were mostly nautical tomes and manuals, though I did spot a collection of sea stories. He set the first book down on the counter.

"Do you keep a log of the items you purchase from sailors?" he pursued.

"Course we do. We're not total fools."

He set down another volume. "Did you work here before your uncle died or did you come afterward?"

"I worked at Bryant and May's match factory, but I worked here as well now and then. Why should Uncle Lazlo hire someone when he can squeeze the work out of his only living relative, right?"

"Did you happen to notice a young Chinaman here around that New Year's Day? I suspect he might have been looking through these very books."

The girl thought for a moment. "Nah. Sorry. Can't recollect offhand. I wasn't here all the time, you see. Used to have a life, I did. Not like now. I'm about as dusty as these bleedin' books. I might as well hop up on that shelf you just emptied."

Barker set another book on top of the growing stack. "Is there a chance I can take a look at the log of incoming items?"

"Not a chance. Not for two boxfuls of musty books. Not for all the musty books in London."

"What about something more . . . expensive?" Barker

began to look about the shop. "Then can we call it square?"

"Now you're talkin'."

Barker walked slowly through the room, examining sextants, harpoons, and fishing nets. Finally he looked out the front window.

"The jacket in the window, lad. Bring it here."

I obeyed and went over to the window. I unbuttoned the sealskin jacket and brought it to my employer, leaving the headless dummy naked.

"It looks rather small," I pointed out as I handed it to him.

"You surely don't think I would wear this thing. I am purchasing it for you."

"Me!" I protested, but Barker had already thrown it over my shoulders. It was pure white, made of the pelts of baby seals. I didn't approve of killing the poor beasts just to make a coat, but I knew better than to protest in front of Barker. He was on a case and would not have cared if the coat were made from kittens.

The girl broke into a grin and even gave a whistle. She had very nice teeth, I noticed. "Oooh," she said to me. "Don't you look flash?"

"May I see the log now?" Barker asked her.

"Not so fast, your worship. Ain't seen as much as a sou yet. Three pound even for the coat; three, one and six for the rest. A girl's got to make a living."

"Three pounds for a coat?" I asked as I took the money from my pocket.

"Where else in London are you gonna find sealskin?"

"Thomas," Barker said, "pay the girl."

"I don't believe I caught your name," I said to her.

"Don't believe I threw it your way. It's Hestia Petulengro. Hettie to my friends. I don't number private detectives among me friends."

"The log!" Cyrus Barker boomed. His patience had come to an end.

"All right!" she bristled back at him. "Keep your shirt on! Is he always like this? You poor blighter. The log is back here."

She took a large book from behind the counter and set it in front of Barker. While he examined it, Hettie and I played involuntary peekaboo. I looked at her; she looked away. I looked at Barker and felt her eyes on me, then I looked up and it started all over again. I fancied half the East End might be in love with her.

"Here!" my employer said a minute later. "Luke Chow (D) *Ajax:* one sailors' kit; one knife; one book, Chinese. Taken in New Year's Day. What does the *D* stand for?"

Miss Petulengro seemed disposed to argue for another item, then changed her mind. "Deceased. My uncle often bought dead sailors' effects from the ships that came through, regular-like. I do remember when that book came in, because it was an English sailor, but the book was Chinese. Come to think of it, it was a funny little book, full of stick figures fighting and foreign letters."

"Do you have the sailor's name?"

"No, we don't ask. Not everything that comes in was purchased legally."

"What became of the book?"

"Uncle Lazlo sold it later that day. I remember him re-marking on it, wondering who'd buy such a thing."

"Did he say who purchased it?"

She shrugged.

"Have you ever heard of a Mr. K'ing?"

The girl suddenly went cold. She gathered her shawl about her. "Here now, there's no need to be bringing him into this."

"So you know of him."

"This is Limehouse, mister. He owns half the district."

"Did you know Inspector Bainbridge?"

"Oh, everyone knew old Bainy. He ran Limehouse like a machine. Bit rough if you rubbed him on the warp instead of the woof. He investigated my uncle's death."

"Do you get ruffians in here?" I spoke up, remembering the toughs I had seen in Bethnal Green.

"Not this side of Limehouse Causeway. This is triad territory, but I'm sure you know that."

"Did Inspector Bainbridge ever come back and question you about the case or mention any leads?" Barker asked.

"He'd check on me from time to time. Even made him a cuppa tea once, but I don't appreciate having policemen underfoot. Never did find my uncle's killer."

"You live over the shop, then."

"I own this whole building," she said with some pride.

"Your uncle gave it all to you in his will?"

"He did. Fair and square. Not that it's been a great and glorious thing, being a shopkeeper, I might add. Sometimes I wish I was carefree and working in the factory again. I'm just scrapin' by here, except for when private detectives come in and want questions answered."

"Agents," Barker corrected. "We are private enquiry agents. Now tell me, did you have a close relationship with your uncle?"

"Not especially close, no. I came to live with him about five years ago, after my parents died."

"What sort of fellow was he?" Barker asked.

"Oh, you know the type. All oily and smiling this side of the curtain and a regular tyrant behind it. Smack! 'Get me my dinner, girl.' Smack! 'These taters is cold!'"

"Where were you the night your uncle was killed?"

"Do you think I did it, then? Are you saying it was me?"

"Of course not," Barker assured the girl. "I meant to ask why were you not in the shop."

"It was New Year's Day. I was out with my friends. As I said, I used to have a life. I wasn't going to work no holiday just to add to his coffers."

"Did your uncle mention an appointment?"

"Sure he did. Eight o'clock appointment to get robbed and killed. I thought you might be a cut above the regular police. Your clothes are better, but these questions are weak stuff."

"Very well, Miss Petulengro. Are we square?" Barker reached up and grasped the brim of his hat, inclining a few degrees from the vertical. It was his interpretation of a sweeping bow. He is not as a rule demonstrative. "I thank you, miss, for your time. Come, Thomas."

We quitted the shop. I stole a final glance at the girl as we left. She smiled at me with satisfaction, but then she was several pounds richer. I'm sure there were many weeks she didn't make that much profit.

Outside, Barker huddled in an alleyway out of the wind and lit his pipe. It took a few matches to get it going and when he finally had it lit, he held up the matchbox. It read Bryant and May.

"They are the toughest girls in London, lad, the matchstick girls. They work hard and they entertain themselves boldly after hours. They are known for their impromptu fights away from the factory. Hair pulling, eye gouging, scratching. Miss Petulengro had a scar on her chin I'll wager she received in just such a fight."

"She's certainly bold," I said.

"She is that. I believe she is hiding something. She's intriguing under that red hair of hers."

"Intriguing, yes," I replied, still thinking of her.

"Not that kind of intriguing, Thomas. You are as quick to fall into love as Robby Burns. I was considering having you take Miss Petulengro to dinner and questioning her further, but now I am beginning to have doubts."

"I'll keep my wits about me, sir, I promise. But why didn't you question her more just now?"

"Because I would have to buy the entire shop to receive answers to the questions I have. It will be less expensive to feed her."

I had to admit, there was good sense in that.

11

———— ❈ ————

SOMETIMES THINGS FALL THROUGH THE CRACKS
for all our efforts. After the funeral, the visit to K Division,
Coffin's penny hang, and the more than fascinating half
hour in the company of Miss Hestia Petulengro, we had forgotten something important. Back in our residence near the
Elephant and Castle, our butler would have awakened from
his drug-induced sleep to find himself alone.

I have to say this for Jacob Maccabee. He has backbone.
Did he send word to the office and say the patient was
being neglected? No. He shaved and washed his face and
combed his hair. He changed out of his sleeping suit, and
when it became obvious that he could not get a pair of
trousers over his bandaged leg, he slit a perfectly good pair
and pinned them together after he got them on. Then, despite an aching limb, a pounding head, and Dr. Applegate's
admonitions, he attempted to go about his daily duties.
When Barker and I arrived about six o'clock, there was the
faithful servant, resplendent, preparing dinner, and pretty
much all in.

"What in blazes!" Barker thundered. "Get back in bed!"

"Sorry, sir," Mac said, toppling forward in a faint. We carried him to bed again.

Applegate arrived about an hour later. I was sure we were going to get a hiding with Mac dressed for work as he was, but he just shook his head at our unconscious manservant.

"Butlers make the worst patients," he informed us. "Sometimes we have to tie them to the bed. You'd think they would relax and enjoy a needful rest, but no. Someone might be pilfering the sherry."

Mac got a helping of laudanum for supper which left me to finish dinner, since Barker had a constitutional enmity to his own kitchen.

In my year of service, I had cooked a few meals for Barker. The previous year, in a cottage near Liverpool, I'd made rabbit stew with only a few bits of fur remaining in the dish. He hadn't complained, but then, he wouldn't. Now I was in a respectable kitchen and I wanted to prepare something edible, possibly even delicious. After all, Mac had just rather shown me up in the duty department, and I was already in disgrace after nearly losing Harm.

I learned something that night: it is not easy to prepare a meal one-handed. A one-armed man has difficulty cutting a loaf of bread or setting a table. Luckily, Etienne Dummolard was a genius at creating meals that could be served without much preparation. As Barker's chef, he had been coming here for years, commanding the kitchen in the mornings and leaving meals for us the rest of the day while he worked at his restaurant, *Le Toison d'Or*. At six thirty, when I called the Guv down for dinner, the table was full of silver, steaming dishes, and a good cobwebby bottle of *vin rouge* I found in the cellar. Barker chewed his way through the meal without comment. He ate the bread I'd cut, he drank the wine I'd opened and poured, and he ate the meal I'd slaved over as placidly as a Guernsey cow would chew his evening cud. After that, he left the room without a word. I was beginning to think Mac's position a little more difficult than I had been led to believe. The other thing I hadn't counted on was that I would be cleaning up afterward, with only one good arm.

When I was finally done, I locked up for the night and turned down the gas. I went upstairs and changed into my night attire, then I lay back on my pillow and stared at the ceiling with its rows of alternating beams and plaster. I was done in and it wasn't even eight thirty. I picked up my Mencius, which was such a sleep-inducing agent it might have been used on Mac instead of the laudanum. The next I knew, there was another commotion downstairs.

I jumped from the bed again. An hour and a half had elapsed, according to my clock. I looked about for some weapon and realized there was nothing in my room that would serve. Perhaps an irate assistant would be enough. I went downstairs.

"Thomas!" Etienne Dummolard greeted me from the back door. Four large suitcases stood at his feet.

"Etienne! What are you doing here?"

"What does it look like I'm doing here, imbecile. I'm moving in!"

I had never felt so relieved in my life. Dummolard could take over Mac's duties. I wouldn't have to cook another blighted meal.

"But what of the restaurant?" I asked. "What of Madame Dummolard?"

"She is here with me, of course!"

The back door flew open and in stepped Madame Dummolard, in a traveling cloak and hat, six feet in height and suitably proportioned.

"Mon petit chou!" she cried, and surged forward to plant a kiss on both of my cheeks. I might have restrained her, if only for the sour look Etienne gave me during the demonstration, but Madame is unable to be restrained. She prattled on in a stream of French so quick I only caught every tenth word, and fussed over the state of my arm.

"It is good to see you again, madame, but why are you here?" I managed to get in.

"Ah, Thomas, when M'sieur Dummolard told me the grievous state of affairs, I said, 'Mireille, you must go and do what you can, you and your big, strong husband.'" The latter was directed to Etienne with a caress on his stubbly chin, which cheered his mood somewhat.

"This is the domain of M'sieur Mac?" she asked, reaching the front hall, with me still in her clutches.

"Yes, but I don't think—"

She pushed open the door and walked to the bed where Mac lay, still in his suit and insensible from the opium. She clucked her tongue at the poor fellow's injuries. Then she summed up.

"I am ready," she announced. "I believe I can do good work here."

"What kind of work is that, madame?" I asked.

"Ozkippur," she announced solemnly.

"I beg your pardon?"

"I will be your *ozkippur.*"

"Oh, I see. I don't know if Mr. Barker wants a house-keeper, but I am sure—"

"They arrive tomorrow morning."

"Who does?"

"My girls, of course. A maid, a nurse, and a char. I can get more if we need them."

"But Mr. Barker must first agree to it. I mean, who shall be paying for it?"

"That does not matter at all. Etienne will pay for it all," she said breezily.

"What?" Dummolard demanded behind me, and before I could move I was being buffeted between the two of them as they commenced a rapid flurry of French like volleys of gunfire. Barker must have been able to hear all this two floors up but was too sage to come down. The fight ended as abruptly as it had begun, though I wasn't sure who won the argument.

"Our room, it is up on the first floor, no?"

"We have a guest bedroom there, yes. It is at the end of the hall."

"Take me there. Etienne, stop standing there looking sour. Make yourself useful. Carry the luggage."

I led Madame Dummolard to the guest room, down the hall from my own. It was clean and serviceable, but it was obvious that it lacked a woman's touch.

"It will do," she pronounced. "We have had worse, have we not, Etienne? I shall bring some things to make this room pretty. Put the first of the suitcases down there, Etienne. *Non, non,* not there, *cheri.* Over here."

I left them to it and fled the room. I made it all of about

two steps, for in order to return to my room I must pass the staircase that led to Barker's aerie. There was a pair of slippers on the stairs, slippers with feet in them. The rest of my employer was cloaked in shadow. I made out his form, sitting on one of the steps with his elbows resting on his knees and his fingers knit together in front of his face.

"Lad."

I came up a few steps. "Yes, sir?"

"Is that *she*?"

"Madame Dummolard? Yes, sir."

"What is she doing here?"

I explained what I took to be the situation. Afterward he sat for almost a full minute in thought.

"I suppose it solves the situation, after a fashion," he said, "though it is not without problems of its own. I do not have time to interview servants. We shall try it for now. I do hope Madame is not talkative in the mornings. I detest vivacity in the morning. Good night."

As it turned out, we saw nothing of her during breakfast. Three servants arrived that morning, one to look after Mac, one to clean the house, and the third to wait upon us. The char was a stout and hardworking Irish girl, and the nurse was English, but the maid was very French. I waited for the impending disaster, but she served breakfast without a word and Barker could not fault her anything. When he went out to look at his garden, Madame emerged from the kitchen and spoke to the maid in whispered French. Then they disappeared before the Guv returned. We struggled into our coats and left, like any other morning.

•   •   •

"Lad," Barker said from behind his desk once we were seated, "I need you to go to Fleet Street this morning. Visit the General Register Office and take down whatever information you can on all deaths occurring around early January 1884. See if there are any unusual deaths in the days before and after New Year's. Go to *The Times* and compare your facts to the reports in the back issues. Have you got that?"

"Yes, sir," I said stolidly, but inside, I felt it was the best possible news I could hear.

"Have yourself some lunch while you're out," he said, crossing to his smoking cabinet for the first pipe of the day. "We cannot have you digging among all those musty records on an empty stomach."

Outside, I hailed a hansom cab, glad to quit the office. Employment and employers are good things on the whole, but there's nothing better than to slip the knot and get away for a while on some errand or other.

A half hour later I was settled in a room inside that large pile of graying stones they call the Register Office, which contained the information of every birth, death, and marriage in the great capital of the empire. Here, in this impersonal hall, one's entrance into the world was carefully recorded, as well as one's exit. Here one's joining in marriage was noted, and generations of Londoners can trace their ancestry through the aging pages of endless record books here, shelf after shelf and row upon row. I could see why some people would find this boring, going over dull records with their officious jargon, but I couldn't help seeing what was really recorded: the miracle of birth, the mystical union of two people, and the eternal mystery of death.

I love research. Cyrus Barker's idea of a fine time might be grappling a felon to the ground and clicking the darbies on his wrists, but I much prefer the collecting of cold, hard facts in libraries and public record offices until I've methodically built up a mountain of evidence that will prove someone's guilt.

I took down the volume of deaths for December 1883 and January 1884, very conscious of the passage of time. December 1883 had been a few months after my sentence was completed and I had just come to London. It seemed a long time ago, now. Had Quong's killer been waiting an entire year like a coiled spring ready for the text to show itself before striking again? Surely the book could not be that vital, could it? It looked to me to be little more than a few scribbles and stick figures.

I copied everything into my notebook and as I copied, I read. Quong had been found dead on the second of January, 1884. Quong, Chow, and Petulengro had all died within a few days of each other. They had died in various manners, however, and some might have been considered natural causes. Quong had been shot; Chow had passed away mysteriously on the line in Coffin's penny hang; and Petulengro had died from a blow to the neck during a robbery. The common thread running through all the deaths was the location, Limehouse, and the inspector in charge of the investigations, Nevil Bainbridge.

I began investigating other murders that had occurred around the New Year. Lord Saltire had passed away in Park Lane but only after a protracted illness. Two children died stillborn that night, and one poor urchin had died of exposure, for it had been bitterly cold. There had been a woman stabbed to death in Whitechapel, but her killer, who turned out to be her common-law husband, had been apprehended. Lastly, a sailor in Millwall, the Isle of Dogs, had died in his bed. There was no need to record any of these cases in my notebook, as they had no bearing on the case, or so I thought until I was in the act of closing the book and my eye ran across something.

I pulled the book open again and almost frantically flipped through the pages. Yes, my eyes had not been deceiving me. The last fellow, Alfred Chambers, had passed away on the second of January of renal failure in the company of his wife. People die of kidney failure every day, I'm sure, but Mr. Chambers had been a first mate aboard the *Ajax*. I took down the entire report, though the death did not occur in Limehouse and was not investigated by Bainbridge.

Happy that I had uncovered something of possible interest, I made my way over to *The Times* and was soon in the back issues room, looking for reports of the killings. I only found two. One read "Chinese Found Shot in Limehouse Reach," while the other read "Chandler Dies During Robbery." Apparently Chinamen dying in penny hangs and men having kidney failure were not considered newsworthy.

I closed my notebook and devoted my attention to the idea of lunch. I found a pub in Fleet Street where all the journalists went, and had a nice steak and kidney pie and a cup of coffee. On the way back, I dawdled for a while in the bookshops of Charing Cross Road. Afterward, I went back to the office and found myself crowded on the doorstep by Inspector Poole. I opened the door for him, and he took one of the chairs in front of Barker's desk, while I sat at my own. Barker seemed not to have moved since I left. Goodness knows what he had done or if he had eaten lunch. If he kept this up, Jenkins would have to dust him.

"Terry."

"Cyrus," Poole said. He looked as tight as a coiled spring. "I thought I would tell you that we're letting Ho go free tomorrow."

"I see," Barker said. "There was no reason for having arrested him at all."

"You know what sort of odd characters go into his place," Poole said. "Anarchists, socialists, communists, exiles, Lascars, Orientals—"

"Enquiry agents," I put in.

"Lad," Barker warned. "Ho is not responsible for who walks in his door, Terence. He does not advertise in radical newspapers or cater to criminals. He runs an honest tearoom."

"I have information that he has close ties with a criminal named Mr. K'ing. In fact, Commissioner Henderson believes it is possible that Ho *is* Mr. K'ing."

Barker grunted. "That will be news to both of them. I never thought I would credit Henderson with too much imagination."

"We've taken good care of him," Poole insisted. "Better than most foreigners by a long chalk. Of course, anything you can do to help us in our enquiry would be helping him, as well."

"I see," the Guv said. "You want me to do your work for you, then you'll release him."

Poole frowned. "Look, Cyrus, I don't think you understand how close you are to being arrested yourself. The old man's considering it even now. There are many at the Yard who think that you killed Bainbridge yourself, you and the nipper here."

"Nipper?" I interrupted. "There's no need to be—"

"Look, Cyrus," Poole went on, as if I weren't in the room. "I'm up against it. You have no idea what sort of pressure I'm under to solve the case. I need help. I thought we might share information."

"'Share,' is it?" Barker asked. I noticed his Scot's accent always got a bit thicker when his blood was up. "You mean, you tell me what I already know, while I give you what has taken me days to uncover?"

For once, Poole smiled. "Something like that." It broke the tension. We all chuckled over it. Even Barker gave up his stony reserve.

"What thought you of Bainbridge's blotter?"

Poole tugged at his side-whiskers. "If what Bainbridge thought is correct, all the deaths that occurred just after New Year's may have been the work of one killer, though he didn't know who it was. We have your assistant, Quong; the Chinese sailor Chow; and the Gypsy who ran a chandler's shop, whose name I won't even try to pronounce. Beyond the fact that they were all foreigners, the only connection they seem to have had was a book. The book, the book, the bloody book! Didn't you say in court it was a boxing manual? Who kills three people over a boxing manual?"

"It's a rather special manual, Terence," Barker explained. "It teaches, for one thing, a way to disrupt the body's internal functions, killing someone without a sign."

Poole grunted in disbelief. "You mean like the Chinaman, Chow, dead on the line without a scratch."

"Precisely."

"If such a thing existed, it could change my work considerably. How would we know a common heart attack from murder?"

"It gets worse," Barker said, crossing his arms. "Death need not be instantaneous. With the training from the book, one could disrupt a system—let us say the circulative system—of someone in the morning merely by touch, and that person could die that night after a normal day's activity. Or the next day or a week later."

"Fantasy," Poole scoffed. "It's all Chinese bugaboo. I don't believe a word of it."

"Admittedly, I only read it in the book. I wouldn't believe it myself without more proof."

"I might have that proof," I muttered.

They both looked at me, and it was a moment before the Guv spoke. "Explain."

"Well, sir, I came across another murder, I think. It happened the second of January. A sailor named Chambers was found in his bed, dead from kidney failure. The inquest the next day ruled natural causes, but Chambers wasn't just anyone. He was a first mate aboard the *Ajax*. I think he might have spent his first night ashore at Coffin's with Chow. Chow might have given the book to Chambers for safekeeping, warning him that if anything happened to him to get rid of the book quickly.

"Chambers got rid of his effects the next day at Petulengro's after Chow was found dead. I've got it all in my notebook and was going to type it up for you."

"See that I get a copy," Poole said.

"Certainly."

There was a pause, and I got that feeling along my spine that things were about to get tense again.

Poole took in a bushelful of air and blew it out. "So, where's the book, Cyrus?"

"Don't ask me that, Terry."

"Where is the book?"

"Are you asking me for Scotland Yard or the Foreign Office?"

"The book is evidence in several murders now. We must have it."

"As you said, it's just a book."

"Then give me the blasted thing!"

Barker tilted his head back, as if looking up at the ceiling. "As I said before, I don't have it to give. It is not currently in my possession."

The inspector pulled one of Barker's cigars from the box on his desk and bit the end off savagely before lighting it. Blowing out a puff of smoke, he leaned back in his seat. "I don't believe you."

"You know I deplore lying," the Guv said. "A man's word should be his bond."

"That doesn't mean you wouldn't lie if it were important."

"I am not lying to you, Terry. I do not have it."

"But you did," Poole insisted.

"I did."

"What did you do with it?"

"I gave it to a Chinaman."

"Quit playing games with me, Cyrus!" Poole snapped.

"There are over five hundred Chinamen in Limehouse. Which one did you give it to?"

Barker said nothing.

"You know there's only so much I can do to protect a friend," the inspector went on. "If the Foreign Office told me to tear apart your offices, I'd have to do it. If they said, 'Toss this fellow into Wormwood Scrubs,' I wouldn't be slipping you a key."

Barker's silence was worse than any words that might have been said.

"Have it your own way, then. If you want things official, then official they shall be." Poole got up and stubbed out the cigar in the ashtray on the desk. "Your cigars are stale," he complained.

On his way out, he buttonholed me. "I want a copy of that report. In fact, I want a copy of all the reports you found."

"They are a matter of public record," I retorted.

"You're as bad as he is!" Poole bellowed and went out the front door with a slam that rattled the Constable hanging in our waiting room.

Jenkins gave a low whistle from the outer room. "Hope he's off duty soon," he pronounced. "There's a fella what needs a stiff drink."

Barker picked a cigar from the box and ran it under his nose. "They cannot possibly be stale. They are from Lewis of St. James's." He emptied the ashtray into the bin under his desk. "Now, where were we?"

"Thumbing our noses at Scotland Yard."

"Don't be cheeky. Type up those reports, there's a good lad."

As I inserted the first sheet of paper into the Hammond, a thought occurred to me. I knew who had the book. The only two Chinamen he'd spoken to that he knew were Ho and Old Quong. I'd been by the Guv's side whenever he spoke with Ho, but I had been on the table when he had spoken with Old Quong. There was no doubt about it in my mind. The bonesetter had the text.

12

———◦———

WHAT CAN YOU INFER," BARKER ASKED ME, "from the deaths of Luke Chow and Chambers?"

"Well, sir," I said, "both men appeared to have arrived at the hang in good condition, so they must have been killed by whoever is after the book."

"And yet—" Barker prompted.

"And yet the killer must have already had knowledge from the book, in order to kill them in that manner. So what did he need the book for?"

"Where did he get the knowledge in the first place?" Barker continued, ignoring my question.

"Perhaps he read it in the monastery. Perhaps he was a monk."

"Not necessarily. I had the opportunity to examine the book the evening we first received it. There was a page missing, a very important page, I believe. If Luke Chow were going to attempt to sell the book to someone, he would have to give them a page from the text in order to prove its authenticity. Let us say Luke Chow came across the text in the archives and alerted someone willing to pay for it. It's possible he let him in late one night and they decided to steal it. They had some sort of falling out, after the two monks were killed. Chow ran off with the book and hired himself aboard the *Ajax* bound for London. But the murderer discovered Chow's destination, arrived on a faster ship, and was waiting for him."

"That's a long way to come just to get hold of a book. Why bother?"

"You have hit it squarely, Thomas. Why does he need the book? What is his purpose? Answer that and we'll find our man."

"Is it really true that he can kill someone just by touching him?"

"According to the text, it's more than touching. It creates vibrations that disrupt energy in the body."

"Are you going to keep the text?" I asked, then wished I hadn't. Sometimes I speak without thinking, despite all the warnings the Reverend Spurgeon gives us about guarding one's tongue.

"I'd sooner keep adders in our bathhouse."

"But you do still have it," I said after a pause.

"Now, lad, you heard me say that I do not have it."

"I thought you were just putting off Scotland Yard. So I suppose Dr. Quong has it."

"I didn't say that."

"Then who has the book?"

"You're starting to sound like Poole," Barker said, leaning back in his chair. "Best not to ask, Thomas. If one doesn't know, one cannot be forced to say under oath or torture. Get to work on those reports now. I am most anxious to read about the death of the mate from the *Ajax*."

I was just beginning my report, intent on getting every jot and tittle down just right, when in the outer office Jenkins gave a sudden cry.

"Sir!"

Before I even moved I heard the soft swipe of a pistol clearing leather. Barker raised his Colt revolver as if from out of nowhere and set it down on his desk. The Guv has a holster built in underneath his chair. What passed for remarkable in other people was a necessary commonplace in his little world. He knew someone dangerous might come in, and naturally he would require a pistol quickly. Things in drawers were clumsy to get in and out, but a holster under the seat was sensible. I didn't have one and had to retrieve my Webley from one of the upper drawers of my rolltop desk. At least I had had the foresight not to lock it.

They came in then in a leisurely fashion, three of them: a big man in front and two smaller behind. Street toughs. They wore sailors' bell-bottomed trousers and hobnailed boots that clicked so loudly on the wood floor I feared for it. The ones behind wore pea jackets with knit caps, while the leader was clad in a long black coat of waxed cotton. Under it he wore a fancy waistcoat and a silk neckerchief. The large expanse of shirt between tie and waistcoat was not especially clean. He wore a brown bowler with the lowest crown I'd ever seen, and when he removed it, I saw that the sides of his head had been shaved, leaving a bushy brown strip down the center and a pair of thick side-whiskers that seemed to hang like pothooks over his ears.

"Here," he said in a raspy voice. "There's no need for

breaking out the ironware, Push. I've come to see if we can transact some business."

"Patrick Hooligan," Barker said in greeting. "And how is the Hooley Gang?"

"It hain't been a good season, but things is looking up." Hooligan eased his bulk into the leather chair in front of the desk and crossed a boot across his knee, revealing a brass toe cap polished to a high gloss. "Not that I'm complaining, mind. May I?"

Barker pushed the visitor's cigar case toward him an inch. "Help yourself."

"Always liked a good smoke," the tough said, coming up with a large knife. I leaned forward, my hand on my pistol, while one of the boys eyed me threateningly and reached into his own pocket. I thought mayhem might occur. Instead, Hooligan sliced the end of his cigar off and put the knife back in his coat. I noted he didn't offer his subordinates anything. Just then I realized who they were. These were the lads I'd seen the morning I had been chased out of Limehouse. This man must be their leader.

"Business, you say?" Barker asked, after the tough got his cigar going.

"Yer. Got anyfing to drink 'round here?"

"The Rising Sun is around the corner."

"The street says you're a bar of iron," Hooligan said around the cigar. "Can't be bent. Reg'lar churchgoer. That's all right. Got no use for it meself, but I can work with it. I got what you might call a business proposition."

"Have you now? I'm listening."

"Word in the East End is that you came into a bit o'

property afore some other blokes did. Blokes who've been huntin' it for months. Now if you was to have it—and, mind, I ain't saying you do, but if you did—what might yer be planning to do with it?"

"First of all, Mr. Hooligan, let me say that the property you speak of is not in my possession."

"Naturally," Hooligan said.

"But if it were mine to do with as I wish, I would return it to the monastery in China from which it was taken."

"Having made no profit on it at all?" our guest demanded, clearly aghast at the thought. "You've been awastin' too much time in church, m'lad. You're a straight arrow and a scientific fighter, but you got no head for commerce. What'll you get out of it, I ask yer? Not enough to pay your scrawny clerk in the front room or your scrawny 'sistant in this one. They're undernourished, is what. Pathetic."

I bristled at the remark, but the conversation continued without my opinions.

"And look here, unless you take it yourself, how many eyes'll see it before it reaches China again? If it ever does, which I doubt. You may think you have Limehouse sewn up, but it's still a big world out there."

"I've got associates in China," Barker said, "who will safely get it back to the place from whence it came."

"That's as may be, but you still have to get it there. I seriously doubt it's gonna be easy even to get it outta London Town."

"What have you heard?"

"Enough. There's a book. Dunno what it's about or what it looks like, but someone's willin' to kill people in order to lay hands on it. The Chinese government wants it, the Foreign Office wants it. Scotland Yard wants it, and Mr. K'ing wants it. I find that all rather interesting, as a business-man, you understand. Rumor says half a dozen people have been killed over it. Why, there's only twenty or thirty people murdered in all of London in a year. That's a powerful lot of killing to find one book."

"And how are you involved?"

"I'm involved, Push, because it's my territory. My *new* territory. You see, I've begun expanding on the north side of the river."

"You're a Surrey man from the south side," Barker said. "Mr. K'ing will not like it."

"K'ing doesn't worry me. He's all mirrors and smoke. Got himself a reputation among the Blue Funnel crowd and a good racket goin', everyone tithin' reg'lar to him like he was some kinda church, but it's a good thing I'm a charita-ble man, else it would be a rough time for heathen foreign-ers dockside. *All* of them, if you get my meaning."

"Speaking hypothetically, how many men could you lay hands on for such an action?" Barker asked.

"The Chinks ain't exactly made themselves welcome here. I could get upwards of two hundred in a day, three if I'm willing to extend myself. Got friends in Liverpool and Manchester, I do."

"But no plans."

"None yet," the gang leader said, dumping an inch of ash in the ashtray on Barker's desk. "Not until I talked to you."

"So what is the proposition?"

"I want to broker a deal. I'll go to K'ing and say you're willing to hand over the book, if the Chinese government chokes up enough of the ready to suit us. Who knows? K'ing might even put forth the money himself and hope for compensation from the empress later. Then he can go back to Peking and live like a lord the rest of his life."

"Leaving Limehouse to be looked after by you and your associates."

Hooligan grinned. One of his teeth was gold. "The people there'll need protection, of course, and they're already used to payin' for it. It would be a pity to just waste it. It's the law of supply and demand."

"You've thought this out well," Barker stated, his fingers tented in front of him.

"Well, I ain't had me much book learnin', but I got smarts. Got to survive in the streets."

"So, Mr. Hooligan, what is to keep me from merely going and brokering the deal with K'ing myself and cutting you out entirely?"

"Glad you asked, and, by the way, this is information I am givin' you for free, which you may not live to hear again, so pay attention. Word is that old K'ing is layin' for you. Don't know what it is you done to set him off, but set off he is. He's been spendin' money like water preparing for the New Year's festival next week, but some of my informants tell me it ain't goin' to be the usual entertainment."

"Talent?" Barker asked, with one of his cold smiles.

"Circus freak show, if you ask me."

"I see. Thank you for the tip."

"Now what about my proposition?"

"I'm sorry. I shall have to decline."

Hooligan knocked off his cigar ash again. "Shoulda expected it. You know you won't get penny on the pound if you give it to the government, nor none of the credit, neither."

"I realize that."

Hooligan turned his head toward his subordinate who stood by the window acting as lookout. "Hey, Benny, what's that word that means you do things for the public good and not for money?"

"Altruistic."

"That's the word. You are altruistic, Push, and as a citizen of metropolitan London, I'm glad you're looking out for my welfare. But you got no head for business. When you've failed and gone, I'll have to buy these offices and turn them into something useful like a public house or a gin shop."

"I've no doubt you shall turn a profit," the Guv stated. "I thank you for the tip and hope you are not offended at my declining your offer."

"You know old Patrick Hooligan. Always has another card up his sleeve. I owe you a bit o' thanks anyway."

"How so?"

"For involving old Bainy. Now that he's dead, the Reach is wide open. All the boundaries is gone, and that Scotland Yard prig—what's his name?"

"Do you mean Inspector Poole?"

"That's the man. Poole is too busy trying to find the killer to mind the store. There's enough smash and grab goin' on to make K'ing and me both rich men. But with Bainy gone, it's a cinch one of us is eventually going to get greedy, and devil take the hindmost, if you get my meaning."

"I see."

"Look, if you change yer mind, just stop by the Elephant and Castle of an evening. One o' my boys'll be there. C'mon, lads, I'm parched. Let's go over to the Sun for a whiskey."

"Thank you again for the warning," Barker said as the man rose from his chair.

"Anything for a white man," Hooligan said. "It's us or them, or to put it more plainly, it's us, period."

They clicked and scraped their way out. Jenkins came in from the outer room while Barker dumped the contents of his ashtray into the dustbin under his desk for the second time in an hour.

"Look at the state of this floor," Jenkins complained.

"Interesting fellow," I remarked, as I slid the pistol back into my drawer.

"Indeed."

"What was that he meant about the Elephant and Castle?"

"It is his base of operations."

"It's practically on our doorstep," I pointed out.

"Aye, it is."

"You know the thought occurs to me that he might have shot Bainbridge himself, and we're blaming someone for his death who left London months ago. It's awfully convenient. He could also have come from the Elephant and Castle and tried to burgle our house."

Barker nodded. "Very devious, lad," he said, leaning over and holstering the gun under his chair. "Let us leave before we are interrupted again. Have you got that address in Millwall?"

"Yes, sir."

"Then you are free to go. It is your half day, after all. I shall pay a visit to Chambers's widow."

Barker always knows how to twist the knife. "I've got nothing going on, sir. May I join you?"

"As you wish."

The widow Chambers lived in a row of brick houses on Mellish Street where every house was identical to the next. If we hadn't had the exact address, we would never have found her.

"Mrs. Chambers?"

The door had opened and Mrs. Chambers was holding a wiggling infant in a blanket, while behind her, several dirty-faced children were sticking their heads around for a peek at the visitors and talking to each other.

"Mrs. Chambers as was," she said. "It's Mrs. Lynn now. Who wants to know?" The woman turned around abruptly and bawled behind her. "Will you shut up back there? Can't you see I'm a-talkin' ter gentlemen?"

"We are private enquiry agents, madam," Barker said, "investigating several murders that may have been related. One of them was your late husband."

"But he weren't kilt," she insisted, wiping a strand of hair out of her eye and hefting the child higher with her knee. "His kidneys gave out."

"True, madam, but another crewman from the *Ajax* died the night before, also apparently from natural causes. It is suspicious."

"'Ere now. You two ain't from the assurance companies, trying to put the screw on my husband's money, are you?"

"Not at all, madam, I assure you. We're investigating another case entirely. I only have a few questions."

She thought, as well as she could while holding the

baby, which had begun to whimper. "I dunno. I got on with me life."

"It is good that you have, madam. But, just a few questions, in his memory?"

I admit, it was an imposition. Who knew what pandemonium was going on behind that door? I fancy she might have been a beauty once, years ago, before the bloom had gone off her, when she'd gone from being Chambers's best girl to Mother. The years, the poverty, the grind, and, of course, her first husband's death had all taken their toll.

"Very well," she told Barker, in the same way she must give in to a child's request. "But make it quick, please. This un's 'ungry."

"When your husband returned from his last trip to China, did he seem at all secretive?"

"Yes, he did. Said some Chinaman on board had died from the ship. I thought he was carrying on a bit, I mean, he worked around 'em alla time, but he never chummed up with one afore. Said he 'ad some business to attend to, oh so important like. 'Susan, I 'as business to attend to.' I gave him an earful, out drinking our money away with his mates at night, and now he 'as business in the day, leaving me with a household o' brats. 'Maybe I 'as business to attend to myself,' I says. 'Y'ever think o' that?' But 'e wouldn't back down this time. That weren't like my Alf. 'E generally backed down."

"So, did he transact his business?"

"He did. Then he came back with flowers for me. Musta sold something to have enough for a bit o' flowers. I'd cleaned 'im out afore 'e left. Never trust a sailor with money, they go through it like water. Anyway—hush, child—I wasn't gonna let 'im get off with buying me hothouse flowers 'stead o' tellin' me where 'e went. It might be dangerous."

"What did he say?"

"He didn't say nothing. That weren't like 'im, neither. He shut up tight and I couldn't get nothing out of 'im. Went to bed mad, we did. That was the worse thing. We went to bed mad and 'e never woke up again."

"Did he make any sound during the night?"

"He cried out in the middle o' the night and said a word or two in his sleep, but never woke up. I could tell 'e was ill, but I didn't know what was wrong or what to do. Then 'is kidneys failed 'im, and the blood, oh lands, it was everywhere. Soaked the bed so bad it couldn't be cleaned. Had to throw it out. Nasty, terrible way for my Alfred to die. No dignity. Hush, you!"

The latter was directed toward the child in her arms, who was alternately wailing and blubbering. Mrs. Chambers—or rather, Mrs. Lynn—seemed to care not a whit that her youngest was crying. Her mind was back on the events surrounding her first husband's death.

"'Ere now," she said. "Are you saying there is some connection between Alf's death and the Chinaman's?"

"It is possible."

"Natural causes, they said. You think they're wrong?"

"That, too, is possible. It's certainly strange for two men to die of natural causes within twenty-four hours of their arrival in England."

The woman juggled her baby. "Keep me informed. I may have to speak with my solicitor. Alf didn't leave me much besides brats. I deserve some compensation. I figure the Blue Funnel can afford it."

"No doubt."

By this time, the infant had gone from mewling to full-throated screams. Barker judged he'd gotten what he came for and began to back away. Just then the woman turned the baby around and I was never so shocked in my life. The baby was Oriental.

"Thank you, madam. We'll let you get back to your bairns."

We walked a few streets. I tried to keep silent, but I couldn't. "I thought she said her married name was Lynn."

"Ling, not Lynn."

"Why would she marry a Chinaman, sir?"

"They have a reputation among East End women for being good husbands. They work hard, don't drink, and rarely beat their wives."

"But socially, sir—"

Barker gave a short cough that passed for a chuckle. "This is the East End, Thomas, not Kensington. People do what they can to survive."

"All those children and then a little Chinese brother," I mused.

"I'm sure there are a number of pastors willing to solemnize such a union, but if I may say it, lad, you're still rather naive. Many of the unions in this area are common law only, and some families have a farrago of children."

We had passed into West Ferry Road, talking of East-West relations when our minds were suddenly brought forcibly back to the case. A couple of Asian roughs, looking no more than eighteen, came running down the street, chasing each other in high spirits. They barreled into us and would have continued had the Guv not laid hands on the second one. It was one of the oldest dodges in London. The second was a pickpocket, and Barker caught the hand in his coat. That might have been the end of it, but the second snaked his thin leg around his companion and laid a round-house kick that caught my employer in the chest. Barker staggered back into a ragged beggar seated against a wall. The latter, in a shapeless coat and hat, put his hands up to ward off my falling employer, but the two men fell over each other. The youths, free again, ran down the street.

"Hey!" I cried. "Come back here!"

"No harm done," Barker said, rising and dusting himself off, setting the beggar and his cup as they were. I knew what the Guv would ask before he said it, and dropped a shilling into the cup.

"Dratted pickpockets," I grumbled. "The town is rife with them."

"That is too much of a coincidence for mere pickpockets, lad," Barker said. "I think it more likely to be another attempt by Quong's killer to lay hands upon the text."

13

BARKER BLEW THE STEAM OFF A CUP OF COCOA. The heavens over the waterfront had opened up again and we had taken refuge in a confectioner's shop. There were no public houses in sight, and the shop afforded some degree of comfort and respectability. The cocoa warmed me better than a pint of bitter could, but the sight of Barker sipping on his cup of Fry's was certainly a novel one. As a rule, he did not care for sweets.

"What did you think about Poole's theory that Ho is Mr. K'ing?" I asked.

"It is erroneous but not entirely preposterous. Ho has always run deep. There is an underworld in China of boxers and bodyguards and secret schools of martial training and Ho has always been involved in it."

"How did you meet Ho, sir, if I may ask?"

Barker put down his mug and wiped his mustache. "It was during the Chinese Civil War. Hong Xiuquan, leader of the rebellion, was out to destroy the monasteries at the time. He believed in a mangled form of Christianity, with himself at the right hand of God. Like most fellows my age, I joined as a soldier. One day, we were marching through a village outside Yangan when we came upon an army of rebels set- ting fire to a temple and killing the monks. Now, General Gordon was a Christian but he couldn't stand by and watch a group of monks being slaughtered, even if they were Bud- dhists. He led us into the fray. What we didn't know was that there was a second army behind the monastery.

"We fought all day and most of the night. There were heavy casualties on both sides. We had rifles and bayonets to their spears and arrows, but there was plenty of smoke from the burning monastery, and we fought at close quarters. By the end of the night, between my wounds and sheer exhaus- tion, I could hardly hold my rifle. I wandered among a sea of corpses, blood up to the horse's bridle, as Revelation says, and the only living man in sight was a monk coming toward me with a spear in his hand. When he got close enough, he threw the spear at me. I ducked, amazed that he'd done it, after I'd just tried to save his monastery. What I didn't know was that a wounded rebel was standing behind me with a broad sword, preparing to hack off my head. The spear caught him full in the throat. After all this time, I can still picture the look of surprise on the fellow's face.

"The monk was Ho, of course. His head was shaven and he wore a long saffron robe splashed with gore, but you would have recognized him. He was only in his twenties, but I was not more than seventeen, myself. He put his foot on the chest of the freshly killed rebel soldier and pulled out the spear. We stood and watched the monastery burn. His first words to me were, 'Perhaps this is a sign that I was not meant to be a monk.'"

I smiled at that image, and then asked, "What shall we do about Mr. K'ing?"

"There is nothing for it, lad. We shall have to beard the fellow in his den."

"Perhaps Ho could furnish an introduction."

"That would compromise Ho and possibly endanger him. Surely this fellow has a dwelling in Limehouse and an office where he conducts business. There must be someone who knows where he lives."

"Dr. Quong?" I asked.

"Quong is an honorable man. I would not feel right about approaching him with such a request."

"Jimmy Woo, then."

"Excellent. I believe he is the very man. As an interpreter, he must travel all over Limehouse. I believe the rain has stopped. Let us go to the Asiatic Aid Society and see if we can find him."

The Asiatic Aid Society was an organization much like the more-well-known Strangers' Home, whose purpose was to care for aged or infirmed Eastern sailors who had found themselves washed up on our Western shores. Located in East India Dock Road, the building may once have been the mansion of an admiral in the days of Napoleon and Wellington. Now its halls were given over to aging lascars in the early stages of dementia and sad, neglected-looking Chinamen in bath chairs. There was a smell in the air of mold and dry rot, Asian food, and the sickbed that my nose didn't like and my stomach cared for even less. The atmosphere was bleak and oppressive. I hoped our time here would be brief.

Sometimes I forget how deeply ingrained Barker's faith is and how seriously he takes it. Perhaps it is because I've been present on so many occasions when he has had to resort to violence. To him, it must have been the most natural thing in the world to drop down on one knee beside an old Chinaman's bath chair and converse quietly with him in Chinese. He actually fussed over the toothless old fellow, pulling up the blanket which had fallen around his knees, making some remark that made the old man's eyes light up. The old salt, who had been lethargic when we came up to him, began to chatter to the Guv animatedly, nodding his head so his straggly beard wagged. He raised a finger, deformed and crippled from arthritis, and pointed down the hallway with a yellowed nail. Barker stood, they bobbed respectful bows at each other, and we proceeded down the hall.

"It is a pathetic end, lad," he commented as we passed down the corridor, "but with no living relatives, he's better here than in China."

We found Woo in an office off the hall. He was helping a sailor process paperwork at his desk and waved us to a pair of chairs. He got out a seal and appended his name to the side of a document in red ink. Then came the prolonged leave-taking with the individual, with all its bows and grins. Being Chinese, I realized, is all about protocol.

"Good afternoon, gentlemen," Woo said, greeting us. "Managed to stay out of the wet? It's raining cats and dogs, I said to myself this very morning. What can I do for London's illustrious enquiry agent?"

"We were wondering if you are acquainted with a merchant in Limehouse known as Mr. K'ing."

Woo's hand, which was constantly in motion when he

talked, stopped suddenly, and he tried to cover it up quickly by shooting his cuffs and adjusting the stickpin in his tie.

"Really, you know, he's just a myth. There's no such animal, I assure you. He's just a creation thought up by certain merchants hoping to keep some of the dockside gangs at bay."

"Inspector Bainbridge thought otherwise," Barker pursued. "He even provided a sketch for us."

Woo blinked twice behind his monocle. "Wouldn't know about that, myself. I can only say that I've never met him, and if anyone would know about him, it would be me. You mark my words; he's just a clever ploy on the part of merchants to draw some people in and keep others out. Mr. K'ing does not exist."

"I see," Barker said, but I was certain he thought otherwise. "Do you work here all day? When do you have time to discharge your duties to the Foreign Office?"

"I am in and out of the office all day and much of the night, as well. My work here is not suitable for my needs and so I must supplement my income with odd jobs. For example, I gave a reporter a tour of Darkest Limehouse just the other day."

What needs did Woo have? I wondered. Obviously his tailor was one of them. His cravat and handkerchief were silver today, with a black cutaway and striped trousers.

"How is Mr. Campbell-Ffinch of the Foreign Office faring these days?" I dared to ask.

"Oh, he's managed to successfully alienate most of Limehouse. I do my best to temper his remarks, since he doesn't realize what gross insults he gives everyone. Poor chap, he's doing more harm than good."

"When did he arrive in London, Mr. Woo?" Barker asked.

"Just plain Jimmy will do. Let's see. It was after Christmas last year. No, it must be two years ago, now, since it is February."

"So Campbell-Ffinch has been on this case for over a year? The Foreign Office must be more forgiving than I thought."

"Don't think they haven't threatened him, but I gather he's furthered a few other cases in and around this one, through his bullying tactics and his group of Old Boys. I don't believe the needs or desires of the Imperial Government come at the top of the F.O.'s list of priorities."

"What about yours, er—Jimmy?"

"You mean regarding the Finch? That's what I call him—the Finch. He sings and blusters all day, but no one really pays attention. He treats me abominably, but the F.O. compensates me for it. I've had worse employers. One merely has to understand that he's going to take his frustration over his own inadequacies out on you." He eyed my employer. "Do you mind if I ask you another question, the one everyone in the district is dying to know? Do you have any Chinese blood? Are you one of us?"

"Yes."

Woo actually stopped and took Barker by the arm. "Really? You're Chinese?"

"Yes, I really do mind if you ask me another question."

I saw Woo hesitate a moment, then he threw his head back and roared with laughter. It rang false to me, but that was the impression all Chinamen gave me: that they laughed when they had been caught out or embarrassed.

"Good one, sir. Didn't know you detectives had such a sense of humor."

"Enquiry agents."

"So sorry."

"Shall you return to China someday, Mr. Woo?" Barker asked.

"Oh, I do hope so, sir. I miss the old place, Shanghai, Peking, the beauty of the Sung Mountains."

"Ah, a northerner," Barker was quick to say. "I've only been to Peking once to aid the Dowager Empress, but I found it spectacular. You must be very familiar with the Forbidden City."

"Of course. I see we understand each other."

There it is again, I thought to myself, *that phrase.* First Barker's friend Huang Feihong used it in the letter and now Woo. What did they understand now?

"It must bring back good memories for you," Barker continued.

"I look forward to the day when I arrive in Peking again and can see the roofs of the city. Shall you return yourself, sir, and continue the legend of *Shi Shi Ji?*"

Barker actually thought over the question. "I consider myself a resident of the world, Mr. Woo, but I must admit I also have a soft spot for China. Perhaps someday I shall return, at least to visit."

"I think sometimes I could just jump aboard a ship and say good-bye to London, even after all these years," Woo said, "but then I come to my senses and remember I've got responsibilities here."

Woo showed us to the front door and we passed a group of old salts content to sit around the square tables, playing endless games of mah-jongg. It was pretty to look at, but it made chess look as easy as draughts by comparison.

"Well, I must take my leave. The Finch expects me to translate for him within the hour, and, if I know him, I'll be fetching and carrying, as well. Pleasure seeing you chaps again."

Off the fellow scampered like Alice's White Rabbit. He really was one of the most eccentric fellows I'd ever met. Barker and I walked several streets to the tram, which took us out of Limehouse again.

"What did he mean by the two of you understanding each other?" I asked.

"Have you noticed Woo's voice?" my employer asked.

"It is rather high and strident."

"The Forbidden City is not open to normal males, since it contains the Prince's wives and consorts. It is heavily populated and run by eunuchs."

"Are you saying?"

"Yes. To anyone familiar with China, the voice is a dead giveaway."

"He's a . . . castrato?"

"Not castration, lad, I mean a complete sacrifice." He made a cutting gesture with his hand, like a cleaver.

"My word!"

"It is the price young men in China must pay if they are intelligent, talented, and ambitious."

Ambition is one thing, I thought, *but that is a price I consider too dear merely to get ahead.*

14

THE NEXT MORNING, THE SABBATH, I STOPPED
just long enough to down a cup of coffee and snatch a
brioche before stepping outside. My employer was direct-
ing one of the workers in how he wanted the algae removed from his fish pond before it froze, with the aid of a
long-handled bamboo rake. He stopped on seeing me and
gave me an appraising look. I had grown very good at esti-
mating his moods based upon the raising and lowering of
the brows behind his spectacles and the crinkling of his
eyes at their corners. He shot a glance toward his Pen-jing
collection, and I followed his gaze to where Miss Winter
stood in her heavy veil, brushing Harm on top of a flat-
topped rock Barker used to prune his miniature trees. The
dog, at least, had manners enough to yip a greeting at me
while Miss Winter brushed the dog's fur as if I weren't
there. It was chilly in the garden that morning and I didn't
merely mean the weather. I waited until I received the
smallest of grudging nods from my employer, who went
on discussing the removal of the algae, as if it required
Pythagorean mathematics. It was all the permission I re-

quired. I took off my hat and offered my most sincere bow.

"Miss," I ventured, "I apologize for the unfortunate turn of events of three days ago. It was not my intention to enter into a disagreement with your maid, and the circumstance that resulted in her lying on a mudflat was entirely an error in judgment on my part. I was concerned over the welfare of the dog, you see, which of course, was stupid of me, for he obviously could not have been in better hands."

The woman stood there stock-still, as they say, with her brush still buried in Harm's fur, while I waited, hat over my chest, for her forgiveness. Ducking one's ladies' maid in the river was certainly a breach of etiquette, I reasoned, but it was not exactly a crime. Not an unforgivable one, anyway. Would she accept my apology?

She stood there a moment or two, lost in thought. Finally, she finished her stroke, set the dog on the ground, and put her brush away in a little leather box she had brought with her. Even from a distance of five feet, her veil was impenetrable, but as I was noting it, she leaned forward and lifted the heavy tulle from her face.

"I have no maid, Mr. Llewelyn," she stated.

A shiver ran down my spine that wasn't due to the fact that it was cold in the garden. How was I to know that the Chinese girl I had fought and the girl who tended after Harm at our home once a week were one and the same?

"I—I'm so sorry," I stammered.

She said nothing but regarded me out of black, almond-shaped eyes. I wanted to protest, but couldn't find the words. How could I have known? For that matter, what was a Chinese girl doing dressed up like an Englishwoman—though I had to admit she was attractive in her close-fitting widow's weeds. Some movement of my face must have betrayed my thoughts, for she suddenly stepped forward and before I could move, slapped my face hard. It reminded me of the fact that I myself had already been ill-used. True, I had tossed her in the Thames, but she had half kicked me down a stairwell, not to mention trying to scratch my eyes out. I thought we were about to have another set-to, but thankfully Barker had finally finished communicating the exact formula for extracting algae from a fish pond and came up beside me.

"Miss Winter, I believe you have already made the acquaintance of Mr. Thomas Llewelyn. Thomas, may I present my ward, Miss Winter, or as she is known in Chinese, Bok Fu Ying."

All fierceness deserted her face, as a cat retracts its claws, and she curtseyed graciously to me.

"How do you do?" she asked without a trace of an accent.

"I'm pleased to make your acquaintance. Did you say *ward*?" The last, of course, was directed toward the Guv. A full year's service I had put in, and never once had he mentioned having any such thing.

"Yes. I am her guardian," Barker stated, as if it were the most logical thing in the world, and perhaps it was in China. "I have been for over five years now. Miss Winter is in mourning. She was betrothed to my late assistant."

The young woman cast down her eyes and seemed to retreat into herself.

I believe until that time it hadn't really registered in this poor brain of mine that Quong had been a real person. I sleep in his room, even have worn his coat and hat a time or two, but there was nothing personal to remind me of his having come before, no photographs or mementos. Certainly nothing as personal as a girl he had left behind. *Poor fellow,* I thought. He once had an interesting career and a beautiful fiancée, and then one day he came across that blasted text and by end of day was a corpse floating in Limehouse Reach. So much promise of a good life, ended too soon.

"I regret your loss, miss. I've heard nothing but good things about Mr. Quong since I came here."

The girl bowed her head gravely, and there was nothing left to be said. She left in her carriage while Barker and I walked across the road to the Metropolitan Tabernacle. Spurgeon preached upon forgiving thy neighbor. I wished Miss Winter had been in attendance.

After lunch, a joint of mutton in herb sauce prepared by Madame which was at least as good as her husband's, Barker reached into the sideboard and pulled out a large pad of paper. "Get out your notes, lad, and see if you can reproduce Bainbridge's blotter. Perhaps it will give us some clue as to who the killer is."

"Yes, sir," I said, and set to work. I had no training in art beyond a lesson or two in draftsmanship during my school days, but I persevered for over an hour, copying with my notebook in front of me, using both it and my memory to copy Bainbridge's work as closely as possible.

When I was finished, Barker waved me out of my chair and propped up the tablet against the back. Then he pulled the visitor's chairs away from the desk and we sat down and looked at my work, or more precisely, my interpretation of Bainbridge's work.

"This entire sketch is about Hestia Petulengro," he stated. "She is key to this entire picture, and yet she has little or no connection to the book that I can find. There can only be two reasons for her to be here on the blotter. Either she is actually key to this investigation and we don't know how, yet, or—"

"Or," I said, continuing the thought, "Bainbridge had some sort of infatuation or relationship with Miss Petulengro. I notice he didn't dare try to reproduce her face, as if he were not worthy of the attempt."

"I'm afraid you are correct. These initials in the corner are personal rather than professional. It is a schoolboy's habit to turn the object of one's affections' initials into a talisman, copying them endlessly. And him a married man. Och, this is not pretty, lad."

I was about to say, neither was Mrs. Bainbridge, but that was not fair. Instead I concentrated on some of the other figures in the drawing.

"Sir, most of this is very much connected to the murders. Here is Jan Hurtz, lying dead, and here is Luke Chow, hanging on the lines. And this fellow with the hat and fur-collared coat is Mr. K'ing. You will note that he's not even looking at Hettie Petulengro. I don't think he knows her."

"I do not believe Inspector Bainbridge was entirely forthcoming with us, lad, or entirely honest. He had secrets of his own, such as why he was content to be working down here in Limehouse the last few years. He and I had a working relationship but not a friendship such as I have with Terence Poole."

"But, sir," I pointed out, "you got into quite an argument with Poole just the other day."

"That proves it, lad. Friends can shout at each other and express their opinions and know their friendship will not be affected by it. It was different with Bainbridge. We aided each other, but we were competitors. He wanted to solve the case himself. He was not about to hand it over to a private enquiry agent. He needed me because he had to know what had been pawned. You saw that he tried first without us. Anything he said to us, then, is suspect. If, for example, he could have connected the murder to K'ing and then brought him in, he would be a hero at the Yard."

"Are you saying he might have forged such a connection? That he was dishonest?"

"I would not cast aspersions upon the dead, not without evidence, anyway. I do not know his character. In my discussions with Poole, I gather he didn't know him well, either. Bainbridge kept himself to himself."

"Perhaps not with Miss Petulengro."

"Yes, we shall have to speak with her again but not just yet. I shall have to think how best to go about it."

We gazed at the picture again for a moment. The Guv leaned forward and tapped the paper with a thick finger. "This fellow with the menacing look, what did the constable say his name was?"

I consulted my notebook. "Charlie Han, petty criminal, connected with the betel nut trade. What is betel nut, sir?"

"It is a mild narcotic. Now this other fellow, the bearded one leering at her, he looks unnaturally stiff. Was he that way in the original picture?"

"Yes, sir."

Barker scratched under his chin in thought. "His eyes look out of focus, though his expression is fierce enough.

This is an odd shadow along his neck. Could I see your original sketch?"

I showed him the notebook.

"You know, lad, I don't think this is a shadow at all. It is a bruise. This is Miss Petulengro's uncle, drawn from death. I still see no reason for the murder of Mr. Petulengro, unless it actually was a robbery. Quong had already purchased the book. I doubt the killer would have murdered him out of pique."

I let that sink into my thoughts for a while, then didn't care at all for what came back. "Do you think Miss Petulengro killed him herself and made it look like a robbery?"

"It is very possible, lad. She had several motives. She feared for her safety. She inherited a good business. She got out of matchstick making, which is a dangerous occupation."

"So she is a viable suspect."

"I would say yes, except for the method of death. She is a bold, feisty girl. I would have taken her for a stabber. Do you remember the row of clasp knives in the case? She would have gone for one of them. A club is not her weapon at all."

"But it was Inspector Bainbridge's weapon," I said.

"Yes, lad, it was. He was a devil with a truncheon. But if he were after the text he still had no reason to kill Lazlo Petulengro. Of course, there is another possibility, that they planned Petulengro's death together."

"Mind you," I said, "there is no motive I can see in either of them killing to find the text. I don't see how they would benefit."

"True," Barker conceded. "There is even the possibility

that the shop was in fact robbed and he was killed by the thieves, as it appeared. Chandleries are often robbed by the very sailors who frequent them, and New Year's is a common time for robberies."

"So, you're saying Mr. Petulengro was either killed by his niece, Hettie; Inspector Bainbridge; both of them; the nameless killer we are after; or the thieves who appear to have broken in."

"Aye. Or someone else."

"Someone else?" I cried. "Who is left? The Lord Mayor?"

"I have not asked for his alibi, lad. No, I am talking about our fierce friend, Mr. Han, the other man leering at Miss Petulengro in the drawing. I believe we shall have to track the fellow down and ask him some questions. I suggest we not be gentle about it."

Just then Jenkins brought in a message. Barker scrutinized it and then nodded his head in approval.

"Mr. Han must wait," he said. "This is from Poole. The Yard has finally released Ho."

15

WE PULLED UP IN FRONT OF NEWGATE PRISON
and alighted from the cab. I was less than comfortable being
here, even if it was only to pick up someone else. Newgate
had the dismal atmosphere of my own Oxford Prison. I had
not the quickening of heart I sometimes felt when entering
Scotland Yard. In its place was a kind of institutional misery.
I felt wretched just seeing it but wasn't going to admit it to
Barker, who sat waiting patiently.

I turned the case over in my mind. Barker had possessed
the text for almost twenty-four hours before he'd passed it
on to his "Chinaman." I'd assumed it was Old Quong, but
now I considered the possibility that it had been Ho. Perhaps Ho was merely holding it for my employer. What
would the Guv do with such knowledge? He would not
wish the text to fall into the wrong hands.

"So, what is your position, sir?" I asked. "Is the text evil,
or is it merely knowledge?"

"You are in good form today, Thomas," he said after a
moment's silence. "You have put your finger on the very
question that I have been contemplating."

Just then, Ho came out of the bowels of the building looking his usual, truculent self. He and Barker nodded, and I followed them out into Newgate Street. Out at the curb, a cabman slowed when he heard Barker's sharp whistle, then sped by when he caught sight of Ho. Luckily, a second driver was not so reluctant. We clambered in, and within a few minutes were headed out of the City into the East End.

Barker stopped the hansom a street or two away from Limehouse Reach. West Ferry Road was a row of tenements on either side. Ho got out of the cab and shuffled along with his head down and his hands in the pockets of his quilted jacket. At one door, he stopped, pounded twice, then immediately proceeded on his way. A few doors down on the opposite side of the street, he repeated the action. One of Ho's waiters shot out of the first door, pulling a coat over his tunic. The teashop owner knocked on two more doors in the street, and by the time we reached the alleyway Ho's restaurant occupies, we were followed by almost a dozen men. The Chinaman slipped a small key from his pocket into the door's padlock and opened it. Then we followed him inside.

No one needed to light a lamp at the entrance, but for once we needed one at the end, because the tearoom was unlit. The room had a stale odor of trapped tobacco smoke and cooking oil. Waiters and cooks lit gas lamps and immediately began heating water to begin the process of cleaning. The room was still set up for the inquest, and we began to move tables and chairs about to a semblance of their former arrangement. Even I, with my one good arm, pushed a chair or two into place. The odor of stale smoke gave way to strong bleach and soap as the kitchen was treated to a hot scrub. I heard the cooks in the back begin talking in Chinese and laughing as they worked. Ho came out of his office and bellowed something that silenced everyone. If I had thought being incarcerated had not affected Ho, I was mistaken. It had made him even more surly, if such a thing were possible.

Barker clucked over the Pen-jing tree, which had gone without light or water for days. He carried it out to the entrance, cold as it was, to see if sunlight might revive it while Ho lowered himself onto the cushions behind his desk and began running a wire through his smoking contraption.

"Were you in any way mistreated?" I asked.

"I was," he answered. "Food very bad."

"It always is in prisons," I said from experience. "And they half starve you, as well."

"No bath for days. I feel very dirty."

"I'm sure the Guv would want you to use the bathhouse tonight."

Ho shook his head while he stuffed his water pipe with tobacco from a glass jar. "There are bathhouses in Limehouse." The tearoom owner sat with his hooded eyes closed, savoring the smoke from his pipe. I thought as long as I was here, I would ask him some questions.

"Have you ever heard of a fellow named Charlie Han?"

"Betel nut," he responded without opening his eyes.

"Yes. The police are looking for him in connection with the case."

"He won't be found if he does not wish to be found."

"That sounds like Mr. K'ing," I said. "Does Han work for K'ing?"

"Han works for Han. I'm certain he is paying for the

privilege of working in triad territory. No one lives or works here who does not pay Mr. K'ing."

I reached into my pocket and, taking out my notebook, flipped it to the page containing the sketch of the man in the Astrakhan-collared coat and wide-brimmed hat. I set it in front of Ho.

"Is this a good likeness of Mr. K'ing?"

The hooded eyes twitched and opened a little. A plume of smoke issued out of the corner of his mouth. He grunted.

"Does that mean yes?"

"Stop bothering my smoke with questions! You know it is K'ing. Is this the only copy?"

"No. The original is at Scotland Yard."

Ho closed his eyes again.

"Did you know Quong well?" I asked.

"I knew him," came the reply.

"Do you know Dr. Quong?"

"Very well. Personal friend."

"How did you—"

"Questions, questions. All the time questions. Talk less, listen more. Let me smoke in peace! I have wheat cakes to bake."

"Of course," I said, getting up quickly. I'd strained his patience to the breaking point, but then I didn't think his patience was particularly great.

I found Barker kneeling in the alleyway, fussing over the tiny potted pine.

"Is it dead?"

"It has suffered deprivation, but the branches are still supple. I believe it shall come through alive."

Six people were dead, at least, and my employer was concerned with a shrub.

"Ho says he knew of Charlie Han but doesn't know where he is now. He also said he and Dr. Quong are good friends."

"I already know that, Thomas. You should have let him smoke."

I sighed. "It's hard to tell what to do with the Chinese. There's so much protocol. I wouldn't want to set back Anglo-Sinese relations."

"I doubt there is any way to set them back further. Right now the Western powers are carving up China in the name of imperialism. Even young countries such as America are joining in. There is a town along the north coast of China, I hear, built by the Germans using Chinese labor, that so replicates their country, one would swear one was in Bavaria."

"I had no idea," I said.

"Aye. But everyone is working under a misapprehension. They are assuming the Dragon is dead, but it is like this Pen-jing tree. It only sleeps. One day, the Dragon shall awaken and when it does, God help us all. It shall feel as though Armageddon is upon us."

"You think there shall be war?"

"Oh, there shall be war. You may be sure of it."

"Between China and England?"

"England, France, Germany, and all the others that are attempting to interfere with China at the moment. They don't trust one another, but they'll band together if it is in their interests."

"Wouldn't that be a slaughter?" I asked. "After all, the Europeans have guns."

"Yes, but the Chinese have superior numbers, and if they were trained in *dim mak,* they would think themselves invincible. They would fight like devils."

"When might this happen? Soon?"

Barker shrugged. "Who can say? Soon, if the aggression gets worse. What concerns me is that if there is a sudden war, we have half a thousand Chinese within a few miles of the royal family. If just one of those five hundred has the knowledge of *dim mak,* then I am justified in fearing both for the monarchy and also for the innocent citizens of Lime-house."

"Might the government round them up?"

"I would hope so, rather than face a purge of the district by the citizenry after a clash overseas." Barker looked down and ran a hand over the back of his neck. "But perhaps it shall not come to pass. Let us concentrate on the present and see if we can ferret out Bainbridge's killer before he harms anyone else."

16

IN THE PREDAWN HOURS OF THE NEXT MORNING, I was awakened by a sudden sharp crash outside my door. I cursed myself for a fool for not keeping some sort of protection in my room. I opened my door cautiously, ready for anything. As it turned out, I was ready for anything but what I found there.

Cyrus Barker was in his nightshirt lying across my sill. The porcelain chamber pot he had carried from his room upstairs had shattered on the polished floor, spilling its contents. The liquid, even by the low light of the turned-down gas jets, was a dull rusty color and thick as blood.

"Sir!" I cried, going down on one knee and trying to lift his head with my one good arm. Barker was unconscious. It must have taken all he had to climb down from his upper chamber. I placed my hand on his chest, fearing the worst, but though faint, I detected a beating heart. What could I do? If I didn't act quickly, my employer, my mentor, the man to whom I owed practically everything, would be dead.

There was a sound on the stair, but it was only Harm.

He took in the scene before him with his bulging eyes, seemed to gather himself for a moment, and then raised his head and howled the most mournful wail I had ever heard from an animal. I can only compare it to the funereal dirge of a bagpipe. It was obvious that Harm thought his master dead.

"What has happened?" Mac called up from the foot of the stairs with a thrill in his voice that told me he expected the worst.

"The Guv has passed out in the hall," I cried.

Mac managed to hobble up the stairs with the aid of a walking stick, just as the door opened behind me and Madame and Monsieur Dummolard emerged. They had taken the trouble to don proper dressing gowns and slippers. On seeing the sight, Dummolard let out a remark that should not be repeated in English or French.

Mac reached the landing and surveyed the scene. "This is bad," he stated. "You had better call Dr. Applegate."

"Of course," I said, and took the stairs down three at a time. The Harley Street physician answered the telephone as soon as I was put through. I was not at my most coherent, but somehow I managed to communicate the direness of the circumstances and he rang off, saying he would be along in a few moments. I looked at the clock in our hall. It was shortly after five in the morning. Then I ran upstairs again.

Barker still had not come around. He is a man known for his immobility and yet seeing him there so inanimate was unnerving. *What if he died?* I wondered. *What then?* My mind leapt ahead to the funeral, the settling of the estate, the selling of the house and dismissal of his servants, myself included. How could I bear to be cast adrift again, after all this? Surely Fate could not be that cruel.

Madame Dummolard was already soaking up the mess on the floor by laying towels across it before sweeping up the shards of pottery.

"Do we dare move him to a bed?" Maccabee asked. "I cannot bear to see him like this, prostrate in his own hall-way."

"We had better not risk it. Applegate lives but a few streets away. He should be here soon," I answered.

The doctor arrived in ten minutes, commenting that we were keeping him busy these days. He authorized Barker's removal to his bed upstairs and it took the five of us to carry him there, slack-limbed as he was. Applegate then herded us out before examining his patient. Mac, Dummolard, and I stood in the corridor uncertainly. Barker was our leader and now we were left without direction.

"Let's have some coffee," I suggested.

"*Bon!*" Dummolard responded, relieved at having something to do.

The four of us went down into the kitchen, where Dummolard boiled coffee on his gas stove while I wrestled with my inner demons. At the moment, they were conjuring images of Barker's funeral. Would it be a big one when the time came? Barker, if he even made plans, would have favored a brisk, businesslike affair at the Baptist Tabernacle. As far as he was concerned, his soul was in heaven and his body was merely so much humus to be set aside, awaiting the Second Coming. I had no idea where he might wish to be buried, perhaps with his ancestors in Scotland. There were many that were indebted to Barker, including the

Prince of Wales himself, who might be desirous of attending. Then there were the Chinese who would wish to be there, led by his very own ward. As for me, my life would be shattered, as it had been shattered when I had lost my wife. I managed to take hold of myself. After all, the man was not dead yet.

The Dummolards and I were seated at the deal table in the kitchen. Madame Dummolard poured coffee for all of us and we sat in woeful silence.

"I'm sorry," I said finally. "This whole thing has me out of sorts."

"That is understandable," Mac replied, and for once he unbent a little. "I cannot believe this is happening. He has not been sick once for as long as I have worked for him, going on five years."

Just then Dr. Applegate came into the kitchen. Mac poured him a cup of coffee and he fell into the unoccupied seat.

"His condition is very grave, gentlemen," he said, running a hand over his features until they were ruddy. "His kidneys are failing. I do not understand it. He is a very healthy man. I won't be coy with you. Cyrus Barker is at death's door. But we won't give up without a fight, will we?"

It was then that the last piece of a puzzle clicked together in my head. The sailor Chambers had died from kidney failure. This was no accident. It was *dim mak*. I thought back to the two youths who had tried to steal his wallet. Had it been they? No, more likely it was the innocent-looking beggar they had knocked Barker into, the one who had reached up and caught the Guv, with both hands against his back as they fell over. He had been dressed in a long hooded cloak and shapeless hat, obscuring his face, and now, a day later, the Guv's kidneys were giving out as if his insides were made of clockwork gears and the hour had tolled.

I leapt to my feet, suddenly sure of what I must do. Mac and the Dummolards looked up in astonishment.

"I must go," I said. "Etienne, find whatever weapons you can. Get them from Barker's bedchamber if you must. Mac, fill your shotgun and guard the front door. I must leave and this is just the sort of opportunity the killer might use to attack the house again. I'll be back!" Then I turned and rushed out the back door.

I ran through the streets, raising the eyebrows of the few people out on this slowly dawning morning. My plan involved getting to our horse Juno as soon as possible. As I ran toward the rising sun it occurred to me that the murderer, whoever he was, was winning. He had killed Quong and shot Bainbridge, downed Mac and now he had even brought down Cyrus Barker. If anyone had a chance of besting the killer it was Barker, and right then I felt as if his life or death was in my hands. The only man who could possibly save Barker's life, if in fact it were savable at all, was Dr. Quong. Somewhere in his antiquated shop with its bowls of roots and bottles of herbs and its pins, there might be a cure. I had to get to him and bring him back as quickly as possible.

I slid on a patch of ice and nearly fell but righted myself and kept on going. Finally, I arrived at the barn. As calmly as possible, I told the stable boy to saddle Juno, for he was as head shy as the horse. He got her tacked up in record time, after I offered him a half sovereign. As sedately as possible under the circumstances, I climbed into the stirrups as the boy opened the livery doors.

"You've wanted a good gallop for weeks now, girl," I said in her ear. "Now is your chance."

I kicked her and she leapt forward, her iron shoes ringing off the roadway. We galloped along the Borough High Street past rows of anonymous houses. I felt the pent-up energy in Juno being released and the fierce joy of having something useful to do. I understood it because I felt it myself. Between us we swallowed up the streets as we headed toward the river and the bridge that spanned it.

London Bridge was nearly deserted as I urged the horse on. By now, Juno and I had become a single entity. A policeman blew his whistle at me, but I cared not a whit. We squeezed between a couple of draft horses, who voiced their displeasure, and went flying down Gracechurch Street.

"Good girl! Excellent!" I cried into her ear and then I brought her into an easy canter, for she couldn't keep up this pace forever. We trotted through the City and increased our speed again once we reached Commercial Road. A little more than half an hour after I had left, I was beating on Old Quong's door.

"Dr. Quong! Dr. Quong! Are you there?"

I assumed he lived above his shop and that he would answer my stout knockings, but there was no answer. It hadn't occurred to me he might not be home. Perhaps he was out on a call somewhere. I knew not what to do but climbed back onto the lathered bay and began circling the streets of Limehouse. I found him on the fifth or sixth street I passed, sitting on a small stool in the street getting the top of his head shaved by a Chinese barber. I pulled up so quickly, the barber nearly cut off the doctor's ear.

"Dr. Quong, come quickly. Barker has been stricken. It is his kidneys. I think it is *dim mak.*"

"*Dim mak?*" the doctor said, wiping his forehead with a towel. "You are certain?"

"Very. He hovers near death. If anyone can save him, it is you."

"Take me home. Must get bag." He used the barber's folding chair to climb behind me.

Juno's energy was flagging on the way back, but she came from good Thoroughbred stock and had hidden depths. We did not equal our time on the journey back to Newington, for the town was well awake now and the traffic heavier. Some were stopping to watch two men, one in a cast and the other an Oriental, on the back of a sturdy mare galloping through London. By then Juno was bathed in sweat and there were flecks of foam on her bridle.

We finally reached the Elephant and Castle and I pushed myself off as I reached the familiar alley behind our house. I unlocked the moon gate and tied up Juno there before I hustled the doctor over the bridge and through the back door.

"What's going on here?" Applegate demanded when the two of us, weary and disheveled, reached the top of the stairs.

"Tell me, doctor," I said, "do you despair of his life? Be honest, I beg you."

Barker lay in his bed, his lower torso wrapped in a towel and his skin slick with sweat. Applegate looked at him and frowned.

"Answer me, please!"

"Very well, then, yes, I despair of his life."

"Then let this fellow have a try. His name is Dr. Quong. He is a Chinese herbal doctor and he cannot do anything to worsen Barker's condition. I believe, sir, that my employer has been attacked by a secret Oriental method and the only cure is from an Oriental doctor."

"I've been treating Cyrus Barker for five years now," he growled. "I've fixed lacerations and broken limbs and busted heads. But I'll admit I'm beat. I do not know if there is a cure for this, but if this fellow can find a way, he may try. May I watch?"

Old Quong nodded to him but pointed at me. "Him stay. You go out."

After all this I was being tossed out on my ear. "Wait! Can't I—"

"No!" both doctors barked.

"Hang it!" I cried and went downstairs.

"What is happening?" Mac asked as I reached the hall.

"Ask them!" I snapped and went outside into the garden. I had to see to Juno or she would take ill in the cold. I led her to the alley and back to the stable. Once there I removed her saddle and blanket and began rubbing her down. I could have bade the boy to do it, but I needed to do something as much as Juno needed it done. I rubbed and combed her until her muscles, which were bunching and shaking in her breast from the cold and activity, finally began to relax. Then I filled up her hay box and water bucket, shoveled out her stall, and put down fresh straw. Normally she is stall shy, unwilling to be locked in the small enclosure, but for once she went in without protest. She was all in, and nearly asleep before I left the barn.

I returned to the house praying that God would spare my employer. Surely it made no sense to take him when he was doing so much good. I admit he could be a martinet at times, but he was exceedingly bighearted. There was nothing that if I convinced him I had the need of he would not buy, and the very best, too. If there was a benevolent God watching out for us, surely the world would be poorer without this one man struggling down here, this Noah among the forsaken, this Quixote tilting at windmills.

17

An hour later, Dr. Quong was closing his lacquered case full of bottles and tonics and Dr. Applegate was latching his bag. They had reached a truce, if not exactly a friendship, and both had other patients to see. Mac's nurse was now looking after her new charge on the upper floor and I had a chair drawn up by his bed.

I reached across to lay a palm on Barker's forehead and found it hot to the touch. Under that placid exterior, my employer's body was in a pitched battle for its life.

"S'truth," a voice spoke behind me.

"Hello, Jenkins," I said, not looking up.

"'E ain't dead, is he?"

"No, not dead. Who told you he'd been hurt?"

"Inspector Poole stuck his head into the office. He'll be along in a bit. Word got to Scotland Yard, I think."

My mind filled in the blanks after that. I must have been seen and recognized riding into and out of Limehouse. Barker had told me once that information traveled fast in London.

"What?" I asked. Jenkins was speaking to me, but I was lost in my own thoughts.

"I said what'll I do? The office?"

"What about it?"

"Should I keep it open or refer cases to Hewitt?"

Hewitt was another enquiry agent who sometimes took the cases Barker was too busy for.

"For now, just take messages," I said. "And put that out!"

Even if I hadn't smelled the cigarette, I knew he had one. It was like a sixth finger in his right hand, though he limited himself in the office to a few each day. I watched him take a last lungful like a diver before he went under the water, then cross to the dormer window and toss the fag end out into the street. He leaned forward and exhaled through the inch of space between the window and the ledge and then he came back and regarded Barker's still form solemnly.

"Never seen him like this," he said. "No tie with the pearl stickpin. No Windsor collar. The least we can do is comb his hair." Jenkins reached into his pocket and removed a small comb, running it through Barker's hair. It made me think of corpses, and I wanted to reach over and stop him but stopped myself instead. Jenkins was worried as well and this was making him feel he was doing something, even if it did send a chill up my spine.

"Can't the doctor do anything?" he asked.

"We've had two in," I said, saving for myself the fact that one of them was a Chinese herb healer. "I think the immediate danger has passed, but there is no telling when he shall awaken."

"Hard times," Jenkins said.

"Indeed. Are you going back to the office now?"

"Yes, sir."

"Why don't you lock up at five? No sense staying open late. We've already got a case we're working on."

"Thank you, Mr. L." Jenkins left the office at five thirty every workday, bound for the Rising Sun public house where he held court. "I could use a drink after this."

Going down, I met Inspector Poole on the stairs. He looked strained, as I suppose I looked myself.

"I need to speak to you," he said, taking my arm.

"I'm sorry," I said. "I don't believe we have a suspect for you just yet."

"I'm not here for that. I understand the house was broken into and your butler injured."

"Yes."

"And now this. I don't believe all this Oriental mystical nonsense, but would you say Cyrus's injury was probably due to this case and the book?"

"Probably. I'm not certain how yet and won't be until I speak to Mr. Barker, but it has to be more than a coincidence, wouldn't you agree?"

"I would. I want you to know I'm putting a pair of constables in the area until further notice. Good men. They both saw time in India."

"Thank you, Inspector."

He sighed and shook his head. "I can't believe this. I'm going to catch this fellow, just you wait."

Having had his say, I saw him to the door. My view of the street was obstructed by the large black growler he had come here in. He climbed inside, then smacked the door of the vehicle with his hand. "Limehouse!"

"Was that Poole?" Mac asked from the doorway of his room. He was still in his dressing gown and leaning on a pair of crutches.

"Yes. He's sending two men to keep an eye on the house."

"Good!" Mac responded. "Though I don't think the fellow I encountered would be dissuaded by a couple of constables." Mac gestured to me, so the maid in the drawing room couldn't see. He brought me into his room and closed the door. "The maid is getting on my nerves," he said. "She was entertaining at first, if a bit Frenchy, but with the Guv hanging on for life upstairs, it's maddening being ten feet from the door and not being able to answer it. The killer could stroll right in and kill us one by one."

"I don't think it's as bad as that," I said.

"I can almost get about, I think," Mac continued, ignoring my remarks, as usual. "We could get by with just the charwoman for a few days. I know the governor cannot make any decisions. Do you think we should ask Madame Dummolard to pack up her maids and leave?"

"Are you going to ask her?" I countered. "Even the Guv was afraid to turn her down. She is a formidable woman. Besides, I don't think the thief or killer will come back as long as the house is teeming with people. I say let Barker tell her when he is himself again. I'm sure you can get on for a few more days having your cushions fluffed and your meals fed you by maids."

"They're using the wrong polish on the floors," he complained. "And if they move one paper up in the Guv's rooms, I'll be the one swinging for it when he wakes up."

He closed the door, leaving me alone in the hall. I turned,

planning to go upstairs again, but I stopped as Bok Fu Ying came in the back door.

She stood in her black bustled dress with her hands folded in front of her, looking forlorn. I should have alerted her that Barker had been injured, but it had not occurred to me. I walked down the hallway to her and took her hand.

"How is my guardian?" she asked.

"Ill, but not gravely, I think. Dr. Quong has been here. Come this way."

I led her upstairs. I thought she was prepared to see the Guv, and I think she thought so herself, but she still stiffened when she first saw Barker.

"What is wrong with him?" she asked.

"It is his kidneys."

"Kidneys. That is serious, is it not?"

"Very serious," I answered.

She nodded and after a moment a tear or two fell down from her lashes, missing her cheeks entirely, breaking into droplets on her collar and glancing off. I reached for my handkerchief and held it out, but she took no notice, keeping her eyes glued to Barker. Finally, her lids fluttered and she accepted my proffered handkerchief.

She broke down then completely, crying silently, as if making noise were forbidden. I helped her down the stairs, saying whatever soothing words came to me. I led her into the kitchen and seated her in one of the chairs by the window. Dummolard was mid-puff on his short French cigarette in front of the cutting board and he looked at us in surprise.

"Etienne, could Miss Winter have a cup of tea?" I dared ask. It was an unthinkable breach of the chef's unwritten rules, I knew, but this was an emergency. I waited a second while he considered verbally dicing me like a clove of garlic. Finally, he gave a Gallic shrug, turned, and put the teapot on the hob.

Miss Winter coughed and spoke, her voice hoarse. "I apologize. Forgive my emotion. He is all I have now. I lead a very circumscribed life."

"I quite understand."

"He simply cannot die. If he does, I shall die myself, and then who will look after Harm?"

"You think very highly of that dog," I said, trying to distract her from talking of death. For one thing, I couldn't definitely say Barker wouldn't die, though I hoped Old Quong or Applegate would relieve all our minds soon.

"I have to, you see," she answered. "Da Mo owns me."

"Da Mo?" I asked. "Who is Da Mo?"

"The dog. His Chinese name is Da Mo."

"What do you mean, he owns you?"

"I mean I belong to him. I was given to Sir by the Dowager Empress to look after him. I am the dog's slave."

"His slave?" I could not believe my ears.

"Of course. He is an imperial dog raised by the Dowager Empress herself and is entitled to a slave. If I had performed my duties unworthily or displeased him in any way, or should he sicken and die, I would have been beheaded in the Forbidden City."

"That's monstrous!" I couldn't help saying. "It is barbaric!"

"It is the way," she said as if that excused it. "Sir was

obliged to accept me and to see to my needs, but when we left China soon afterward, he gave me a writ of freedom. Slaves are not acceptable in modern England, he says, but he was not obligated to take such good care of me and to make me his ward. He is a noble man."

Dummolard reached between us and set a cup of tea in front of her. "Here you are, mademoiselle."

"Thank you, Monsieur Dummolard. It is good to see a familiar face on this cold, inhospitable day."

The Frenchman nodded gruffly and left me to look after the girl with a look that said, *Be careful or you'll answer to me.*

"May I ask how you and Quong met?" I asked.

She smoothed her skirt carefully and took a sip of her tea. "He used to work in his father's shop and when he heard Sir was the famous *Shi Shi Ji,* he made bold enough to ask if he could become his student. I was living in the house then, looking after Da Mo and the Pen-jing trees. We began to greet each other when he arrived. Sir must have noticed. He rarely misses anything, for he likes the nuances of life. He considered for a while in his private way, then invited Dr. Quong to tea in the small pavilion at the back of the garden. I remember that day well. They had pots of tea and wheat rolls and discussed our future together."

"You mean that it was an arranged marriage?"

"You make that sound like an evil thing," she said. "We trusted them implicitly, and it was obvious to them that we cared for each other. We benefited from their wisdom and experience.

"At that time, Sir considered hiring an assistant, saying that in his work two were often safer than one. He proposed to Dr. Quong that his son first go to live in Three Colt Street, and after he became Sir's assistant, he came to live here while I stayed in Limehouse among my own people, with the doctor and Uncle Ho visiting me occasionally to see after my welfare. Naturally, I would have been happy to marry right away, but he was a virtuous young man. He did not want to rely on the largess of his father or my guardian but to make his own way in the world.

"Sir opened new opportunities for him, but I do not believe my fiancé intended to stay an enquiry agent forever. He ranged all over Limehouse looking for possible business opportunities. He read widely and interested himself in the affairs of our people in London."

"You make him sound very serious," I said.

"He was serious," she admitted, "but he clothed his manner in humor. When we stepped into a shop he spoke to the owner, making jokes with him and passing the time of day, but when he left he could tell me what new stock had come in and what was selling well. He knew the name of every merchant in a street. Often someone wished to hire him, but Shao Zu felt an obligation to stay with Sir until he had acquired enough money for us to be married."

"You must have been distraught to lose him."

"I cannot describe the misery to you of that terrible waiting and then the news that he was found dead. I thought my life was over. Many times since I have considered taking up the knife and doing away with myself. I thought I had nothing to live for. And now my guardian stands upon the brink of death. I do not know how I can stand it."

I looked at Dummolard, who had been listening to the tale with such rapt interest his cigarette had become one long ash. Like myself, he felt for the girl. The cook tossed the end of his cigarette onto the slate floor and left the room, shaking his head, leaving me with the bereaved girl.

"Don't worry," I told her. "He will get well. Dr. Quong will make sure of it."

She nodded and wiped her eyes with my handkerchief, which must have been sodden by then. I couldn't bear the thought of this girl giving way under her burden and killing herself.

Just then the door to the kitchen flew open and Madame Dummolard came in.

"Ah, *ma petite!* I just heard you were here. Don't you worry. M'sieur Barker will be well again before you know it." She held the crying girl to her. Bok Fu Ying looked like a doll in her arms.

Harm scratched on the back door. I got up to open it and followed him out into the garden to allow the women some privacy.

It was cold and starting to snow outside, but it felt good after the stuffy heat of the kitchen. Everything was dormant save for the plants in the greenhouse. There was a thin ring of ice around the perimeter of Barker's artificial pond, but spotted goldfish were coming up for the morsels the gardener had tossed in.

I wandered among the grass-ringed stepping-stones and reached the small bridge. There were stone newel posts on both sides, with a small figure atop each one. My hands ran over the cold surface of the carved stone and the fierce faces of the creatures. Lions. They were stone lions. I looked back over my shoulder. The dormer windows above looked like a pair of eyes staring down at me, the glass as black as the Guv's spectacles.

"Wake up," I murmured. "Please, sir, wake up."

18

———◦———

A FEW HOURS LATER, THE MAID CAME UP THE stairs, interrupting my reverie. I had been sitting and staring into the fire in Barker's hearth for who knows how long, worrying.

"Monsieur Llewelyn, there is a visitor."

"Send him away," I said. "There have been too many people up here already."

"But he is not here to see M'sieur Barker. He wishes to see you."

"Show him to the library, then. I shall be along in a few minutes."

Who wished to speak with me? To tell the truth, I didn't much care. I would go downstairs and tell whoever it was to go away. I wasn't expecting a friend.

Israel Zangwill rose from the fireside chair in the library as I entered. His hat was on his knee, mottled with melting snow. It was early afternoon and yet Israel was here, instead of at his position at the Jews' Free School.

"What are you doing here?" I asked.

"I started a new position, Thomas. I have given up teaching," he said, a smile on his Pucklike face. "I have become a reporter for the *Jewish Chronicle*."

"That's marvelous, Israel. Congratulations." I shook his hand. "No more first period gymnastics for you now, eh?"

"Exactly. Who is the new maid in the hall and what has become of Mac?"

I explained the immediate situation and Israel took it all in.

"So he was attacked in Limehouse, you say. Does this have anything to do with a fellow named Mr. K'ing?"

"How on earth do you know about K'ing?" I asked. "His name is hardly spoken above a whisper."

"I've been investigating him for an article after a few of our crowd lost a painful amount at fan-tan. I suppose telling the *Chronicle* was a way to get even."

"You haven't by chance been given a tour of Limehouse by an individual named Jimmy Woo?"

"'Individual' is a good word for him. Yes, that was me. He showed me all over the district until I mentioned Mr. K'ing. Then he shut up so tight I might as well have stuck a cork in his mouth."

"K'ing has that effect on people. Woo says he doesn't even exist."

"He exists, all right. He owns an opium den in Pekin Street."

"How did you come by that information?"

"I'm a reporter. I bought it. I thought your employer might be interested, though I didn't know he was working on a similar case."

"It's just the sort of information he's been looking for, but I doubt he'll be up for several days, if at all. He hasn't woken up since he was attacked."

"Drat!" Zangwill said. "I spent my last shilling on the information and now I can't even afford to get inside. You're the only fellow I know with both the courage and the ready to go there with me."

"I'm sorry, Israel, but I can't leave Barker's side, and, besides, you shouldn't be going to an opium den. It's dangerous and terribly addictive."

"Oh, I'm going, all right. I have to. My employment depends upon it. I rather sold it to my editor, you know, 'Sinister Oriental, pipe of poppy, white slave trade' and all that. I've got to go through with it. I've rather burned my bridges behind me."

"I wish I could help you, but Barker's health, his life is too precarious now." I studied my friend. "I can't believe you threw over a good position."

"It is your fault," he retorted. "You are the one that got me thinking. You're always doing important things, risking life and limb daily, and what do I do? I wet-nurse a group of children. It was stultifying. This last week has been the most exciting of my life! If I have to visit an opium den or stalk Limehouse for an underground criminal leader to get a story, I shall do it."

"Your parents must be livid."

Zangwill gave me a pained smile. "They are not overjoyed, but it is already done. If I fail, I shall have to find other work, but I refuse to fail. Look, supposing this place is pertinent to the case and you're spending precious hours here when you could be solving it. How would you like to serve your employer a finished case on a platter when he wakes up?"

I shook my head. "Sorry, Israel. The Guv would caution me just as I am cautioning you. Slow down and think this over."

He ran a hand through his shock of curly hair. "I have an idea, then. I won't go tonight if you go with me tomorrow night. Your boss might wake up in the morning. I really need your help. If you don't go with me, I shall have to take Ira."

Ira Moskowitz was a close friend of ours. He is built like a sack of potatoes and would be of no help at all in a desperate situation.

"All right, all right," I relented. "I shall go with you tomorrow night if Barker's condition does not worsen or if he wakes up and feels it is the right thing for me to do. But I've already made one mistake in this case and I do not want to make another if I can help it. You're not actually going to smoke the stuff, are you?"

"Surely you don't think I'm the sort that would go to such an establishment for pleasure."

"No," I said, "just to beard the most dangerous man in London in his den."

Zangwill leaned forward. "Do you really think he is the most dangerous man in London? Oh, I like that phrase. I simply must use it." He pulled a small pad from his pocket and made a notation in pencil.

"You're treating this like a game, Israel," I told him. "K'ing is very real and, I suspect, very dangerous. I, for one, would not care to be under his scrutiny."

"Look, we'll go in and buy a few pipes. It's not illegal and we won't smoke them, though people do it all the time. I'm more interested in what goes on behind the opium den than what occurs inside it."

"That's what I am afraid of."

"Tomorrow, then," Zangwill said as I saw him to the door.

"Very well. Tomorrow. Where and when?"

"Pekin Street. Let us say seven."

Dr. Quong arrived about an hour later. He tried a different kind of needle treatment this time, involving small cups with holes in the bottom through which the needle was passed. A bit of cotton on the end of the needle was ignited, which sucked the air out of the small chamber and adhered the cup to the skin. In ten minutes, Barker was covered in little glass cups.

"It doesn't hurt?" I asked.

"I would no hurt *Shi Shi Ji*," Quong said. "He will find my son killer."

"When can I get this cast off?"

"You Westerners all the time hurry. Chop, chop. Cannot rush healing body. Chinese medicine work slowly but good."

After he had pulled every pin from Barker's body and massaged a bottle of liniment into his back that turned it bright yellow, he left us alone. Harm came in, sniffed at everything, and hopped up on the corner of the bed. He put his almost chinless head on his paws and sighed.

"I know how you feel," I told him.

At a loss for what to do, I explored the books on Barker's shelves. The walls slope from the apex until they meet a line of low, long bookcases on both sides. They contained mostly religious texts. I pulled an old copy of *Pilgrim's Progress* from the shelf and reacquainted myself with Chris-tian, Mr. Worldly Wiseman, and my personal favorite, the Slough of Despond. Barker stirred and sighed in his sleep twice during the evening but did not wake up. I debated sleeping in a chair but allowed the night nurse when she arrived to shoo me off to bed like a mother.

The next morning, Barker was still profoundly asleep, one foot firmly planted in this world and the other in the one to come. I was sure he would have woken by now. Was he getting better or was this bad news? Applegate came midmorning and spoke cryptically. He said the Guv was doing "as well as can be expected," but would not make any further comment. I asked if I should go out and pursue an inquiry that evening involving the case. He said he thought that the fresh air would do me good.

The way it is described in the guidebooks, one would think Limehouse a kind of Brighton-on-the-Thames instead of a worn-down and bedraggled district with outdated sewer systems and buildings teetering on stilts by the edge of the river, a constant source of worry for the Lord Mayor.

Arriving at my destination, it occurred to me that it takes a certain measure of courage for a man to go to a place that might be dangerous and another measure before going in. I had brought the first but I was not positive about the other.

"Does this place have a name?" I asked Israel, for I saw no hoarding bidding people to enter, nothing save for a small gas lamp over the entrance door.

"Jimmy Woo says this place is called Inn of Double Happiness," Zangwill said.

"This is an inn?" I asked skeptically. It looked more like a house of assignation to me.

"How should I know?"

"Are you sure about this, Israel?" I asked as we stared at a flickering gas jet over the door.

"Yes," Zangwill said steadily, then wavered. "Well, sure-ish."

I felt as if we were schoolboys daring each other to go into a deserted house. "There's no way you could impress the editors at the *Jewish Chronicle* with some other story?"

"Not unless I can create a hair-raising account of the annual meeting of the Daughters of Judah that would thrill the world in its entirety. How is Mr. Barker doing?"

"He is . . . recovering."

Zangwill played with his upper lip, a habit he has when he is debating something. It was accompanied by a tapping of his foot, much in the way Harm jerks his leg when I scratch his stomach.

"Let's go in, then," he finally said.

"Yea, though I walk through the valley of the shadow of death—"

"Stop that!" he said and began moving forward.

We clattered down the steps and flung open the door, where we were greeted by a wall of smoke that had size and shape and atmosphere. My companion plunged into it and I followed, my hand in the pocket of my coat where my pistol lay in its built-in holster. Now that I was about to do it, I felt even more the foolishness of it, but Zangwill had gone in and I couldn't let him go it alone. Cautiously, I slipped into the smoky darkness.

The reek of opium assailed my nose. Its sweet, cloying odor is so unpleasant I felt I could detect the lightest whiff miles away. It clawed at my throat and I knew I'd need several baths and my clothes several washings before the smell would go away. Zangwill and I passed through two rows of double berths, all of them filled. Most occupants were Chinamen and other Asiatics, but there was the odd European. I stopped to gaze at a man in formal attire, his top hat pulled down over his eyes and his long pipe on his chest. He could be dead and I'd be none the wiser.

I passed an alcove festooned with old sail material tied up with bits of rope like a curtain. A candle was lit and a woman was sucking in smoke. She stopped and regarded me a moment. She was dark and had a hooked nose and large hoop earrings, but I could tell nothing else—her age, her nationality, why she was smoking opium, how she got here. Her eyes followed me as I moved, and then she reached out a clawlike hand to me, a longing for who knows what? I shook my head and her hand fell. She sucked in more smoke and I continued on my way.

"Amazing," I heard Zangwill say through the smoke a few steps ahead of me. "To think we're in London."

The room opened out at the back. There was a small bar made of crude wood; a staircase going upward; and several old, mismatched chairs. The area was lit by a single gas lamp, but the darkness encroached upon it and herded it into a small circle. An Oriental, little more than a boy, came forward.

"No," I said, "I'm not smoking."

"No smoky one pipey?"

"Yes," Israel ordered. "One pipey. Do we pay now?"

"No, no, no, later. You sit there. I bring pipey."

Zangwill sat down on the dirty sheets of one of the berths, and I pulled up a chair beside him.

"It's not too late to leave," I told him. "When he comes back, I'll say we changed our minds. We can go over to the Barbados for a cup of coffee and—"

"No, I must go through with it," Israel insisted. "This is just as it was described to me. Turn your chair 'round and keep an eye on that stairwell. I believe the insidious Mr. K'ing's lair is up those steps."

The boy brought the pipe and lit a match for my friend, who was then forced to suck in enough smoke to keep it lit. I watched the little bead of gummy opium bubbling in the bowl of the pipe.

He coughed a couple of times. "It's not exactly a clay pipe at the Barbados," he squeaked. "This stuff tastes terrible." He put the pipe aside when the boy left.

"So, you have quit teaching and become a reporter," I asked. "What else has happened since we last met?"

"I've met a girl, a corking girl. Her name is Amy Levy. She is a poetess and a member of the Fabian Society."

It was quite unlike him to talk about a girl. "A poetess, eh?"

"Yes. She is very modern, one of these new women."

Just then an Oriental man came down the stairwell,

looked at some figures in a ledger and returned upstairs. If that was Mr. K'ing, I was not impressed. He was all upper teeth and Adam's apple and very little chin. He looked nothing like the portrait Bainbridge had left us.

After a while we fell into a reverie. I hadn't reckoned that the combined effluvia of so many pipes would be almost like having one of my own. It began with pinwheels at the corners of my vision. Before I knew it, I was having a headache and feeling woozy.

"Llewelyn!" a voice spoke into my ear. I opened my eyes, though my sight wasn't very clear. It was the chap in the top hat, who had been lying in the bunk against the wall. He had thrown his hat back and he looked familiar. "Llewelyn," he repeated, shaking my shoulder.

"Mr. Forbes?"

"Pollock, old man," he corrected. "So what are you and your friend doing here?"

"Friend?"

"You need some air, I think. In fact, you both do. Help me get him on his feet."

We got on both sides of Zangwill and lifted him up. He was nearly insensible. Forbes reached into his pocket and a rain of coins jingled down onto a rickety table. Then we opened the door and met the bracing cold air.

Outside, the snow had stopped, but a misty haze had formed in the cold air. It felt good coming out from the infernal stench of the den. *Inn of Double Happiness, my eye. Double Misery, more like.* I needed a few breaths before I could walk, but I wasn't sure I could trust Zangwill to stand upright. We led him down the street a bit and propped him against a building. Then I did the same for myself.

It felt as if someone was squeezing the bridge of my nose with a pair of pliers. I was nauseous, too, and felt I might be sick, but managed to get hold of myself. We were just about to step into the street when a horse and cab nearly ran us down. I fell back against the wall, my heart racing. It had been close. The four-wheeler came to a stop in front of the den and the door opened. Could it possibly be?

A form was getting out of the cab, a black shape, a shadow until he turned around and his face was illuminated by the meager gaslight from above the door. A broad-brimmed hat, Astrakhan-collared coat, thin face, Chinese eyes, thin mustache. It was Mr. K'ing.

"There's your man," Forbes said in a low voice.

K'ing settled his coat about him and turned, speaking to someone in the cab. A second fellow stepped out, a figure in dove gray. It was the last person I expected: Jimmy Woo.

We leaned against the wall in the shadows. K'ing and Woo spoke to each other for a moment in Chinese, and then Woo bowed and walked off in the other direction.

Forbes kept his head down, covered by his top hat, but I was staring straight at Mr. K'ing when his eyes swept the street and locked onto mine. Surely he couldn't see us in the shadow, could he? His face hardened and I thought we were caught for certain, but he turned and stepped briskly down the steps into the inn.

Forbes breathed out and coughed. He breathed in quickly and began coughing again. Finally, he pulled a hand-kerchief from his pocket and clamped it over his mouth. Slowly, the spasms passed. I pretended not to notice and let the man retain his dignity. I owed him that and more.

"That was close," he finally gulped.

"Do you think he saw us?"

"Who can say?" Forbes said and hefted Zangwill again.

"Thank you for coming to my aid," I told him. "What were you doing there?"

"Keeping an eye on things," he said cryptically. "What about you and this fellow?"

"He's a reporter and a friend of mine. He is doing a story on Limehouse."

"This is the sharp end of the sword, old boy," he said. "Couldn't you just take him to a noodle shop or a fan-tan parlor?"

"Exposing K'ing was going to make his career."

"More likely it would end it. I think Mr. K'ing might have an opinion on whether or not he would care to be exposed."

"Woo," I remembered. "He was with Jimmy Woo. What does that mean?"

"You will have to ask your employer that question. Cab!"

We caught a cab and shared it as far as Whitehall and Israel's lodgings. We didn't speak much. I still had pinwheels in the corners of my eyes and was half asleep. In fact, I think we all were. When the cab stopped, we got down and I waved to Forbes, who tapped the brim of his hat with his walking stick.

A few more streets, I told myself. *A few more streets and I will be home.* I kept seeing K'ing's eyes boring into mine.

19

Ho APPEARED ON OUR DOORSTEP THE NEXT morning. He had never been to the house, at least not since I had been in Barker's employment. I took him upstairs, not realizing I was making a mistake. He watched Barker silently for a while, then lit three joss sticks with a match and set them in a holder he'd pulled from his pocket. Having done what he came for, Ho nodded and left the room. I followed him down to the ground floor, which is where the trouble started.

Dummolard came out of the kitchen and caught Ho's eye. He came hurtling after the Chinaman and the two began shouting in two different languages. I thought for certain they would come to blows as they bellowed at each other like bull elephants.

"Gentlemen, please!" I cried, but they paid me no attention. Things might have deteriorated further if an even more formidable adversary had not joined the fray. I'm speaking, of course, of Mireille Dummolard.

She came out of Mac's room, where no doubt she had been feeding him sweetmeats and reading to him from Mrs.

Braddon, and began spitting French phrases in rapid succession like bullets from an American Gatling gun. Both men tried to retain their sangfroid in the face of such a barrage, but it was only a matter of time. In half a minute the men were standing with their heads down, looking like schoolboys caught pulling the tail of the vicar's cat. Ho slinked out the back door while Madame Dummolard marched her husband into the kitchen.

I sat down on the first step of the staircase and held my head. I didn't want to be in charge anymore. I believe life had been less taxing in Oxford Prison.

"I say," Mac called from his bed. "Was that Ho?"

"It was."

"You can't put him and Monsieur Dummolard in the same room, you know. They always fight. It's a feud of long standing."

"Thank you for warning me," I said.

There was another rap at the door and the infernal girl reached for the handle again.

"No!" I cried, arresting her in mid-gesture. "No more visitors. We are declining all visitors today save Mr. Barker's doctors."

"How do you know it is not the doctor?" the maid asked in her accented English.

"Applegate has a nice brougham with a white mare. The other doctor is a Chinaman. If there is no white mare at the curb and no Chinaman, that door stays closed. Do you understand?"

"*Oui,* monsieur," she said with a short curtsey.

I walked toward the kitchen for a cup of coffee, realized the Dummolards were still arguing in there, then considered going out somewhere for some peace and quiet. There was nowhere to go. Instead, I climbed the stair and sat down at Barker's bedside, flipping open the copy of *Pilgrim's Progress*.

"Hello, lad," said the still form on the bed.

"Sir!"

"Was that a fight I heard downstairs just now?"

"Yes, sir," I said. "I'm so glad you are awake. Ho showed up and got into it with Etienne. Then Madame Dummolard came and lit into both of them. I thought I was going to have to send for the police."

Barker grunted from the bed. "You were never warned about them," he said, his voice weak.

"Not until after the fact."

"How long have I been asleep?"

"More than two days."

"Blast," he murmured.

"Your kidneys almost failed, sir. Do you remember?"

"Vaguely. Let me think a moment."

I allowed him the silence. It was good to have him awake again, cogitating. I helped him take a sip of water and then sat down with the book in my hand.

"Death touch," he finally said. "Was Applegate here?"

"He was, sir."

"Applegate could not save me from a death touch. He wouldn't know how."

"No, sir, but I brought Dr. Quong here, as well."

I think I actually surprised him. He spent another moment in silence working it out. "Good, lad," he finally said. "Very astute."

"Thank you, sir," I said.

"That's the first sensible thing you have done this entire case."

"Yes, sir. Sorry, sir."

"I suppose I should be dead now had it not been for your quick thinking. Confound it," he said, showing a little of his normal spirit. "So many hours gone out from under us, and me as weak as a kitten. Tell me what has happened while I was . . . resting."

I related everything chronologically from the time I'd found him unconscious in the corridor until he woke up: calling Applegate, fetching Old Quong, Jenkins's arrival, Poole putting a guard on the house, Bok Fu Ying, Zangwill's news, our visit to the inn, Forbes helping us—everything.

"It appears you've had a time of it."

"Yes, sir."

"I should have realized what had happened. I was caught out."

"You cannot anticipate everything, sir."

"You can if you're wise enough," he said. "Old Quong. Bring him here. I need him. Harness Juno and take the cab. Inform him that I need a good marrow cleansing."

"Yes, sir," I said and went downstairs. There is nothing like being the bearer of good news. Mac shouted a hurrah from his bed, Madame and Monsieur Dummolard stopped arguing long enough to hug each other as well as me over the news, and Harm seemed to understand intuitively and flew up the stairs to his master. Stepping out into the morning air, I made my way to the stables, thinking to myself what a good day it had suddenly become.

Juno seemed to sense it as well. She nickered as soon as she recognized me and the boy was muttering under his breath by the time he had her in the traces, so impatient was she to begin. She broke out through the front door as though it were the gate at Ascot. I was hard-pressed to keep the old girl reined in the entire way there, but I must say she looked beautiful in the sunlight with her bay coloring and glossy sheen. She kept her head high and her steps brisk all the way there.

I tied her to a pole outside Dr. Quong's herb shop. Inside, the old man was talking to an elderly female customer but stopped when he saw me.

"Awake?" he asked.

"Awake."

"Ah! I come, then," he said, concluding his business with the woman.

"He said something about marrow cleansing," I told him when we were alone.

"Ah, yes. Very good, very good," he said, and began to throw preparations into his bag. "You bring your horse again?"

"I brought a carriage, actually."

"Good. Horse is no good on old man's bones."

If it was an unusual sight to see a Chinaman on the back of a horse and rider charging through London, it was equally novel to see one in a hansom cab. In a few moments, we were on our way to London Bridge and points south.

Eventually I pulled the cab into the alley behind Barker's house. I led the doctor up the stairs, stopping in my room to shake off my coat. I found Barker's stair blocked when I arrived, however. Ho had returned and now straddled the bottom step of his staircase, arms crossed and feet splayed.

"Let me pass," I said.

Ho shook his head. "He cannot be disturbed."

I was going to say something but stopped short. There were strange sounds coming from upstairs in Barker's voice. I wanted to go up to see what was happening. Instead, I asked Ho directly if he could tell me what was going on.

Ho looked up at me as if deciding whether or not explaining was worth the effort. After all, I was a barbarian and would understand imperfectly. On the other hand, like a gadfly, I refused to go away. I would stare at him until I got an answer, some sort of answer, anyway.

Ho's face screwed up as he tried to concentrate. He is an ugly brute, if one can say that of an associate. His general expression and demeanor are as if he is deciding how best to gut and serve you. It was possible he might give up the explanation before it began.

"There are certain tones and sounds that affect the organs of the body," he finally replied. "When one repeats these sounds, it is like giving yourself an internal massage. His kidneys have been damaged and Dr. Quong can only do so much externally."

"Is it like the internal exercises he gives me?"

"Much more advanced."

"What if—"

"What if you do not ask so many questions."

I gave it up, realizing he wouldn't let me upstairs. "I'll leave you to your guard duty, then."

Dinner that night was coq au vin. Though it did not diminish my opinion of madame as a cook, I am not in favor of wine in food. Perhaps I was nettled. Barker did not come down, of course. The maid brought a tray up, but Ho merely looked at the food as if it were poisoned and sent it back. It was a good thing Etienne had gone back to his restaurant.

Ho finally summoned me to the room around seven. Barker was sitting up, or rather he was kneeling on the bed and sitting upon his crossed ankles. He was shirtless and his head was down as if he were asleep. I crawled into a chair and tried to be as unobtrusive as possible. The marrow cleansing, whatever it was, had ended, but the Guv looked all in. His skin was slick with sweat. Was he sleeping? Meditating? Dr. Quong had his bag at his feet and was watching Barker intently, as was Ho.

Several minutes later, Barker raised his head and looked over at me. "Bring the carriage," he said weakly.

"Sir, aren't you too ill to travel?"

"Do not argue or question," he said brusquely. "What must be done will be done. Bring it 'round to the front door."

"Yes, sir."

I went downstairs, but before I went to get my coat, I knocked on Mac's door. I needed reinforcements.

"He's going out," I told him, after he had hopped to the door.

"Out? He cannot possibly go out. He just woke up!"

"That is what I said. He insists. I've been ordered to get Juno and bring her 'round the front. Can you have a word with him?"

"I shall try."

By the time I returned with the cab, Ho and Dr. Quong were helping Barker out the front door, holding him up at the elbows, despite Mac's protests. They climbed in with him and we bowled off into the night.

Branching off Commercial Street a half hour later, I dropped Quong and Ho at the tearoom and at Barker's orders took him on a long and leisurely circuit of Limehouse. He had both hands on the head of his stick and the tip was between his shoes, but he looked as if he had just enough strength to sit upright. I had the trap up and could see him nodding to passersby. What was he getting at, traveling so far from his sickbed? Didn't he know how close he had come to dying?

I paraded my employer through the district. At Pekin Street, just across from the Inn of Double Happiness, he rapped on the trapdoor. I pulled over to the curb, or what would pass for one; Limehouse did not have such genteel modernities. He ran a lit vesta over the bowl of his pipe and took a puff. Like a flue, the smoke shot up in front of me. Barker got down from the cab and walked slowly to the wall, turned, and leaned against it.

"May I help you?" I asked.

"Stay there," he said in a low voice.

He stood and smoked for a quarter hour, eyeing the opium den across the street and no doubt being eyed in return. After another five minutes, the door to the den down the steps opened, but no one came out. It was black as pitch under the dancing gas lamp. *What a perfect spot for an execution,* I thought. *One bullet and all K'ing's troubles would be over.* Nothing happened, however. No one came out and Barker did nothing more remarkable than to take another match to his pipe in the shelter of a doorway as hyperborean winds whipped through Pekin Street. I would have expected a flying knife, at least. Barker knocked out his pipe and attempted to get back in the cab. It took him three tries.

"Home?" I asked pointedly.

For once I knew exactly what he was thinking. He wanted to go to Ho's but knew he didn't have the strength to travel up and down those stairs or through the long passage under the Thames. Reluctantly, he grunted his assent.

"Come on, girl," I told Juno.

Soon, we were home, where Madame Dummolard and the nurse took charge of our employer, while I saw Juno bedded down for the night. On the way back, I got up my courage to ask Barker what he was doing, traipsing about the East End straight from his sickbed. That was the plan, but like most best-laid schemes, it went agley. The Guv was asleep when I got back. No doubt he had fallen asleep the moment his head hit his pillow.

What would cause a man who had just had his kidneys fail him to get out of bed and travel somewhere, and when he got there to merely smoke a pipeful of tobacco and leave? It was a message for someone, I knew, either for Mr. K'ing, since he had stopped across from the man's place of business, or for the killer, if they were not one and the same. The message was that Cyrus Barker had not been put out of commission. Barker needed to show his strength by going to the Inn of Double Happiness. It was spitting in the eye of all those who thought him down for the count.

Well, we showed them, I thought, as I got ready for bed. He gave more than a few people food for thought tonight. They had counted him out, but they were wrong. Cyrus Barker was back.

20

THE NEXT MORNING, I FOUND BARKER IN HIS BIG
Georgian bed with the heavy damask curtains drawn back.
He was leaning against a nest of cushions with newspapers
from the last few days spread about and a pot of tea on a
tray in front of him. I was glad to see he was not getting
ready for work.

"Did Dr. Quong order you to bed, sir?" I asked.

"He did," Barker said. "I might ignore one doctor, but
when they collude, I am forced to obey. Look at this!" He
pointed with scorn at a small vase containing a rose on his
tray. Barker kept no roses in the greenhouse and it was February, so it must have been brought in from a hothouse
somewhere.

"Very nice."

"Nice," he repeated, as if the word were poison in his
mouth. "I presume you and Mac have reached an understanding with Madame Dummolard's staff while I was—"
He couldn't finish the sentence.

"I cannot speak for Mac, sir, but I've been too busy or
worried about you."

"She is driving me mad."

"Madame?"

"If she is not hovering about, her maid or nurse is. The fair sex will fuss over a fellow when he is ill, I suppose, but flowers are not a good sign. Next they shall voice concerns over the arrangement of the furnishings."

I had a mental picture of a woman, any woman, telling Barker where to put the sofa and could not help smiling. The first thing to go, I speculated, would be the collection of antique weapons he kept on the red walls of his bed-chamber. Madame could not do it, but I knew there was a certain widow he visited from time to time who might.

"What else have you been doing with yourself?" Barker asked. "Have you pressed your suit with that Petulengro girl?"

"I haven't taken the opportunity of your sudden attack to go out spooning every night, sir, if that is what you are implying. Your health and your visitors have kept me occupied," I said, ignoring his jibe.

"Something about the gypsy shop owner's death still jars me. She is hiding something. I think you should buy her dinner."

"Dinner?"

"I am not saying you should make a habit of taking suspects to dinner, but it seems the best way to get her to talk, short of buying up her entire stock piece by piece."

"I see. You still count her a suspect then?"

"I do not imagine she killed the monks in the monastery in China, but I assume she is capable of shooting a gun in a tunnel. You have got to understand these matchstick girls, lad. They are rather hardened."

"So, who are the suspects?"

"Ah, no. You'll not be catching me out that way. You have been in charge for a few days. You tell me."

I ran my hand across my face a couple of times to give myself time to think. "Well, Mr. K'ing, of course."

"Why do you say that?"

"You don't think so?"

"I did not say that, but you cannot just say he is a suspect. You must say why we must consider him."

"Very well. He is the leader of a criminal organization in London. I don't think anything of such a magnitude would happen in his district without his having a part in it."

"Perhaps. Continue."

"There's that fellow on the blotter. The betel nut man."

"Charlie Han."

"Yes. He is a known criminal. Bainbridge seemed to think him dangerous and so far we have not been able to find a trace of him."

"How would you proceed?"

"By finding out how long he has been in London?"

"Excellent. Who else?"

"Campbell-Ffinch. He has been in town the proper amount of time and is extremely anxious to get the book."

"And?"

"Jimmy Woo, I suppose. He seems to know a lot of what is going on in the Asian quarter and he has been here for a long time."

"We should check that."

"What if all these murders are really not the work of one man? We've got different methods, different times, and even different countries. How do we know the killer of the monks in the monastery over a year ago is the same fellow who shot at us last week?"

"You make a good point," Barker conceded. "In defense, I can only say that those who kill once often kill again and that I sense I am on the right road here."

"I still wonder what his motive is," I said. "Why does he want the book so single-mindedly? Having lost it, most people would have given up by now."

"It is an Oriental trait to wait patiently but an Occidental one to hang on out of sheer doggedness. All shall be revealed in the fullness of time."

There was a footstep upon the stair, and the maid appeared with a tray in her hand, an envelope upon it. Barker took it from her with a slight glare in her direction, then ripped it open. He extracted a piece of paper and began reading.

"What is it?" I asked.

"It is a court order giving permission to search my home." He turned to the girl. "Tell Madame Dummolard we will have supper as usual. If they are going to search my house, I wish them to see that we are not inconvenienced in the least."

The maid curtseyed and left.

Inspector Poole and Campbell-Ffinch were suddenly at the top of the stair and were taking in the sight of Cyrus Barker in bed, surrounded by walls bristling with weaponry.

"Very impressive," Campbell-Ffinch said, but whether he meant Barker at home in his Regency bed or the collection of weapons, I couldn't say.

"What is wrong with you?" the Foreign Office official demanded.

"I had a set-to with your killer. I am on bed rest for a day or two."

"Did you see him? Did you see who it was?"

"No, drat the luck."

"Did he get the text?"

"It is not in my possession," Barker declared. "Feel free to search the premises, since you have already obtained legal permission to do so. I hope you have more profitable subjects of inquiry, for I assure you that these next hours shall bear no fruit."

Campbell-Ffinch pulled two more envelopes from his pocket with a gesture of triumph. "I have two additional court orders: one to search your offices and another for the property you own in Three Colt Street."

"I also keep a horse and carriage in a stable a half mile from here. You might get an order for that, as well."

"If necessary, we shall," Campbell-Ffinch said. "I must say, I do not care for your attitude, Barker. You've lost an assistant and an acquaintance, yet you still appear as obstinate and uncooperative as ever. I only hope your fee is sufficient to assuage the inconvenience I'm going to put you through."

"It is a small book, sir," Barker replied, "but you are fortunate. England is a small island."

"If it is here, we shall find it!" The official scowled and marched down the stairs.

"I'm sorry about all this, Cyrus," Poole said. "If there were any other way . . ."

"I understand, Terry. I am not blaming you."

"Why not just give him the stupid book? What could it hurt?"

"You do not know what you are asking. If Campbell-Ffinch throws me in jail and takes all that I possess, it still would not be as catastrophic as if he had that text. And let me be firm about that, even with you. I do not have possession of it."

Poole gave me a look of utter misery.

"Don't look at me," I told him. "I cannot help you. I have no idea where the text is."

The inspector gave a shrug and went downstairs. A few minutes later I heard Dummolard below. They had dared enter his domain without permission. Poole returned a few minutes later.

"Cyrus, I must ask you to restrain your Frenchman."

"As you see," my employer replied, "I am incapacitated. If you can induce him to climb the stair, I shall instruct him to allow the search, as long as you do not go poking fingers into his pies. Etienne is very sensitive about his crusts."

I couldn't help it. I snorted. The Guv is a very serious person most of the time, and one might feel he has no sense of humor, but being pressed by some authority brought out a touch of drollness in him.

Poole scowled at me and I shut up. "If he gives us trouble, I'm taking him to A Division for questioning and possible charges of assault."

"You shall have to take that up with him," my employer said. "He is capable of making his own decisions. Arrest him, if you like, but my experience of Dummolard has been that he is generally uncooperative."

"I wish I had never heard of that blasted book," Poole grumbled.

"There," Barker said. "We agree on something."

Poole went back downstairs.

"Where were we?" Barker asked.

"I don't recall. How are you feeling, sir?"

"Rather weak, I'm afraid, and my kidneys hurt. I shall be glad when Dr. Quong returns."

"Sir, does Old Quong have the text?"

"Best not to ask, lad. You wouldn't want to perjure yourself in the dock under a barrister's questioning, if it comes to that."

There was a scream down below and a second torrent of French, female this time. Barker chuckled, then winced at the pain. A few moments later, a beleaguered Poole returned.

"Cyrus."

"Madame Dummolard is at present my housekeeper, Terry," the Guv explained. "It is her duty to keep house. Perhaps your constables are not returning the items they are searching to their original positions. You should either instruct your men to be more careful or carry her up here bodily, and I shall instruct her to be more helpful."

"I think you are enjoying this."

"My home has been invaded and yet you complain about resistance. If it is too much trouble, go back to Whitehall and leave us in peace."

Poole shook his head and went downstairs while Barker returned to his newspapers.

"What are you reading, sir?"

"Stead's article in the *Gazette* about Khartoum. Parliament simply must consent to send a force to retrieve Gordon's body."

Gordon, of course, was General Charles Gordon, who

had fallen with his troops in January in the Sudan. News had arrived that he had been slain by the Mahdi's Muslim warriors. Gordon's likeness had begun to appear in placards and magazines and in photographs in shop windows. England likes its dead heroes even more than its live ones. I remembered Bainbridge had mentioned his name. His nickname was Chinese Gordon. I wasn't well schooled in Chinese history, but as I recalled, he had defended Shanghai against the Chinese rebels some twenty years before and Barker had fought with him. "Did you ever meet the general, sir?"

"I served under him," he said. "We were called the Ever Victorious Army—Chinese troops led by English and American officers at the behest of the Chinese government."

"How did you get mixed up in all that?" I asked.

"I was working on the docks at Foochow when the entire south was overthrown. My parents had died of cholera a few years before and I made my way to Shanghai to try to locate my elder brother, who was at a private school for Europeans along the Bund. I finally found him, but he was keen to join the fighting and soon I found myself with an English unit as an interpreter while my brother helped the Americans. The armies split up and I never saw him again."

"My word."

"Yes, the Americans accused England of aiding the secessionist side in the War Between the States. There were two civil wars going on at once. In the chaos after the English and Americans split, Gordon was assigned to my regiment. He was unaccustomed to leadership and something of a Christian mystic, but he had a way of inspiring the troops. He was fearless, walking into battle as if God Himself was protecting him.

"After three years fighting, we finally broke the back of the rebel forces and routed them. The rebel leader died, killed himself some say, and that was it. Gordon was decorated and sent home to England a hero. I understand his straightforward talk earned him enemies in the War Office and he lay fallow for many years until he was finally offered a chance against the Mahdi's troops. It was suicide, lad, a shabby way to treat one of England's greatest leaders of men."

My mind was taking it all in, a young, impressionable Barker and a valiant leader in war-torn China. I had to say something or he would close up on me again.

"So when did you meet the Dowager Empress?"

Barker ran a hand over his brow wearily. "Some other time, lad."

Some other time, I thought. *It's always some other time.*

21

BARKER EXPECTED ME TO EARN MY SHILLING.
There would be no hanging about the house waiting for
him to need something. I went to the office by cab, bundled
up and under cover from a light snow.

Once inside I watched the snow stop and start, paced,
and waited to see if someone needed an enquiry agent. No
one did, or perhaps they merely put off their need for our
services to a more clement day. If so, I thanked them, much
preferring to sit inside looking out at the swirling flakes in
Craig's Court than to be out in them.

The morning dragged on until lunch. I skipped around
the corner to the Sun, which was full of Yard men, and had
some beef from the joint and a half pint of bitter. All too
soon I was nipping my way back again.

The post was barren of interest that day and though I
tried to ponder the case, my brain was preoccupied. I was
never so glad for six o'clock to come 'round. I had successfully whiled a day of my life away doing absolutely nothing.
I rather envied Jenkins as he ran out the door at five thirty.
At least he had somewhere to go.

•   •   •

Back in Newington, Barker had had a day as exciting as mine, though he'd been able to rest through most of it. He resisted Madame Dummolard's offer to bring up his meal and insisted on dressing for dinner. The nurse attempted to help him, but the Guv ordered both women out of the room, with less than the usual politeness he granted the fairer sex. Once downstairs, he looked almost like his normal self, though a trifle gaunt.

"We shall be going out again tonight, lad," he informed me as we helped ourselves from the sideboard. "I've received a message from Forbes. Campbell-Ffinch shall be boxing, and I want to see him fight. It shall be bare knuckle and therefore illegal."

Late that evening Barker and I took a hansom cab to Victoria Station where we boarded a train bound for Wimbledon to attend the match. Secretly, I was hoping to see Campbell-Ffinch grassed or at least to see his supercilious expression wiped from his face.

This was one of those instances where being a private enquiry agent was better than being an officer of the law. Were a constable to stumble upon the scene he could only arrest a fellow or two and let the rest of us go. None would cooperate, some would lie, and the few detained would be released in the morning. We, on the other hand, could walk among the participants and learn what there was to learn.

We arrived at a public house with the promising name of the Ring. There are many types of public houses, according to the interests and dispositions of the proprietors, and this one was a sporting pub. Prints of famous boxers of the past lined the walls, going back to Mendoza, along with reliquaries the Roman Catholic Church could not have preserved better: Jack Randall's shoes from the 1820s, a bust of Bob Gregson from the Royal Academy, and a loving portrait painted on a Staffordshire jug of the great Dan Mendoza himself, heavyweight champion in the days before gloves and rules, a glorious time which shall never see its like again, at least according to the publican. A great boxer, he assured us after Barker had struck up a conversation with him, even if the famed man had the misfortune of being a Jew. Our host was the sort of fellow who believed every English youth should be six feet in height, a good twelve stone at least, and muscled like a plow horse, and any deficiencies were due to Norman blood or other generational mistakes.

Barker had made a radical change in his attire: he was wearing a diamond-set horseshoe stickpin. It is funny how the least thing will allow one to fit in. He went from sober private enquiry agent to sporting enthusiast in a moment, and his entire personality changed.

"I heard a rumor," he said, leaning over the bar, a bundle of energy, "that there might be sport to be had in this neighborhood this evening, if one played one's cards right. My friend and I have come an awfully long way at a chance for a flutter."

"We might be able to accommodate you and the young gentleman," the publican said with oily enthusiasm.

"Yes, we were just at the Athletic Club the other day, watching the most pathetic match between Strothers and Carson. Twelve rounds. They weren't even hurting each other! It was as if they had taped cushions to their hands. I started talking about the old days and some of the great fights, such as Cribb versus Molineaux, Randall versus Mar-

214 __ **Will Thomas**

tin, and Sayers versus Heenan. My poor friend here has never seen a bare-knuckle match, a true gladiatorial contest, and I promised him I would take him to see one if we had to leave England to do it."

The publican ran a thumb across his lower lip with a canny look. "I don't think a man would have to go as far as that to see a good matchup."

"That is what my sources have told me."

"Oh, really now?" he said. "And who might these sources of yours be?"

"I am not at liberty to say," Barker said, looking offended, though I knew it was an act.

"You'll have to tell me if you want to see some blood sport," the man pressed.

"I do not put the finger on my friends," Barker continued to insist.

"Suit yourself, then. I never said nothing about nothing." And with that, the man began wiping the counter with a towel. He'd brought us some Watney ale, which was better than the house deserved. We each took a pull from our tankards and let the matter cool for a moment.

"Oh, very well," the Guv said to me. "If you're going to give me that look. It was McLain that told me about the . . . meeting."

"Handy Andy?" the man spoke up. "He's out of it!"

"Aye, he is out of it, but he is not dead, yet. He still hears things. Word says this Campbell-Ffinch fellow can fight. A real up-and-comer."

"They don't call him the Hammersmith Hammer for nothing. Time!" The latter was bawled over our shoulders to the crowd.

"So," Barker said, putting down his half-empty pint glass and wiping the foam from his mustache, "were one interested in what you so rightly call blood sport, where might one go?"

"Watch and learn, gentlemen," was all the response we got. "Watch and learn."

The clock struck eleven and the lot of us were ejected at closing time. This was not your average closing, however. There were over fifty of us standing in one or twos along the old road, stamping our feet in the cold. The pub owner locked his door with a flourish and led us down the road for a quarter mile. It must have been an odd sight for someone in one of the cottages along the way, half a hundred marching along silently in the dark. Well, almost silently. Everyone had been drinking, after all, and looking forward to a fight.

I had heard somewhere about clandestine fights that sometimes they took place in the middle of the roadways, the better to vanish if constables should appear. Surely that would be in warm weather, however. Were I a professional fighter, there wasn't enough money in the Bank of England to make me take my shirt off outside that night. Things improved considerably when the publican led us up to an ancient-looking tithe barn and opened the time-sprung doors. The fighters were already in their places, warming up. There were several lanterns lit, but they dared not risk any sort of fire in the dried-out structure, so it was very cold inside the building.

Campbell-Ffinch looked a worthwhile opponent, I'll say that for him. Were I a betting man, I'd put my shilling on him. Stripped to the waist, in his silk drawers, long hose, and boots, he looked formidable. He was brown all over, and where there was brown, there was muscle, too. He seemed to glow with health, and as he shadowboxed, a fine layer of steam rose from him like from a Thoroughbred after a run.

As for his opponent, I've seen one like him in every village: big-chested, bigger bellied, spindle-shanked, and past his prime. He was the sort that had shown promise once, but it had all been brawn, and he'd never developed the brain to go with it.

The publican showed a flair for sportsmanship and an ability to ape his betters in the boxing fancy. He announced the fight as if it were a national title event, and to his way of thinking, it was. The sport of bare-knuckle or old rule boxing had been declared illegal and could not now bring together champions from all over England as it once had. Campbell-Ffinch, the Hammersmith Hammer, was called the champion. The contender's name was not worth remembering, but his moniker was the Titan of Tunbridge Wells.

Our host was kind enough to point out the bookies whose takings would provide him his fee, no matter who won that evening. We were one of the few in the crowd who did not partake, but we were not conspicuous about it. The attention went back to the center of the ring, where the boxers were given the rules. A man at the side of the room rang a bell and the fight commenced.

I had boxed a little when I was in school, and I had seen a few matches as well. This wasn't like those fights at all. It was more like fighting against a bully when I was a lad. The fists slamming into jaws and stomachs were mostly bone with a thin layer of tissue over it. It hurt to see it. The skin of both men began to turn an angry red. Surely it wouldn't last long. The old boxer was game, I'll give him that, but he was no match for Campbell-Ffinch. It was give-and-take for a while, and then there was a bell.

In the second round, the Foreign Office man's opponent came out, determined to even the odds, but Campbell-Ffinch got him up under the jaw with a juicy one that made him stumble and shake his head. He would have been downed if the bell had not rung again.

The Titan was slow off his stool for the third round, and it became obvious that the Hammer was toying with him. The Titan tried a final desperate ploy and shot out a jab. Campbell-Ffinch's left arm came up, hooked 'round the fellow's wrist, and pushed it down. He stepped in so close, their chests almost touched, and as his left countered any move the Titan might try, his right delivered a vicious hook punch to the Titan's temple and down he went, like a bullock at Leadenhall market. There was no shaking of the head or straining to get up. The man would be lucky if he awoke before mid-morning.

A number of audience members voiced their displeasure, but there was nothing they could do about so short a match. One couldn't exactly complain to the village constable, and if sometimes a match was short, the next might be overlong. So are the vagaries of boxing between two human engines without gloves.

Campbell-Ffinch was pronounced the winner, someone threw a towel over his shoulders, and the Titan's trainer attempted to revive him. Campbell-Ffinch finally saw us and his eyes narrowed.

"What are you doing here?" he demanded.

"Watching a bit of sport," Barker stated. "Good match."

"I do this merely to keep in shape, you know," he said. "Strictly amateur."

Amateur, my eye, I told myself. If I knew my man, he'd wagered heavily on himself and had somebody there to pick up his winnings. He was trying to convince us, because he didn't want us to tell the Foreign Office what illegal activity he was up to. If I knew Barker, he'd keep it to himself. Campbell-Ffinch would be in his debt, and that kind of debt is always harder to work off than money.

"I thought your doctor forbade your getting out of bed," Campbell-Ffinch said.

"I could not resist the opportunity to see you fight. By the way, I apologize for wasting the time of all those good constables this morning, hunting for the text. I assume they never found it."

"I'll find it, Barker, make no mistake about it. I hope you realize you are blackening your name irreparably with the Foreign Office."

"We shall see whose name shall be blackened, sir."

"Wait!" Campbell-Ffinch called, daring to put a hand on Barker's shoulder. "How are you coming along on the case?"

"I should be able to lay my hands upon the man," the Guv said, looking pointedly at the hand on his shoulder, "within a week, if matters unfold as I plan."

"You are certain?"

"Ask for no certainties on earth, sir. I shall do my best and am optimistic." He turned to go.

"What did you think of the fight?" he called out as we left.

"It was unevenly matched. I would like to see you against a better opponent."

"What about yourself, sir? I've heard you are rather good. Perhaps we can set up a match!"

"Ah," Barker rumbled, "but there again, it would be too unevenly matched."

We made our way back to the train station and into a compartment on a train.

"What o'clock is it?" he asked.

I consulted my repeater. "Half past one, sir. That move, sir, that last move Campbell-Ffinch made, that knocked out the Titan—"

"What about it?" Barker asked.

"It was Chinese boxing, wasn't it?"

"Very good, lad. Yes, it was. A hook of the wrist, followed by a simultaneous block and punch. He did it well, too."

"How do you suppose he learned it?"

"No Chinese instructor would teach a foreigner, but the man has eyes and a brain. Perhaps he saw it in a fight and copied the move or learned it from someone unscrupulous, such as a dismissed student. I am certain he would pay well for that information."

"It's far too coincidental, sir. He has to be our killer. He is awfully desperate to lay his hands on the book."

"Perhaps," Barker stated diplomatically.

"Will you speak to Inspector Poole about Campbell-Ffinch's late night activities?"

"No, I want to give Poole a chance to solve this one if he can. Setting Scotland Yard and the Foreign Office at each other's throats will only tie up both agencies."

"More room for you, then," I said.

"I don't need them hampered to find Quong's killer."

"Do you know who it is?" I asked, leaning forward.

"It is still early, lad. One cannot build a house until all the materials are assembled. I counsel patience."

"Yes, sir," I said, "but while we are being patient, we have a houseful of servants and stable fees and other expenses to pay."

"Spoken like an assistant. I thank you for your concern," he said, "but there is no amount I could pay that would equal the sacrifice Quong himself made in my service."

Of course, I had no rejoinder to make to that. After we pulled into Victoria Station, Barker moved forward to get out and I saw him wince, striations in the skin below his black spectacles.

"How are you feeling?" I dared ask.

"The ride has done nothing good for my lower back. My kidneys are still sore, but I take that as a good sign. Things must hurt before they can heal. They must get worse before they can get better."

I stepped out of the station doors and raised my good arm to hail a hansom. I always hate it when Barker sounds prophetic.

22

———◆———

BARKER RESTED MOST OF THE NEXT DAY. HE HAD been pushing himself since he'd first awakened from his injuries. When I got back from the office, Mac informed me that the Guv hadn't even been down to lunch. We were talking *sotto voce* but we should have known the Guv would have heard me enter the house. He called down from the top floor. I set my stick in the hall stand and went upstairs.

My employer was still in bed, clad in his dressing gown. Upon my entrance, he reached into the table by his bed and removed a small daguerreotype, no larger than a playing card. I scrutinized it. It showed a young Oriental with a serious expression on his face against a backdrop painted to look like a Hellenic grove.

"Is this Quong?" I asked.

"Yes. I want you to take it with you to dinner with Miss Petulengro. See if she recognizes it."

"But I haven't asked her yet, sir."

"Then you had better make haste, lad. A young woman as attractive as that is not going to wait for you to get up your courage."

• • •

I slid into the shop a few minutes before closing time, making certain the bell jingled to attract Miss Petulengro's attention. By the time I reached the counter, she came in from the rooms behind.

"Oh, it's you, again," she said, flashing what might be the prettiest teeth in the East End. "What brings you here?"

"I was in the neighborhood and thought I might take the chance that you had not eaten dinner yet."

"Here, I ain't that kinda girl, I'll have you know," she said, putting her hand on her hip.

"Oh! I do beg your pardon! I didn't mean—"

She broke out in a laugh. "Oh, your face. Four shades of red, it is. I meant I ain't the kinda girl you have to impress with a meal, if you get my meaning."

"I see."

"But you might have warned me, you know. I might have made plans of me own. I been asked to dinner twice today already, and I turned them down. What makes you think I'd go out with you?"

"Because being an enquiry agent makes me irresistible to women," I bluffed. "Air of danger and all that."

"Ha! As far as I'm concerned, it's just another name for copper. I suppose your real plan is to open me up and ply me with questions."

"Well, yes, that's exactly the idea, but there's no reason why we cannot do it over a nice meal and a bottle of wine."

"I reckon you're right. Best offer I had all day, I'll admit. Where shall we go?"

"I don't know the East End well. Is there somewhere special you would like to eat?"

"There's a nice restaurant over by Billingsgate where you can get a fish dinner you won't forget. Haven't been there in a while. Will that suit your sensibilities or do you want to go somewhere posh? You *are* dressed like a toff tonight."

"A fish dinner sounds wonderful."

"Perfect. I'll lock up and be down directly."

It was more like ten minutes, but she had transformed into a swan during that time. She'd changed into a long skirt and white blouse with lace at the collar and wrists, covered by a mantle of dark silk paisley that emphasized her gypsy looks. She had pinned back her henna-colored hair and traded the large hoops she wore for a more delicate set of ivory cameo earrings. Her cheeks were flushed but I couldn't tell if it were due to the rouge pot or merely the result of looking forward to a good evening.

The East End wasn't easy to negotiate on a weekday evening. We walked a few blocks until we reached the tram, which took us west a while. Eventually we got off on Commercial Road and hired a four-wheeler. Hettie looked quite beautiful in her evening outfit, and had she behaved herself I'm sure she could have graced any West End establishment. But she wouldn't behave herself, I knew. She was simply too wild. I was certain she could snap her fingers and have a dozen Limehouse denizens at her beck and call.

The restaurant, when we finally arrived, was hard by the Fish Market, in a converted warehouse overlooking the Thames. Inside, it looked more like a cross between a pub and a well-established supper club. As I stepped in, the aroma of melted butter and oyster stew met my nostrils. I had to admit I was hungry.

"'Ello, Eddy, old boy!" Hestia cried out to the maître d', an old gentleman who reminded me of Fezziwig from Dickens's *A Christmas Carol,* round as a ball and jovial as a doting grandfather.

"Why, Miss Petulengro! Bless my soul! How pleasant to see you again! What outrage have we performed that you've stayed away so long?"

"How could you do anything wrong, Eddy? You know you'll always be my favorite."

"I see no other option, my dear," the old fellow said, "than to give you and your gentleman friend here the best seat in the house."

He led us through a maze of corridors full of booths with people dining until we finally came to a set of windows overlooking the Thames, where we were seated. The river, for once, looked almost romantic, and the row of windows looking out on the water made me feel like we were in the stern of an clipper ship. Our table was lit by candles, and it even boasted linen. I noticed not a few eyes upon us, but when one goes out with such a beauty, I suppose one must grow accustomed to that.

"Shall you and the gentleman be having the house dinner, miss?"

"We shall."

"Excellent. I hope everything will be up to your expectations. You, sir. Would you care to see the wine list?"

"I believe," I said, "that such a selection is best left in your capable hands. I would not presume to consider my opinion higher than your own."

"Spoken like a man of discernment. Very well. I am to

be given a free hand, so to speak. Enjoy your meal, and let the courses begin."

"Courses?" I asked Hettie after he had gone.

"Yes. I hope you brought your appetite, ducks. I'm starved."

"Is the food as good as the view?" I asked, looking out at the river.

"Oh, it is. Now I know you have some questions from that boss of yours. Go on."

"If I may, I'd like to begin with your uncle."

Her face turned serious a moment. "Thought you might. I was out celebrating New Year's with some girl friends. Got home late and found the shop in the possession of Bainbridge and company."

"Inspector Bainbridge?" I asked.

"The very same. Me uncle was found dead behind the counter by some sailors who'd been anxious to sell their kit for a night of revels. It looked like a typical robbery. His neck had been broken with one blow. There was a nasty bruise across the left side of his neck, but nothing stolen out of the jewel case or the safe."

"Was Inspector Bainbridge helpful?"

"I don't meant to speak ill of the dead, but Bainy always had an eye on me and I don't think it was a professional one, either. He followed me about and kept an eye on the shop, both before and after. To tell you the truth, I half suspected he did me uncle in. The wound looked just like the mark that club of his would make."

"But why would the inspector want to kill your uncle?" I asked.

"Who knows? Maybe he wanted to make me an heiress so he could marry me."

"But he was already married," I pointed out.

"Oh, I think he'd do in his missus, if it came to that. Not that I asked him to. He was a copper, after all, and not a pretty one like you," she said, and actually reached across the table and pinched my nose. "Lawks, if you don't blush!" She laughed.

The meal arrived after that. Arrived and kept arriving. The fish dinner, which turned out to be famous in the East End, consisted of eleven fish courses aside from the buns and vegetables. There was plaice and sole, sea bass and halibut, flounder, oysters, herring in mustard sauce, cod, eels, whiting, and shad. My dinner companion proved herself an enthusiastic eater. As to drink, I found we each had a goblet of white wine, a glass of porter, and a half pint of stout, to wash everything down with. Had Barker not been paying for the meal, I'd have begun to worry how much it would all cost.

By the end of the meal, I was gasping, "My word. I cannot eat another bite."

"Eddy takes good care of you, don't you agree?"

"He does. I trust this doesn't all come from the Thames."

"Good heavens, no. It comes from Newhaven on the train, first thing in the morning. Eddy hits the fish market early."

"Is that what this place is called? Eddy's? I didn't see a sign out front besides the one saying Fish Dinner."

"I believe its actual moniker is the Billingsgate Family Fish Restaurant and Public House, but if you don't call it Eddy's, you're green."

"I see. All this food is making me drowsy. Would you be interested in a short walk? There is a nice place nearby where we can get a good cup of coffee."

"I'm game for anything."

We received our bill, which was astonishingly inexpensive, I thought, considering all we'd eaten, and after Hettie gave the proprietor a resounding kiss on the cheek, we left. The temperature had grown colder outside and my companion pulled her shawl around her.

"So," she said, slipping her hand under my arm for warmth. "Tell me two things I don't know about you."

"Very well. I am a widower, and I have spent eight months in Oxford Prison."

I thought I'd surprise her, but she merely nodded. "Thought as much. About the prison, I mean. No man with a choice of positions would do what you do for a living. Not men with sensitive souls, like yourself. I can tell that about you. The death of your old lady musta broke your heart. You're very young."

"It happened when I was at university."

"La!" Hestia said. "Look at me. I'm out with a university man. I might have to parade you in front of some of my friends. They'll be ever so impressed."

By now we'd reached Cornhill and I steered us into St. Michael's Alley. I opened the door and ushered her into the Barbados Coffee House, which is as close to being my home away from home as any place in the world. The proprietor took us to a table and I think I rose several notches in his estimation. The old place rarely saw a woman enter its door and certainly none as attractive as Miss Petulengro.

"It's dark as the hole of Calcutter in here," Hettie said

after we'd been seated. Her fingers dipped down into the recess in the middle of the table. "What is this stuff? Smells like tobacco."

"It is. Virginia Cavendish, the best tobacco in London. The warehouses from America and the West Indies are across the way there. Cigars from Cuba, sugar from Jamaica, and coffee beans from South America."

The proprietor returned and presented me with my clay pipe and asked for our order.

"Two coffees, please. Would you like some dessert, Hettie?"

"Nothing, thanks. If I eat anything else, it'll kill me."

After he left, I returned to my questioning.

"It must be a bit strange running a chandler's shop in the Asian quarter. What caused your uncle to give up the traveling life and settle down?"

Hettie took the now lit pipe out of my hands and gave it a preliminary puff. It must have pleased her because I didn't get the pipe back for the duration of the visit. Her smoking scandalized the owner as he passed once, but she tipped him a wink and charmed him out of his surprise.

"The Romany people have fallen on hard times," she explained. "We're being chased out of towns and villages where we were once welcomed. A lot of us have sold off our wagons or left England entirely. Used to be we could get by on mending pots and telling fortunes, going from town to town, but no more. There ain't no profit to be made in it. Pretty soon, you won't see a respectable painted wagon anywhere."

"I'm sorry to hear it. I want you to take a look at something," I said, pulling out the daguerreotype of Quong that

Barker had given me. "This is Mr. Barker's late assistant."

"I remember him!" she said instantly. "Yes, I wondered where he'd gone. We often get Chinese lads in the shop, salivating over me like I was a hot cross bun in a bakery window. Not him, though. He liked books and odd bits. He'd come through regular and check our bookshelf. Educating himself, I reckon. Tried flirting with him once, just a little, to see what he'd do. You'd think I was a live crocodile. He backed out of the shop, he did, like I was going to bite him. He came back, though, the next week, when some new books came in."

"He was engaged to be married," I explained.

"Shoulda known. I take it he passed away?"

"Yes, and in just the same manner as Inspector Bainbridge. Is there anything you've left out that might be pertinent to the case?"

"'Pertinent to the case,'" she repeated. "No, I don't know nothing 'pertinent to the case,' but if I remember something I'll send you a message." I watched her fill the bowl of the pipe and light it with big, smoky puffs. Then she turned it around and slid the mouthpiece with its glazed tip into my mouth as if she were a harem girl and I were the sultan of Persia.

"How big was your uncle?" I asked.

"Pretty big, and meaner than two snakes. One of them Chinamen on top of another's shoulder might reach his neck, but by then he'd have both of them in his teeth like a rat terrier. The only ones I'd say were his match were Bainbridge and your boss."

"What?" I asked. "Not me?"

"Go on," she laughed. "Pull the other one."

When the proprietor finally came to claim my pipe, Hettie handed it to him and patted his hand. One would have thought he was Lancelot receiving a favor from Guinevere. He went back to his corner, no doubt to plan their elopement, while I tossed some shillings on the table and we left. I hoped it wasn't just the cold that made her slip her hand into mine.

I summoned a cab and we took it all the way to her shop. I helped her down and there was an awkward moment in front of the shop. She leaned forward, took my ears into her hands, and put her lips to mine. Two seconds of complete bliss, the kind poets write about, and then she was gone, and I was climbing back into the cab.

"Lucky beggar," I heard from the cabman overhead.

Lucky beggar was right.

23

CYRUS BARKER WAS PACKING WHEN I GOT BACK.
His suitcase was open and he was taking shirts and other
items from a large and ancient wardrobe in the corner of his
room.

"What is going on?" I asked. "Has something happened?"

"Nothing involving the case. I am moving to our chambers for a few days."

"Whatever for?"

Barker pointed to the stair. "That woman is insufferable.
She puts sugar and lemon in my green tea. She moves
things about to suit herself, puts vases of flowers on every
table, and constantly pesters me with questions. She'll never
say one word when twenty will do. If I do not get out of
here, I shall run mad."

"Madame is only trying to be nice," I pointed out.
"When shall you return?"

"When Madame and her army are gone. Things are
working out to your satisfaction, I am sure. All you need do
is snap your fingers and there is a young lady at hand to ro-
mance. And speaking of young ladies, how was your

evening with Miss Petulengro?" he asked irritably, brushing by me to get some ties and suspenders.

"It went well, but nothing stands out as being important over all. I'll remind you that I went out with her at your request, sir."

"I'm certain it must have been a trial for you. We'll discuss it at the office tomorrow, then." He locked the case and secured the straps around it.

"Why not simply tell Madame she and her maids are sacked?"

"That would not be fair to Mac. He is not yet ready to return to his duties. In any case, I like having Etienne here at night, since both you and Mac are indisposed."

"Are you certain you will be all right?"

"Of course. We have a camp bed in the office and a fireplace. Public houses are ready to hand for sustenance, and perhaps I shall confound our killer by moving. At the very least, I shall get a moment's peace."

Madame was waiting in the hall. The door was open, and a cab was at the door. She stood silent and glacial, and I wondered if the two had exchanged words. Etienne came in, frowned as Barker passed with his suitcases, and watched along with the rest of us as our employer left. After he'd rattled off in the hansom and the maid had closed the door, Etienne began a fresh argument with his wife. Mac rolled his eyes and limped back into his sanctum, while I scurried upstairs and undressed for bed.

I had no sooner got under the covers when there came a sound out in the darkness that chilled my blood. It was the long, plaintive cry of a policeman's whistle. Worse still, at the end of it, it broke off and began again, fitfully, as if the officer blowing the tune was being hindered somehow. Something was occurring again outside the house. The only good thing that could be said was that it wasn't happening at two or three in the morning this time.

"Confound it," I said in the corridor as I threw my dressing gown around my shoulders. After this case was over, I intended to sleep uninterrupted for most of a week.

Downstairs, I found Mac with his trusted shotgun cradled in his arms. We unbolted the back door and there we heard the most exquisite words in the English language.

"We've got 'im!" Two constables wrestled with a suspect between them, but they appeared to be getting the worst end of it. One had a missing helmet and the other a bloody nose. The suspect was in bracelets, but Poole had not thought to supply these fellows with much needed leg irons. The chap in the middle was kicking their shins, ankles, and anything else he could reach. He was Chinese and unless I was mistaken, he was the elusive Charlie Han. One constable either lost his patience or finally reached the truncheon on his belt. There was a thump and the struggling fellow went limp. Not so gently, they dragged him over the doorsill into the house and dropped him on the floor in our hallway.

"We need to send for a vehicle," the first one said, while the other—the one with the bloody nose—conjugated various verbs and practiced his expletives while occasionally giving the prone figure a kick.

"We have a telephone set," I said. "I can call Scotland Yard."

The constable was able to handle criminals but not the latest contrivances of the modern age. As he watched, I made the call to Scotland Yard, explained the situation, and requested a vehicle. The chief constable demanded to speak to the constable in charge, who picked up the receiver as if it were a king cobra about to strike, but after a short conversation, during which he shouted into the receiver, we finally got it all settled.

"Blimey," the constable muttered, backing away from the device and wiping his forehead with a handkerchief. "First time I ever tried one o' them things."

"So, who is this fellow?" Mac asked, regarding the still form.

"Dunno," said the second P.C., who'd managed to get half his handkerchief up his nose to staunch the blood. "And I could care even less. Some Chinaman. Found him outside your big round gate, ready to open it. You've had some break-ins, haven't you?"

"Yes, and we've all been attacked, as you can see."

"Would you gentlemen care for some tea while you wait?" Mac offered.

"I could do with a cuppa. What about you, Finney?"

"That would suit me right down to the ground," the first constable agreed.

I reached to turn the unconscious suspect over, but the second constable stopped me.

"Careful there, guv'nor," he said. "He could be shamming. Cut up pretty rough out there."

"Then help me. I want to get a good look at him."

Together we rolled him over. One glance and I knew I was right. He had a head of shaggy hair cut in the European style and one of those Chinese mustaches that don't meet in the middle. It was the last suspect from Bainbridge's sketch, the fierce face.

"Charlie Han," I stated. "He's a known criminal in Lime-house, in the betel nut trade. He's got a large arrest sheet."

"All right, Mr. Han, get up! On your feet. We can't have you a-droolin' on no gentleman's floor."

The half-conscious prisoner raised his head and tried to focus. He looked tough, possibly tough enough to take on Barker in the tunnel or Mac in the study, but the constable's truncheon had done for him.

"Pull yourself together, man," the constable went on, hauling the Chinaman to his feet roughly. I'd have felt sorry for him if it weren't probable he had come to kill us all. Just then the fellow made his move. He swung the constable around until he collided with me and we both went down. With the cast over much of my upper body I could not get up fast enough. Then, as the first constable came forward, Han gave him a strong heel in the stomach. He hadn't reckoned on Mac, however, who cocked and raised his shotgun to his shoulder. With the rest of us temporarily down, Han made an easy target.

"I am very well trained in how to use this weapon, sir," Mac spoke with some authority, "and I am quite willing to use it. I suggest you do not move."

Han must have seen that he was serious. For a butler, Mac can look quite bloodthirsty. I've never seen him so happy as when he was sending a load of buckshot into a crowd of row-dies. Charlie Han settled down and was soon seated in a chair between the two constables with a pair of leg irons about his ankles on loan from Barker's weapon collection. The spirit had gone out of him, I was glad to see. I took the opportunity to go upstairs and change out of my nightclothes.

When the police vehicle arrived, I asked if I might come along. They demurred, but I pressed my attack, pointing out how difficult it was to get a cab in Newington at that time of night. I told them that the owner of the house needed to be told and that he was in the same street but one from Scotland Yard. That is why at near midnight, when all sensible people are in bed, I was traveling in a Black Maria. At least I could say I wasn't the one in leg irons this time.

Promising to return for a statement, I left the constables to handle their prisoner into A Division and popped 'round to our offices on the next street. I gave the door a good, hard knock.

The door opened slowly and I was treated to the sight of my employer in his dressing gown, his hair askew, with a Colt in his hand.

"Are you going to use that thing?" I asked.

"I am debating it. What are you doing here at this hour?"

"The trap is sprung. We've caught a rodent, but whether it is a mouse or a large rat, you must decide."

"It is too late to be cryptic," he growled. "I'll get dressed while you explain. Come."

I went over everything from the whistle I heard in the alley to my knocking on the office door. During it all, Barker was in the back room making himself presentable for Scotland Yard.

"What is your impression, lad?" he asked. "Do you think Han might be the one we are looking for?"

"It's possible," I said. "I must say he put up a real struggle. I wouldn't have wanted to be on the receiving end of that heel to the stomach or fist to the nose, for that matter. And he was reaching for our gate, remember."

"True," my employer conceded from the side room. "He was also one of Bainbridge's suspects. I wonder where he's been hiding himself. Poole's been running a dragnet for over a week now."

He came out, neat as a pin as always, despite the late hour. In a few moments we were walking along Whitehall toward Scotland Yard. It appeared the most peaceful of nights. Everyone was at home asleep in bed, everyone who was not an enquiry agent, that is.

At the station, we made our way through the halls of the Criminal Investigation Department. All had been rebuilt after a bombing had occurred last year, but as Inspector Munro of the Special Irish Branch had threatened, the area where Barker had once taught antagonistics for the benefit of officers had now been turned into offices. One of those offices was for questioning.

In response to Barker's knock, Poole came out and ran a hand through his thinning hair. Evidently, it wasn't just private agents who went without sleep. Poole gave a big yawn and shook his head.

"Have you got a confession?" Barker asked.

"I'm not even sure if this blighter speaks English."

Barker looked in. "His lip is bleeding. Have you beaten him?"

"He hit his mouth on the edge of a chair. He's a bit roughed up, is all," Poole said.

"May I see if I can get anything out of him?" Barker asked.

"Why not, since you *parlez* the jabber."

"Is his solicitor coming," I asked, "or an interpreter?"

"What are you talking about?" Poole asked, puzzled. "He's a Chinaman. We'll tell the legation in the morning. If they want to send someone over, we can't stop them. 'Til then, he's ours."

That was that. There was no use arguing with such logic, or lack of it. We went in and found the man still in darbies, his European-cut coat ripped and his hair looking worse than it had when I last saw him. He looked at us, then turned and spat a big splotch of bloody saliva on the floor. If I expected him to be glad of our arrival, I was mistaken. He looked at us malevolently.

Barker began to speak in Chinese to him, but Poole put a hand on his shoulder.

"Here, now. We're in the Yard, remember. If you're going to go on like that, you'll have to translate word for word for the record."

"Very well." He asked a short question and after a moment's silence, the fellow muttered, *"Hai."*

"I asked him if he was Charlie Han and he admitted it."

Barker asked a second question, but apparently Han thought he had answered enough questions for the time being. He sat in the chair and stared at the floor. He was large for a Chinaman, a few inches taller than I, and strong limbed. I was starting to think we wouldn't get anything out of him the rest of the night when suddenly, the Chinaman gave my chair a solid kick, sending me and my notebook flying into the corner.

By the time Barker helped me up, Han was stretched out on the floor with Poole's knee on his shoulder and was bleeding from the nose as well as the mouth. He was cursing, despite the fact that his cheek was pressed to the floor.

It took me a minute to understand the words he was saying and another to learn that it was me he was saying them to. Just then there was a knock at the door, but we were too occupied to open it.

"What did I do?" I blurted out. "I don't know this fellow."

"You stay away!" the Chinaman continued, once Poole's knee was off him. He was seated now on the floor, blood dripping from his chin, giving me the nastiest look I'd had since prison. "You stay 'way from us. Stay 'way from her!"

The knocking had finally become so insistent Poole was forced to answer it. Something flew into the room like a streak. I thought at first it was some giant bird of prey, but of course, it wasn't. It was Hettie Petulengro and she was angry. Very angry.

24

———◆———

WHAT HAVE YOU DONE TO HIM?" SHE DEMANDED. "You've got him chained up and now you're using him for a punching bag. Three grown men. You ought to be ashamed, you—"

"Who is this?" Poole roared to the sergeant in the corridor.

"Her name is Petulengro, sir. She has been downstairs at the desk trying to find out what happened. Insistent, she was. I thought you might want to see her."

"Sergeant, leave the thinking to me," Poole ordered. "Stay there. We may have to restrain this woman."

"You wouldn't dare!" she snapped at Poole.

"Oh, no? Try me, my girl."

"And you," she said, rounding on me. "What do you have to say for yourself?"

"I don't have anything to say," I told her. "All I've done since I came in here was to take notes and to get kicked out of my chair by this Chinese fellow. What is he to you?"

"If you plan to argue, you cannot take notes," Poole put in, but we were beyond that at the moment.

"He is my—You wouldn't understand."

"What is there to understand?" I demanded.

"He is my . . . common-law husband, I suppose you'd call him."

"Husband!" I exclaimed. "But I just took you out to dinner!"

"Yes, you did. Thank you very much. He is not my husband, exactly."

"Well?" I said hotly. "Is he or is he not?"

Barker cleared his throat and spoke in his low voice. "I believe what Miss Petulengro is trying to say is that she and Mr. Han have an informal relationship. They live together under her roof, where in fact he had been hiding from the police for several days, but there is no legal relationship between them, either temporal or secular. It is common in the East End. She is quite able to accept an offer of dinner. She can even order him to leave if she chooses someone else, though he is not obliged to like it."

The Chinaman, I was upset to see, was having his hair smoothed by Hestia. All my feelings of benevolent goodwill toward the suspect vanished without a trace. I wanted to get a good kick at him myself.

"Well, I like that!" I said. "You didn't tell me I was squiring around a married woman."

"Oh, don't be thickheaded. Pay attention to your boss. He just explained it to you if you would just unstop your ears."

"Hettie," Charlie Han ordered, "do not speak to him."

"Shut up, you," she bawled. "This is all your fault."

"Silence!" Poole bellowed. "If I have to slap bracelets on every one of you I shall do it!"

All of us went silent.

"Barker, can you make head or tail of this?" the inspector asked.

"Plain as a pikestaff. Mr. Han has a personal relationship with Miss Petulengro, and he lives above her shop, but she feels she is still able to . . . to . . . What phrase would you use, miss?"

She thought about it a moment. "Entertain better offers."

"Exactly. She went out this evening with Thomas, in what I assume both agreed was business, but which may have had some private moments as well. After dinner, he took her home—"

"Actually, I took her to a coffeehouse first," I put in.

"Thank you, Thomas," Barker said with what might have been a withering stare behind the lenses of black glass. "So, you took her back to her rooms over the shop. Did you go in?"

"No, sir."

"Did you kiss her?"

"I say, that is rather personal, is it not?"

"It is pertinent to the case. Did you kiss her?"

"Yes, I did."

Hettie smiled slyly at me but said nothing.

"And you, Mr. Han. Were you not in the rooms upstairs?"

"*Hai.*"

"And did you see him kiss her?"

The Chinaman looked downcast. "He no kiss her. She hurry up kiss him."

"I see. What did you then, sir?"

"Run out back door, chop chop. Follow his cab."

"Afoot? It is several miles."

"Nobody give ride to Chinaman, mister."

"You came to a house in Newington."

"I watch him go in big house. I no know what to do. I walk in front of house for ten minutes, then I go 'round back."

"You wished to confront Mr. Llewelyn?"

"No, no. Have chalk. Leave message on gate, 'Stay 'way from girl.' That will show him. I think maybe he stay 'way then, but coppers catched me."

"He didn't do any harm," Hettie insisted. "He was just going to write a message."

"Destruction of property," Poole spoke up.

"Destruction, my bonnet," Hettie replied. "Soap and water would have taken it off in a tick. And anyway, he didn't even get started."

Barker turned to the Chinaman. "Do you have the chalk?"

Han reached into the pocket of his jacket and produced a piece of chalk. Either he was telling the truth or was a very ingenious liar.

"When did you arrive in London, Mr. Han?"

"Two year ago, November."

"I see. When did you meet Miss Petulengro?"

"Two days later," Hettie answered for him. "He and the boys from the *Agamemnon* had gone through their money already, as sailors will. He wanted to sell a jade ring. He was about to go to the Strangers' Home, which is fine if you're ninety. I thought him rather attractive."

Her remark made me angry, I admit, but I noticed that Poole was taking it even worse than I. His lips were in a grimace of disgust.

"You offered him a bed," the Guv continued.

"No, I'm not that kind of girl. My uncle did, in the cellar. He did odd work for him, and attracted other sailors to the shop."

"Did your relationship . . . develop?"

"That's none of yer business, Mr. 'Tec. Oh, sorry, Mr. Private Enquiry Agent."

I almost laughed out loud but stopped myself. She did a very serviceable imitation of Barker.

"Stow the lip, girl," Poole warned. "I have a little cell waiting for you if I need it."

The girl looked ready to take up his challenge, but Barker went on, glossing things over in the process.

"My apologies, miss," Barker said, "Your private life does not interest me, save when it intersects a murder investigation."

"Who said nothing about a murder?" she challenged.

"May I continue? Mr. Han, were you acquainted with Inspector Bainbridge?"

"Yes, suh. He say I no can stay with Hettie after Mister Uncle die. It is unseemly. He lock me up for vagrancy. I get out, get job delivering betel nut, but he 'rest me again. No permit. Lock me up. I get out, get permit, go back work. Here he come again. Papers not in order. Lock me up again."

"He was bullying Charlie something terrible," Hettie threw in.

"Then Mister Uncle be killed. Who is number one suspect? Charlie Han, that's who. I carry flail. 'Spector say is murder weapon."

"Do you have it now?" Barker asked.

"Always have it. Always. Betel nut is dangerous business, need protection."

"Let me see it."

Charlie Han reached into his baggy trousers and pulled out what might be considered a weapon. It was two sticks, each a foot long and about an inch across, with a cord connecting them at one end. They looked harmless enough, I thought, but Poole did not. He took it away from Han, then stepped into the hall to berate his subordinates for allowing a suspect to come into the questioning room without being properly searched.

"This could leave a mark like the one on Petulengro's neck," Barker said.

"'Spector say I killed him, but I no did it. I spend most of night with friends from Blue Funnel. Everybody throw party, so we throw party. Lunnon have two New Years, they say. Mister Uncle got robbed and killed that night. He have terrible temper sometime, but have no reason to kill him."

"One could say that with Mr. Petulengro out of the way, you might gain a great deal," Barker said. "You could gain control of Miss Petulengro's money were the two of you to marry."

"You're thinking like Bainy now," Hettie said. "You don't know nothing. Charlie ain't that kind of boy. He's not the low-class criminal the Yard is making him out to be. He was just a sailor who came here looking for work."

"It is legal to sell betel nut," Han said in his defense. "Plenty plenty people use it."

"So, in essence, you're saying that Inspector Bainbridge was harassing Mr. Han."

"That's right," Hettie said. "He didn't have no cause."

"If he had no cause, why do you suppose he was harassing him?"

"Here, now," Poole butted in. "Nevil Bainbridge was a competent officer. He would not pin a crime on a fellow who didn't give him just cause."

"I dunno," Hettie said, looking up at Barker. "I dunno why he did it. He had it in for him."

Barker stepped forward and loomed over the pair of them.

"I think you do know, Miss Petulengro."

She snapped then. Had Barker not seized her wrists, she would have torn his spectacles off and scratched his eyes out, but her claws looked small and useless in Barker's big hands. Poole got himself in the enviable position of having his arms around her, one hand clasped in the other.

"I believe that will not be necessary, inspector," Barker said. "Miss Petulengro will cooperate. Won't you, miss?"

Hestia Petulengro looked very unlikely to cooperate, but she stared hard into those round spectacles of Barker's, the two of them locked in a struggle of wills.

"There is a saying," he continued. "The truth shall set you free."

All fight went out of her then. She sagged into a chair. Barker did not menace her further, but left her to calm down. He poured a glass of water from the pitcher on the table and gave it to her. After a few minutes she looked more composed.

"Let us start again, Miss Petulengro. Do you have a suspicion of who killed your uncle?"

"Yer. I think I pretty well know who done it."

"Why have you not come forward, then, girl?" Poole demanded. "It was your duty. Had you no wish to bring your uncle's killer to justice?"

"It was Inspector Bainbridge you suspect, isn't that correct?" Barker murmured.

There was silence in the room. Hettie was breathing hard and Barker was immobile, staring down at her in the chair. Poole's mouth was open, and Han had his eyes cast down to the floor.

"I believe it was old Bainy, yes," she said in a low voice.

"You think he killed your uncle and harassed your . . . friend here. Tell me, why do you believe he did it?"

She looked over at Poole, clearly afraid of his reaction. I saw her lick her lips and then she spoke. "Because he was in love with me, that's why."

"I see. And how do you know that was how he felt about you?"

"Because he told me, didn't he? He brought me flowers at Christmastime and poured out his feelings to me. Said he'd throw over the missus and come and take care of me if I'd let him."

"Damnable lie," Poole thundered.

"Take it easy, Terry. Let her speak. Did he later confess he had killed your uncle?"

"No, he didn't, but I worked it out myself, you see. I'd been at the match factory for five years. Most girls only last three. It's rotten work. I'd complained to him how backbreaking and dangerous it was before I knew he had feelings for me. My uncle was a surly old beggar and treated me rotten. He'd even made advances toward me. Bainy knew, because he'd broken up a disturbance at our house more than once. He hated my uncle. I think he knew what a better life

I'd have if he was dead. I wouldn't have to do no backbreaking work and I wouldn't be threatened anymore. But then, Charlie here moved in. The inspector didn't like him at all. After Uncle Lazlo died he started arresting him for just anything. Any crime in the area and he was hauled in as a suspect. He gave him a long record, he did, that made him look bad. Charlie couldn't get work aboard the Blue Funnel anymore, so he turned to betel nuts."

"Get back to Bainbridge," Barker said.

"I'm getting there. He did for him, then, on New Year's Day. Hit him with that big truncheon of his, broke his neck. That's how I reckon it, anyway. I ain't sorry. You gents didn't live with the man. But then, Bainy tried to pin the crime on Charlie here. He knew Charlie carried a flail about in his pocket for protection. Being the commanding officer there, Bainy had him brought in for questioning. But even he couldn't convict him without evidence."

"Look, this is enough," Poole stated. "End of interrogation. You, stop scribbling there and give the notes to me. Barker, I want the two of you in my office in five minutes."

"What about Miss Petulengro?"

"She is being detained temporarily. If she behaves, she might be allowed to leave in the morning. Constables! Separate these two and watch the girl. She has claws."

Five minutes later we were settling into a pair of scratched and rickety chairs in Poole's office. The room was very much like Bainbridge's. I wondered if there was a school of architecture for police institutions. Who chose the fungal shade of gray on the walls and the braided rug on the floor in front of Poole's desk? One could only assume it was a former felon, exacting his revenge.

Poole opened a small box on his desk and removed a cigarette. He lit it up and sucked in the smoke. Then he blew it
out through his nostrils like a dragon and started in on my
employer.

"What in hell was that all about? Are you accusing Nevil
of being involved in the murder we're investigating? Good
lord, he gave his life for this case."

"I have not accused him of anything," Barker pointed
out. "Miss Petulengro gave a private opinion as to what she
thought happened to her uncle. She is not bringing a suit
against anyone."

"She might as well have. You know I can't let this go
now. This will have to go to my superiors who will appoint
an outside investigator into Nevil's actions. What a mess!
He should have known better than to get involved with that
Gypsy minx. And all the while, she was living with a Chinaman! This is a fine hornet's nest you've stirred up!"

"I have a suggestion," Barker stated.

"I'm sure that you do. I'm not sure I want to hear it."

"An investigation would certainly tarnish Bainbridge's
reputation—"

"Tarnish? This is murder we're talking about. It would
blacken it forever."

"And there is no surety that enough evidence would be
able to be collected in order to convict him—"

"That's true. It might just be Miss Petulengro's word for
it. But it would still call into question his character, which is
almost all his widow has to live on, poor dear."

"So, let it lie."

"I'm going to pretend I didn't hear that, Cyrus. You
know I'm a foursquare man."

"Not permanently, Terry. Allow me to investigate a little further. I am not prejudiced against him. I have formed no opinion. If no one feels he or she has been wronged, including the only relative of the late Mr. Petulengro, then why open up a painful and fruitless investigation that shall cost the people of London and tie up constables best used patrolling their beats."

"There is something to that, but I cannot make that decision."

"Let us investigate a little further then, both of us."

Poole had sucked half his cigarette down to ash. He reached toward the ashtray but in doing so, the column of ask broke off and landed on the rug. Poole stomped at it roughly.

"Perhaps."

"I want to thank you, by the way. Your men did a fine job of apprehending Mr. Han."

"P.C.s Horton and Finney are good men," Poole said grudgingly. "With all the action occurring around your place these days, I thought you might need two of our best."

"What shall you do about Miss Petulengro? She might be more cooperative about questioning if you let her go tonight."

"Possibly," Poole said. "But the Chinaman stays until I have everything he knows, including his mother's maiden name, providing Chinese mothers have maiden names."

"Agreed."

"You know, regardless of who killed whom a year ago, Han or that dollymop could have shot Nevil in that tunnel."

"Yes. I had thought of that possibility myself."

"This case beggars all. I wish I had never got out of bed

the day this fell in my lap. It should have gone to Abberline or Swanson. They know the East End better than I. You know what will happen if I bungle this case, don't you? They might take me out of the C.I.D. and put me in charge of Bainbridge's station. A total dead end for my career. I hate Limehouse!"

"How did Inspector Bainbridge get assigned there in the first place?" Barker queried.

"He asked for it, as I recall."

"Did that seem strange to you at the time?"

"It did, but then Bainbridge was not what you call ambitious. It is the sort of posting the younger chaps go for, hoping to get some big case that'll get them promoted to chief inspector. He asked for it, though, and since he had a good record and seniority, they gave it to him."

"If an officer were to fall in love with a girl in Limehouse . . ."

"Stow that," Poole said, putting a hand up. "I didn't hear it. I shall spring her in half an hour, but if she cuts up too fine, I shall toss her right back in again."

"That is your privilege. I am staying at my chambers for a few days. Come by for a chat when you are done here."

We had a hansom waiting when Hettie came out, looking overwrought and tired.

"They're keeping him," she said when she saw us. "They didn't say how long."

"Inspector Poole is a fair man," the Guv said. "If Mr. Han is innocent, he shall be released soon."

"You have a higher opinion of Scotland Yard than I do, Mr. Barker."

"I work with them a good deal, miss. Most inspectors do not take advantage of their position."

"Do you think you can get Charlie out? I know he resisted arrest, but he ain't a bad man. This all sounds awfully complicated."

"Cases often do about this time," he responded.

"You will try to clear Charlie's name, won't you? He's had a devil of a time in England since he arrived. As for you, Thomas, we shall talk later, shan't we?"

I gave her a weak nod. We put her into the cab and she rattled off. Another one came into Whitehall and I secured it, leaving Barker to return to our offices.

I'm normally curious but just then I was too tired to care what might be said when Poole met with Barker. At home I checked that all the doors were locked and turned down the gas in the hall. Upstairs, I changed into my nightclothes again, crawled into bed, and drifted off to sleep, or tried to, anyway. With my cast biting into my shoulder, it was a wonder I got any sleep at all.

25

THE NEXT MORNING BARKER SEEMED REMARK-
ably nonchalant about the events of the night before. The
Guv did not mention his conversation with Poole. He was
more concerned with the morning post.

A pair of letters had arrived, their envelopes highly visible, for they were a deep crimson color and of an unusual
rough texture. One arrived for Barker and the other for me.
We each took one from Jenkins's salver and slit them open,
he with his Italian dagger and I with a more prosaic letter
opener. The inside of the envelope was lined with gilt paper
and the enclosed letter backed with a piece of paper that
matched the envelope. The letter was beautifully executed,
but I had no idea what it said, for it was all in Chinese. I
looked at Barker, who was reading his.

"It is an invitation to a New Year's banquet tonight given
by Ho," he explained. "You have been invited, too, I see. It is
quite an honor. I had not anticipated you would receive one."

"It is addressed to me?" I asked, looking at the letter.
"What does he call me?"

"Little brother."

"Are you seriously telling me that Ho considers me his little brother?"

"Not his, lad. Mine."

"How do we accept the offer?"

"I must respond in kind. Fetch some water, would you?"

Retrieving a ewer from a lacquered tray, I took it out into the yard behind the office and filled it from the pump. The wind snatched the frigid breath from my lips, and the silver ewer grew icy in my hand as I eased the handle up and down. I hurried back inside to find Barker occupied.

There was a small black tray on his desk, a brush, and several sheets of paper. Barker pulled a minuscule bowl no larger than his thumb from a bottom drawer, a tiny spoon, and finally, a box containing a stick of what looked like coal. He was composing a response to the invitation.

Barker picked up the stick and began to grind it against the surface of the tray, which was made of slate.

"Is that ink?" I asked.

"Yes. It is made of soot and resin. Pour the water into that bowl there."

He whisked the ink around with one of the brushes, mixing the water and soot and then pulled a paper in front of him. He placed the brush near the right-hand corner and began to paint.

"What are you writing?"

Barker raised a finger and went back to finish his note. I've noticed his power of concentration was sometimes complete. Chinese calligraphy is something of an art, I understand, and my question was not unlike interrupting an artist at his easel. He finally finished and leaned back to examine the completed letter.

"I have graciously accepted the invitation and thanked Ho for the honor. He is a stickler for protocol." While the letter dried, Barker put the writing materials back. He sealed the letter, affixed Her Majesty's penny effigy in the corner, and gave it to Jenkins to post. Then we forgot the matter for the rest of the afternoon.

As we made our way to Ho's that evening, I attempted to turn the Guv's attention back to the banquet in my usual manner, by hitting him with a barrage of questions.

"How many invitations were sent out, do you think?" I asked.

"Not over fifty. Ho would want it to be exclusive."

"So, it is a kind of party, then?"

"Of a sort, though the meal is the most important part."

We stepped out and found a cab within a few minutes. I pressed him further.

"Will we be the only Occidentals?"

"I would imagine so."

"And the purpose of the event is to celebrate the New Year and the fact that Ho has been released from custody?"

"Correct."

"I don't believe that is the whole story. I admit Ho might celebrate these things, but he has other reasons, I'm certain."

"Very good, lad. I see you are developing your deductive skills. What other reasons might he have?"

I hadn't expected the question to be thrown back at me so quickly. "Well, he's been in jail, which must include some sort of loss of face among the community. He might have a banquet as a show of strength that he has not been inconvenienced."

"Good. Go on."

"He deals in secrets and information. While he was away, it might have gone elsewhere. This meal could be an attempt to bring it back again."

"And?"

I had run dry. I thought for a minute or two. Nothing came to mind.

"Consider Mr. K'ing."

"What would such a meal mean to K'ing?" I asked. "Is Ho trying to say 'We have the same friends and are one' or 'These are the supporters I can take away from you, if I wish'?"

"Surely you know the answer to that question. Think more subtly."

I pushed my imagination as far as it could go. If I were Ho, what would I do with K'ing breathing down my neck? "Both," I finally answered.

"Very good, lad. Now you are thinking like an Oriental."

"Will K'ing be there, do you think?"

"He will be issued an invitation, surely. It is not only given to friends but to all respected members of the Chinese community, even those with dubious reputations."

"Shall Bok Fu Ying be there?"

"Ho treats her as a favored niece, but she is busy preparing for the New Year's festivities. She has been asked to perform. She will not be in attendance."

My mind flitted between two thoughts just then. The first was wondering what sort of performance she would give, while the second was trying to imagine Ho as a doting uncle and not succeeding. Bellicose, perhaps; ungracious, certainly; but not doting.

We arrived in the narrow lane but found it transformed. The broken stone arches overhead were unchanged, but the debris had been swept away and the walls around the entrance given a coat of whitewash. We stepped through the door and found the tunnel lit by two naphtha lamps, and as we progressed down the steps, we found another lamp halfway down. At the bottom there was a red carpet about five feet wide, extending the entire length of the tunnel, with lamps on each side every ten feet or so. There would be no bumping into things in the dark for the distinguished guests, not to mention opportunities for further assassinations.

"Ho is sparing no expense," I said.

"Far be it from him to leave anything out," Barker agreed.

The main dining room had been transformed. Red paper lanterns hung from the ceiling and the walls had large letters cut from gilt paper, which I assumed offered luck and prosperity in the coming year. A long table ran down the center of the room, laden with bowls full of every kind of edible thing imaginable. Each bowl appeared to contain a different ingredient. There were hundreds on that long table, it seemed, and in the very center, given pride of place, a single dish sat on a tray. A very unusual ingredient it was, too, sticks of something that looked like whale blubber.

"What exactly is that?" I asked Barker in a low voice, for the room was quickly beginning to fill with people, all men and all Chinese.

"It is shark's fin," he said, "a great delicacy reserved for the New Year."

I looked at the grayish strips of flesh dubiously. "I don't think I could eat it."

Barker shrugged his wide shoulders. "Suit yourself. It is rather too late for the shark, I fear."

I began to wonder if this feast might not be to my liking at all, and moved closer to the table. The first bowl confirmed my fears. It held what looked like some sort of snake. Another contained what looked like eel. The contents of one after that was more mundane, being slices of raw carrot. There were no prepared dishes, I noticed, such as one normally saw at Ho's. Everything here appeared to be mere ingredients. There were florets of broccoli and cauliflower; bowls of boiled eggs of every size and origin; and Asian delicacies such as water chestnuts, litchi nuts, and bamboo shoots. I saw prawns and chicken, duck and pigeon, giblets of who knows what, beef, venison, pork, and the usual bowl of unidentified meat that I would avoid. As we circled the table, I saw one section was given over to spices and another to sauces of every color and aroma. I was at a loss. How was anyone expected to eat this meal?

The chairs around the tables were quickly filling, and Barker and I took seats. My stomach was telling me either I was very hungry or about to be ill, depending upon what I would put into it.

Ho stepped out of the kitchen then, resplendent in a floor-length gown of green and gold silk, though it was thrown on casually over his singlet and trousers and remained open in the front. Not everything could change, I expect. He began to pontificate in a loud voice while I wondered if it might eventually become necessary in this occupation of mine to learn Chinese. Ho spoke loudly and gestured grandly. I assumed he was greeting everyone and telling them about his unjust incarceration in a British jail.

Mercifully, Ho is a man of few words and soon he clapped his hands and ended his speech. Waiters began streaming out of the kitchen, dozens of them, some obviously employed for this event only. Each carried a large bowl so hot and steaming the waiters needed towels to hold them. Fifty bowls for fifty guests, give or take. Mine was finally set down in front of me. It was full of hot water and noodles, but nothing to flavor them. Slowly light dawned. We were to make our own soup from the dozens of items before us, adding meats and vegetables, mixing flavors, each of us creating our own unique soup.

We waited until all fifty were given a bowl, and one could feel the tension growing in the room. Ho stepped up to the table, raised his arm high, and then barked a word. The room erupted into chaos. The men leapt at the long table of food and began stabbing at the bowls with their chopsticks. I seized my own and joined the fray, spearing right and left. Chicken, prawns, and broccoli went into my steaming bowl. Plover's eggs, bamboo shoots, the fried soy cakes I liked, and a ladleful of the yellow sauce followed. I avoided the bugs and snakes, of course. A water chestnut here, a bit of Chinese cabbage there, a slice or two of leek, half a clove of garlic. I was creating a masterpiece even Ho would envy. Beside me, Barker crowned his own creation with a large slice of shark's fin.

Just when I was about to dig into my wonderful creation, a waiter leaned over and poured oil into my bowl. I looked up in disgust. What was he doing? He had ruined everything. All my work and now I would have to start over.

Barker spoke into my ear as the waiter did the same to his bowl.

"There is a village in China with a factory that has produced earthen bowls for centuries. It is in a small valley with mountains on either side and a river bisecting the town. The factory is on one side of the river and the village on the other. When women prepared lunch every day, it grew cold before they reached their husbands across the bridge. One day, a woman accidentally spilled oil in her husband's bowl and discovered that not only did the oil seal in the heat so it could be carried, but the food continued to cook beneath it. That is how the soup got its name, Across the Bridge Soup. We must let it sit for five minutes, which is just enough time for toasts."

Vessels of plum wine were served. An elderly Chinaman stood and spoke, and we downed our cups. Several toasts followed and I was beginning to get light-headed. Barker gave a toast for both of us and then Ho finished for us all, after which we attacked our bowls.

From childhood, the Chinese are trained to suck noodles. One could stretch a single noodle out ten yards and any Chinese man, woman, or child worth his weight in rice could suck it down in a matter of seconds. I am a rank amateur, but was still willing to give it a try. I launched into my bowl and did not surface for several moments. It was pure ambrosia. I was a genius. Who knew I had such unplumbed depths when it came to creating meals?

Barker had his bowl wedged up under his chin and was shoveling shark meat in like a trencherman while my neighbor on the other side gnawed his way through a glutinous sow's ear. It was a race of sorts. We were a roomful of gluttons. I was glad that there were no women present to witness such a spectacle.

Ten minutes later there were fifty very full and groaning men with empty bowls. Some of us listlessly picked among the dregs at the bottom while the team of waiters brought tea.

"I have never eaten so much in my life," I commented. "I thought I would taste the oil, but I didn't."

"Yes. The nameless woman who spilt oil in her husband's meal deserves our thanks."

The pipes came out after that, for those who smoked. Barker, of course, lit up his Turkish meerschaum while others went for the modern convenience of the Western cigarette. Still others favored thin metal pipes with patterns in cloisonné. Ho brought out his water-can contraption and was smoking it while talking with guests. He worked his way through the room, I noticed, and spoke to practically everyone. I hadn't thought him so outgoing. As for me, I was in a funk. There was a slight ringing in my ears and I found I had been staring at one of the large letters on the wall for several minutes, trying to decipher it.

"I need some air," I said to Barker.

"Good idea, lad. We should take a walk around the district. They should be getting up the decorations for tomorrow."

Just then Ho came up between us. He bowed benevolently to some of the guests nearby. Then he leaned forward and spoke in English, just loud enough for us to hear. "K'ing is up to something. He recently purchased a warehouse in the area and has had carpenters working day and night. English carpenters, who won't reveal his plans to anyone. No one knows what he is about, but something is happening."

"Thank you for the information. I see K'ing never arrived. What of Woo?"

"I did not issue him an invitation. He has seen fit to criticize my cooking, that Peking popinjay."

"We are going for a walk," Barker said.

Ho raised a warning finger. "Be careful," he admonished. "Remember what I said about digging your own grave."

Limehouse had become enchanted that night. Every wall was festooned with messages in gilt and streamers of red paper and firecrackers. Entranceways that no one had bothered to sweep all year were now swept and mopped. The drab and mean streets of the area had become a fairyland, like Andersen's tale of the nightingale, provided one did not look too hard at what lay beneath. I theorized that visitors came here for the celebration each year and never saw its harsher side. Perhaps that was how the district's exotic reputation had begun.

Limehouse was astir, but the killer was not. Apparently, he had taken off the night and that was a good thing, as far as I was concerned. Barker and I were so full, we could not have given him much of a fight.

26

THE NEXT MORNING BEING THE SABBATH, I CROSSED
the street to the Baptist Tabernacle with Barker to hear
Charles Haddon Spurgeon preach. The topic of his sermon
was grace, which to me is always a cheerier subject than
damnation. Along with the sermon came the hymns, which
included "Amazing Grace," Barker's favorite, perhaps because it had been written by a sea captain.

After the service was over and we had shaken the
pastor's hand, we walked back to the house that we were no
longer sharing and ate a solid English lunch of beef and
mash and Yorkshire pudding, like a million other people in
London. It must gall Etienne to cook such fare, without the
chance to toss in a bit of garlic here, a bit of truffle there,
but I would back his roast beef against any Englishman's in
the country.

Barker did not dawdle over tea but went upstairs to
change his Sunday morning coat into a more serviceable
cutaway. He came down a few moments later shooting his
cuffs and adjusting his cufflinks.

"Are you ready, lad?" Barker called up the staircase to

me. One always tries to dress appropriately, but what does one wear to a Chinese New Year celebration? Given the circumstances, I decided to err on the side of caution and wear my overcoat with the lead-lined padding and built-in holster. After all, we were looking for a killer, not merely taking in the sights.

My employer stuffed a finger and thumb under his mustache and emitted a shrill whistle that brought a hansom cab to our curb. We climbed aboard and were soon on our way.

"Are you armed?" he asked.

"One pistol. I couldn't use the other one, so I did not bring it. Do you think tonight shall be important?"

"Yes, I do," he responded. "New Year's is a time to finish old business and begin the new. Alliances are made or broken. Everyone hopes for health and prosperity during the coming year, but I've known more than one life to be snuffed out on such a night and more than one business financially ruined."

After we crossed London Bridge and were in Commercial Street, he went on. "I imagine much of the East End shall be there tonight to enjoy the spectacle. There shall be the usual food merchants and trinkets for sale. There shall also be pickpockets, confidence tricksters, drunken sailors, and brawls. Several West Enders will be slumming, looking for their first taste of opium. Street musicians will abound, as will beggars. Limehouse shall be rouged like an old tart, looking to divert the public, while the merchants of the quarter cosh them and take their money."

We were reaching West India Dock Road when I heard a sound and tensed.

"Gunfire, sir!" I cried, reaching for my pistol.

"No, lad. Firecrackers. They shall be going on all day, I'm afraid. The Chinese have a fascination with fireworks. They believe they ward off evil spirits."

The driver let us down and turned his cab before his horse could panic. One could hear firecrackers going off in every street. We were immediately assaulted by beggar children asking for ha'pennies for a ha'penny dinner. I was reaching for my pocket when Barker stopped me.

"It's a trick, lad," he said. "Off with you! They shall be begging all day from any prosperous-looking person and passing ha'pennies to their parents in the alleyways. They'll earn several shillings by night's end, I'll wager."

Rows of makeshift tables were set up in the street, fluttering with red crepe and silk in the cool afternoon breeze. I stopped to look over a table full of small Buddhas and other Chinese gods of all descriptions, some lacquered red and others a pale green.

"Jade?" I asked Barker.

"Plaster," he corrected. "Probably made from molds and painted not three streets from here."

Long strings of fireworks were suspended from balconies overhead, dancing in the air as they exploded one by one. Envelopes covered in gold leaf hung near the top, safely out of reach but tantalizing to the throng of people below. One Oriental sat at a corner, playing upon a kind of Chinese violin with a bow, his cap in front of him. Half the people of Limehouse seemed to have become food merchants.

Barker was looking around at the crowd, and I knew what he was thinking. It was the perfect time for Quong's and Bainbridge's killer to drill us with a bullet through the forehead from some balcony. I suddenly felt very exposed.

We looked about as we walked through West India Dock Road while hawkers tried to tempt us with games of chance and vendors to sell us things at twice the price they went for on shop shelves the morning before: Oriental dolls, incense, carved dragons, pearls whose authenticity I doubted, silk wallets and scarves, scrolls painted with the symbol for prosperity, novelties, and clothing. The English merchants were not above using the festival to make a few bob themselves, and there were stands selling beer, pork pies, jellied eels, and toffee. A sailor came out of a shop with his sleeves rolled up and a new tattoo on his forearm, the skin raw and red from the needle. He and his comrades were obviously drunk. He would regret today's romp. I hoped I wouldn't, as well.

I felt a hand dip into my pocket and recoil when it came in contact with the handle of my pistol. I spun 'round in time to see a Chinese boy run off, who could not have been more than eleven.

"Quite a to-do," I said to Barker over the firecrackers.

"Yes, it is the only time of the year the district kicks up its heels."

There was the steady clamor of a gong ahead, and Barker and I pushed our way through the crowd to a large intersection. Everyone was milling about expectantly.

The crowd parted as Bok Fu Ying stepped forward into the street. She was without her veil and the plait she wore was down to her waist. She wore a suit of Chinese clothing made of red silk and a pair of embroidered slippers. In her hand was a long broadsword with a red sash. Somewhere off to the right, a band of Chinese musicians began to play a low melancholy tune and she began to move.

The crowd of mostly foreign men watched this representative of their homeland with rapt attention as she spun. The sword in her hand scythed the air left and right, the trailing sash popping like the string of a kite. The blade was extremely thin, though as broad as a pirate's cutlass, and it bent and shivered to and fro as she moved from position to position. It looked like a beautiful dance, or so I would have said a year earlier. Now my eye recognized one deadly technique after another. She could have cut a man to ribbons with that sword, and I could personally attest that she kicked like a Surrey mule.

Finally, she came to a standstill in the center and settled down into a cross-legged position. The music changed and became lower and more eerie. I heard a woman give a short scream of surprise, which set us all craning our necks. The crowd parted and a creature came bounding out, heading straight for Bok Fu Ying.

It was a lion, or at least it was supposed to be. In fact, it was two very agile dancers in a lion costume, a multicolored Chinese fantasy with a huge head, blinking eyes, and a snapping jaw. It looked more like Harm than an actual lion, but then I realized Pekingese are called lion dogs in China, or more exotic still, butterfly lions. The creature charged toward Bok Fu Ying and skidded to a stop. The maiden feigned fear, keeping him at bay with her sword. It pranced about her like a tiger circling its prey. Sometimes both dancers inside would squat down, so that the long fabric of the body touched the ground on both sides. At others, the lead dancer raised the head as high as his arms would reach, the jaws chomping and the eyes rolling all the while. The crowd was enthralled.

Bok Fu Ying dipped, and the lion dipped. She stood and it stood. She turned in a circle, waving her sword, and the lion pranced about her. When it came too close, she smote the lion's foot with the flat of her sword, which made it hop about with a paw in the air while the crowd laughed. The giant head shivered as if the lion were crying. It staggered and lunged toward the crowd as if asking solace, but everyone backed away. Finally, it limped back to Bok Fu Ying and made an elaborate bow in front of the courageous maiden, admitting defeat. In a moment, she had rolled it over on its back and was rubbing its belly as its feet kicked in the air. Everyone, even Barker, seemed to be enjoying the show.

Suddenly, there was an explosion of fireworks from the other side of the street. A new green and red creature appeared then and began to move toward them. This time, it was a dragon. The head was the size of the lion's, but inside the long body, there must have been close to twenty dancers. It took up half the street, zigzagging and curling in a huge circle around Bok Fu Ying and the lion, as it attempted to catch its tail.

The dancers growled in unison as they attacked Bok Fu Ying and the lion. She slashed at its body, but the sword could not penetrate its scaly hide. With one sweep of its tail, it sent the lion sprawling. I could almost believe it real. Bok Fu Ying kept waving her sword at its face, which was vulnerable. The lion attacked, biting the tail of the dragon, which hopped around, trying to get it off.

The finale came when the lion was sent sprawling a second time and the dragon rushed upon the maiden. It reared up as the dancers inside mounted each other's shoulders until the head was a full fifteen feet from the ground.

Quick as lightning, Bok Fu Ying struck. Her sword was thrust into the dragon's breast, using the old theater trick of holding it between a dancer's side and his arm. The creature reared in the throes of death. It danced about like an old tragedian, not having the decency to die until it had milked every last emotion from the crowd. Finally, it reared up and fell forward on top of Bok Fu Ying and there it lay, as if dead.

The lion, acting like a lapdog, revived. It pranced 'round the slain dragon, looking for its maiden. Finally, it seized the tail in its jaws and with a rough shake, rolled the row of dancers onto their backs one by one. I and everyone in the crowd craned our necks. Bok Fu Ying had vanished.

Barker put his head down as if he were listening, then slowly he nodded. I looked behind us and saw four Chinese men in the long quilted coats they favored. My first thought, foolhardy as it may have been, was that we could take them. There were but four, and even if I bested only one, that left three and Barker could easily take twice that many on an average day. Then I felt the barrel of a pistol in my side and realized we had been jugged as neatly as a hare. I put my hands up.

"That is not necessary," one of them said. "Please step this way."

We were herded through an empty-looking warehouse to a spiral staircase going down a floor. After that we were ordered through a grate into a sewer tunnel. A feeling of dread came over me. Nothing would prevent them from shooting us in this godforsaken spot if something we had done had given them reason. I didn't want to end my life in a sewer.

The tunnel, I noted, was dry and must have been blocked up and bricked over some time in the City's past. It had been given a new life, however, as I noticed when we reached the end. Suddenly, the tunnel turned into a hallway, and I took in the incongruous sight of a floor rug and a table containing a small painting of a Chinese scene. It lent an aura of domesticity not in keeping with sewers and pistol-wielding Chinamen. We were waved down the corridor and I felt as if I were walking into someone's home. We passed a room in which four elderly men, like sages come to life from an old painting, were playing mah-jongg. I only got a glimpse before I was prodded in the kidney with the pistol.

"Keep moving," the Chinaman said.

Barker opened the door at the far end, and we followed him inside. A creature screeched as we entered and for a moment I was more afraid of it than the man behind me. I gasped, which must have frightened it, for the animal ran for its cage and flung itself inside. It was a monkey of some sort, with white tufts over each ear like an old Scotsman.

"You have frightened my marmoset," the occupant of the room complained in an abstract way, as if it mattered little to him. I did not have to even look to realize both the voice and the monkey belonged to Mr. K'ing. His face was thin and intelligent, his narrow eyebrows complementing his mustache. He seemed completely at ease. He raised his silk-clad arms and the gunmen searched us and took possession of our weapons.

"My ward," Barker dared command. "Produce her at once."

"She is my guest until this matter is resolved," K'ing answered. "I wanted to show you how vulnerable you are, sir." He turned his cool eyes my way. "So this is the fellow who has caused all this trouble. Did I not see you staggering out of the Inn of Double Happiness with a friend a few nights ago? You are English?"

"I am Welsh," I said, wondering what he meant about my causing all of the trouble.

"English, Welsh, whatever you are, you are not Chinese. I can produce a dozen witnesses who saw you display certain knowledge in Limehouse you could only have obtained in China or have learned from a master, such as the great *Shi Shi Ji*. I believe the incident involved a dog. Several residents were injured. He is your student, is he not, Mr. Barker?"

"He is," Barker said. "The art I have taught him is not Chinese, however. It is Japanese."

"Oh, come," chided the unofficial leader of Limehouse, "are you telling me a dozen people could not tell a Chinese art from the inferior styles of the Japanese?"

"I do. The two arts are similar to a layman, and the fact that Mr. Llewelyn beat them all handily is proof that they were laymen. He is not yet advanced."

"You make a good point," Mr. K'ing conceded. "We shall come back to that later. I have a more important question to put to you, Mr. Barker."

"I know the question. It is why you have brought me here."

"May I ask it, then?"

Barker nodded his head.

"Thank you, Mr. Barker—*Shi Shi Ji*. Are you Chinese,

are you a barbarian, or are you in fact of mixed parentage?"

The Guv did not reply but waited stoically, like Christ before Pilate.

"You will not answer?"

"Certainly not," Barker said. "Having already said I am this lad's teacher, if I admitted to being Chinese, I would be placing a death sentence on my own head. We both know is forbidden to teach the arts to 'foreign devils.' However, were I to admit to being either of the other two, I would thereby dishonor those living masters who have taught me in the past and likely place a death sentence upon their heads in place of my own. That I will not do."

"So, we are at a . . . Forgive me, my English sometimes fails me."

"An impasse."

"Precisely. Thank you. We are at an impasse. Of course, the answer is very simple to find out. I will have my servants remove your spectacles."

"More powerful men than you have tried to do so in the past, Mr. K'ing. I would consider the attempt an extreme insult and should be forced to defend myself. If you attempt to remove my spectacles, I can promise that at least five of us shall be dead in two minutes. I shall, of course, be one of them, but you, sir, shall be the first to go."

"I see. Another impasse. You are leaving me with few alternatives."

"I fail to see why this matter has become your responsibility, if I am not speaking inappropriately."

"You have good manners, sir, whatever your nationality. I am speaking not as a subject of the imperial government but as the leader of a triad. One of my associates has informed me that you displayed the triad tattoo upon your arm the same day your assistant first visited this area. You are, therefore, under my jurisdiction. Before you object on the grounds that it was not the Blue Dragon Triad, I would remind you that the triads are one when rules have been transgressed."

Barker bowed his head formally. "I would not think of contradicting you."

"Very well," K'ing said, leaning forward. "You see, I am trying to be fair. I hope for your sake that you actually are British. I do not wish to take your life or to see it taken, which is the same thing. I am giving you a chance to choose, rather than forcing an answer upon you and causing bloodshed. Which shall it be, Mr. Barker? Are you Chinese or English?"

"I think you know my answer, Mr. K'ing. You've known it for days. I choose the third option. I choose . . . trial by combat."

The Chinese criminal leader gave a wolfish smile. "How do you know that is possible?"

"Of course it is possible," Barker insisted. "It is my right as a member of the triads. The White Lotus Triad, the Green Dragons, and all of the other organizations accept such a trial. Surely the Blue Dragon must do so as well."

"Are you certain this is the way you wish to proceed?"

"Of course," Barker responded. "My other options are death and dishonor. But I am *Shi Shi Ji*. Can you locate a man on short notice who would stand in the ring with me?"

"I believe I have such a man. Very well, the matter is settled. Trial by combat it is. I shall need time to make arrangements."

"And I, to prepare. May I be free to move about the city?"

"Yes, but I am afraid Bok Fu Ying and your associate must stay here as my guests to ensure your return."

Guests? I thought, looking at Barker. He meant that we were prisoners.

"Agreed," my employer said. "What time shall the trial begin?"

"Let us say midnight."

"Very well. I shall return at eleven thirty."

"Yes." Mr. K'ing paused in thought. "As I recall the rules, we are talking about a fight to the death, are we not?"

Barker gave one of his chilling smiles. "Certainly."

"I shall, of course, release Bok Fu Ying regardless of the outcome, but what shall I do with this young fellow, should you lose the fight?"

"That would be left to your discretion, sir."

"Ah," K'ing said, looking at me as if I were a bug to be trod underfoot.

"Until eleven thirty, then, Mr. Barker. It has been a pleasure to meet the great *Shi Shi Ji* face-to-face."

Barker stood, which set off the marmoset again. I turned in my chair with a sense of dread. Barker was going, leaving me here to languish in a cell at K'ing's discretion. The Guv went so far as to lay a hand upon my shoulder, a rarity, indeed. No doubt he sensed my trepidation.

"I shall be back in a few hours, lad. See that they feed you properly or they shall answer to me for it."

Then off he went. Feed me properly, indeed. As if I could eat anything. As if my heart was not in my throat. Barker by all rights should be convalescing from his injuries.

Instead, he was about to have the fight of his life, of both our lives. I realized now what K'ing's men must have been working on so secretly: it was the place in which Barker would fight. That meant that despite his protests to the contrary, K'ing already knew that Barker would choose trial by combat. It also meant that he had had days to find a worthy opponent.

I was imprisoned now in an area of London that for all intents and purposes functioned under the laws of China. If things went according to the uncrowned king of Limehouse, there would be another body floating in Limehouse Reach, where a year before Quong had been found. Possibly three more.

The Thames. It is a serpent that coils through London, and around my life. I had nearly jumped into it once, to kill myself. I had been blown into it once and rescued by Barker, and now my employer was being drawn in again because of me. The outcome of the fight would determine whether my corpse would rest there, yet. We fought not against princes, principalities, and powers, I thought. We fought against Fate itself.

27

BARKER WAS GONE, AND I WAS LEFT ALONE WITH one of the most powerful men in London. He sat in the chair and eyed me appraisingly. I stood and bowed in the English manner, a stiff incline of the head, trying not to show him I was afraid.

"I am your prisoner."

"No, sir," he corrected. "You are a guest in my humble home. Allow me to see to your comfort."

"Ah, but a guest may leave at any time," I pointed out.

"That is so, but then, who shall see to Miss Winter's needs? She is my real prisoner."

"I would like to see her, sir."

K'ing clapped his hands and a guard appeared to lead me through K'ing's "humble home." It was more like an underground mansion. All the rooms were low-ceilinged but so varied that I was certain this could not be the basement of any one building. More probably, these rooms, connected by tunnels, took up much of an entire street of buildings. Most of the rooms were furnished in a manner that was spare but sumptuous. One contained little more than a chair but had an ornate Oriental rug that must have measured twenty by forty feet. Another room contained a series of piers and bridges in carved teak with a subterranean river running through it.

Finally, we came to a door that was locked. The guard unlatched it and ushered me in. In a chair at the far end sat Bok Fu Ying.

She rose quickly when I entered the room, but I could tell she'd been crying. I waited, watching over my shoulder as the guard left the room and locked the door behind us. The room was large and contained a bed, a low table with pillows around it, and a pair of wooden chairs. One would think Bok Fu Ying was a guest save for one thing: guest rooms do not have locks on the outside.

I pulled a handkerchief from my pocket and presented it to her. She obviously had no such article in her suit of red silk.

"They took my sword," she sniffed. "They had pistols. Where is Sir?"

I told her as gently as possible what had occurred and that Barker was back in Newington preparing for the fight at this very moment.

"This is all your fault," she said when I finished.

It was in my mind to defend myself, if verbally this time. I could have said that if she had only told me who she was, we would not have fought, which was the incident that precipitated this entire ordeal. I could have blamed Barker for teaching me things that were forbidden and then not warning me against doing them in Limehouse. I could have claimed that a clash between K'ing and my employer was inevitable and this lost text merely the catalyst. I could have done all these things and passed the blame to another. But sometimes, one must admit one's own mistakes.

"Yes," I told her. "This is all my fault."

She burst into tears again, and, somehow, I had my good arm around her and she was crying against my shoulder. Her silky hair smelled of what I suspected was jasmine, and every paroxysm reverberated through me. The grave reserve was gone because her guardian's life was in danger.

"Regardless of the outcome," I assured her, "you shall be free to go. I assume K'ing will hold to his bargain. If Barker should . . . well, fail, you will be well looked after by his lawyers."

"And you? What about you?"

"Oh, my life is forfeit, I'm afraid. K'ing can do with me as he wills. Not that it was much of a life, mind you."

"Do not talk like that," she said in a low voice.

"My life has been one long series of mistakes," I went on. "You have merely arrived in time for the latest."

"Sir speaks highly of you. He has great faith in you. He says you are 'coming along.' That is a compliment for him."

I directed her to one of the chairs and sat in the other. "I find it amazing that Barker has been informing you of my progress for an entire year, while he has not so much as mentioned your existence to me before last week."

"It is the Chinese way, Mr. Llewelyn. Tell only what is necessary. Be careful in whom you confide."

"*Fide sed cui vide,*" I said.

"I beg your pardon?"

"He has an old wooden shield on the wall of our office with a crest and motto in faded gold. It means 'Trust, but be careful in whom.' I can only assume it means that he trusts you, but he doesn't trust me."

"You have earned his trust," Bok Fu Ying said. "You saved his life, remember? Sir says your main problem is impatience. It is the weakness of the Western world. You came to my door because you would not wait for him to reveal who I was."

"I'm not—" I began, but we heard the sound of the key in the lock.

We both jumped to our feet, but it was only the guard bringing tea and cakes. Miss Winter had a headache and refused the tea. The tension had upset her. I sat and watched over her while she slept on the bed until our evening meal arrived. She talked little while we ate. We were both preoccupied with what would happen at midnight.

Finally, shortly after ten, a guard came and led her away. I demanded to know where he was taking her, but the man spoke no English. At eleven thirty, another came and led me through the tunnel and up into the street again. There was no need now for me to be guarded at gunpoint and the fellow led the way through a crowd of men. Dozens of them, all Chinese, moved toward a warehouse near the river. At some point we all converged, squeezing through a narrow doorway into a building full of benches built around a sunken ring. The seats were quickly filling, but as a guest I was seated ringside. As I came into the circle of risers, I noticed all the wood was new. This ring was what K'ing had hired his carpenters to build, and they must have started close to a week before. It confirmed my suspicion that K'ing must have known all along that Barker would choose trial by combat, despite his show of surprise.

I sat and looked around. Immediately across from me, an arm went up. It was Jimmy Woo, looking beside himself with excitement. I looked away, in any direction but at him. I didn't trust the fellow. He was playing each side against the other and had proven himself unworthy of our trust.

To the left, I saw Ho glowering at me, arms crossed, and in a particularly foul mood. I avoided his gaze, looking for someone neutral and eventually found him, Dr. Quong, looking down into the ring. Then Barker came out in his trousers and gauntlets, looking calm, waiting for his adversary to arrive. Finally, he came and when he did, I felt my stomach tighten.

The Chinese were chanting his name as he came into the ring. He was called Manchu Jack, and he was immense, close to six and a half feet in height. He looked like Mrs. Shelley's monster, save that there were no seams where the cadavers had been stitched together. He was imperfectly proportioned, his limbs overlong, giving him an apelike appearance. His face was all planes and hollows; with his enormous cheekbones and thick, hairless brows, I thought him atavistic, one of the missing links that the Darwinists were always claiming they had found. The front of his scalp was shaved in the traditional fashion, but the rest of his hair hung loose down his back to his waist.

He wore the same pants and shoes as my employer, but he wore a short jacket of white cotton that he quickly discarded by the theatrical method of ripping it off. He turned in my direction as he made a slow circle for all to see. From his muscular chest extending down to his wrists was a tattoo, more elaborate than any I'd seen on Barker or Ho. It was a dragon in a dozen colors, writhing and squirming all over his malformed torso. It was the dragon versus the lion, like the dance we had witnessed earlier. I remembered who had been the victor then.

Just then a door opened in the back. I might not have noticed had not everyone in the room, Barker and the massive Chinaman included, turned. Mr. K'ing came down the aisle and took his place on a slightly raised dais. He wore a Chinese suit, long like a frock coat, over trousers and slippers, all of it of the shiniest black silk. He was accompanied by Miss Winter in a gown of sea green. She had mastered her emotions and looked as cold as ice. They sat down in a pair of elegant teak folding chairs, like portable thrones, and he conferred with several men for a moment or two while Barker stood still with his burly arms crossed, regardless of the blunt spikes on his gauntlets. He was upstaged by his opponent, who began warming up, throwing a hundred or more punches in swift succession. I hated to admit it, but Barker looked a mere juvenile in size next to him. Finally, Manchu Jack's movements came to a close, a flurry of final bets were placed, and Mr. K'ing stood up in front of the crowd.

He spoke in Chinese and no one translated for me, but I am certain it was the customary introduction and explanation of the proceedings. The audience laughed once or twice, making me sure that he added in the politician's usual stock of jokes and humorous asides. It was over in about a minute, and the competitors in the ring bowed to him, then to each other, and then the fight began.

With a howl, Manchu Jack opened his arms wide as he launched an assault. Barker ducked under his arm and walked away as calmly as if he had passed a cow in a field. The monster turned quickly and lunged onto the Guv's forearm, spikes and all. Barker's legs collapsed and he went down, pulling his opponent with him. His foot went up into the center of the dragon tattoo and the hulk was balanced off the ground on Barker's foot for a second or two, before sailing over my employer's head and crumping in a heap in a corner of the ring. There was a burst of cheers, none greater than among those of us who called Barker friend. *Perhaps*, I thought, *he will win this handily and we can just go home.*

My hopes were dashed in the next moment. Back on his feet, the creature swung a hooking punch that Barker could not get far enough away from. It caught him on the jaw and spun him around. I thought he might have broken it, but apart from settling it back into place, my employer took no notice of it. Manchu Jack began to rain blows down on Barker, ones he had used in his opening warm-up, but Barker countered them one after another as if he knew the same routine. The Guv was as stone-faced as ever, while the other fellow looked more and more angry until the veins in his thick neck stood out like ropes.

He lunged for Barker, but in answer, received a glancing blow across his hairless brow, opening one up. Barker was first to spill claret, and some in the crowd began to regret their wagers. The Chinaman was far from down, however, and he walked to the corner where his white coat lay and used it to wipe the blood from his eyes. Barker had proven to him that for once this wasn't going to be an easy win, but I'm sure Jack had more than a few tricks to play before this was over.

I looked over at Quong, who still held the railing and stared over it anxiously. Woo was doing serious damage to his silk gloves with his teeth, and Ho acted as if it were he himself in the ring, on the edge of his seat, ready for anything. Only Bok Fu Ying looked on stoically.

Manchu Jack swung out and Barker leaned away, but it was a feint; with his other hand the man seized my employer's shoulder and pulled him off his feet. In a trice he had Barker on the ground, his knee in Barker's back, near his damaged kidneys, and began pulling back on his forehead to snap his neck. I saw no way for Barker to stop it, but he insinuated his fingers into the laces of his opponent's boot and pulled, rolling both of them onto their sides and then their backs.

Jack seized Barker's head as if it were a melon, but the Guv forced a forearm under his opponent's knee and began to squeeze it with the other. It was a trick rather like one we had played at school, sticking a pencil between a lad's fingers and then squeezing them tightly. It must have been excruciating. The Chinaman let go, and in a moment Barker did, too, rolling back onto his feet again. The big man followed, but he wasn't as sure-footed as before.

Jack tried several jabs like an English boxer, but Barker slapped most of them away. At one point, he grasped one of the wooden buttons of my employer's tunic, and rather than give purchase, Barker allowed the shirt to be pulled over his head, displaying the battleground of scars, burns, and tattoos he had collected over the course of his adventurous life. A murmur of admiration arose from the crowd.

The next blow brought blood onto Barker's cheek, three horizontal marks. Manchu Jack screamed and went into a clawing posture like a dragon, while my employer shifted his weight onto his back foot and the toes of his front, hands extended like cat's paws. Jack uncoiled and attacked, and then they slammed into each other as I've heard the sumo wrestlers of Japan do. The monster seized a kick Barker was planting, but my employer came right over his guard and formed his hand into a beak, catching the fellow in the eye. He'd momentarily foresworn the style of the tiger for the more subtle crane. The huge man growled and tried to grapple with Barker, but his eye was too painful. He threw the Guv down and turned, holding his injured orb.

Cyrus Barker was too professional a fighter to let this opening alone, and there seemed to be no referee present to stop the fight. I watched as my employer rose to his feet and took two steps toward his opponent, preparing to kick him. It was another ruse. Manchu Jack spun around, wheeling his leg out like a log, catching Barker with such force across his legs that he cartwheeled through the air. Another groan went through the crowd as the Guv hit the floor like a sack of grain. *This is it,* I thought, holding my breath.

Reaching down, the Chinaman picked Barker off the ground by cradling his head in his huge hands. My employer hung limp a moment, then his foot came up and gave the fellow a savage kick in the stomach behind him. I expected him to topple, but Manchu Jack absorbed it, grinning menacingly as he encircled the Guv's neck in a headlock. Barker hung a foot off the ground, his feet dangling, as the Chinese wrestler began to squeeze his skull. Barker had his hands around the man's arms, but he could get no leverage. The tension was reaching fever pitch, and I was certain now that we were going to lose this battle. My employer's face had turned beet red and I could see the veins pulsing in his forehead. The Chinaman began shaking him like a dog worrying a rat. All went quiet as I helplessly waited for the sound of Barker's neck snapping.

There was a snapping sound in the silence, but it was Jack who snarled in his throat. Barker's hand had found his fingers and snapped two of them. There was a third snap before the man reluctantly let go. Barker seized the fellow's wrists and braced his feet against the Chinaman's hips, leaning out at a forty-five-degree angle. Then he suddenly pulled himself back into Jack's embrace with a thud. Barker jumped down and turned to face his opponent, his arms raised defiantly, his fingers claws. He'd been silent during the fight, but now he gave a defiant roar.

The huge man frowned and tried to raise his right arm, but he grimaced in pain. He raised his left, but that was too painful also. It took me a minute to figure out what had happened. Barker had broken the man's collarbone with the back of his head. The Chinaman bellowed in anger, trying to throw a kick at Barker, but he ended up falling on his side. My employer went over and put his boot on his opponent's chest, many of the crowd calling for the coup de grâce. Instead, he turned and walked toward Mr. K'ing, raising his fists in triumph. All the men in the room began crying out, myself included, as K'ing stood and acknowledged the end of the match. Barker had won, if just barely. The Guv bowed to Mr. K'ing and limped out of the ring. A litter was brought out and the huge Chinaman moved onto it. It took six men to lift it.

The hall was abuzz with men discussing the fight. Ho had a triumphant look on his face, and I soon found out why when a man came up and handed him his winnings. Had I asked him, I'm sure he would have said he had known Barker would win all along. I was merely glad the Guv had survived.

Straddling the handrail and landing in the ring, I went looking for Barker. It was dark in the short tunnel under the seats, until I came to a fork, going right and left. I tried the right, bursting into a room. A Chinese doctor was treating Manchu Jack's injuries, but Barker was nowhere to be found. I ran out of the room and down the hall to the left, running into a room on the opposite side. There I found my employer, seated at a table, looking rather the worse for wear, while Dr. Quong attended to his wounds. Across from him sat Mr. K'ing himself. They were drinking tea as if the two were old acquaintances instead of adversaries.

Something told me I was being rude, blundering in like this, so I bowed without thinking. Mr. K'ing nodded his head and Barker gave me a wan smile with the corner of his mouth. His jaw was swollen and he had abrasions all over his neck and face.

"Come, sir," Mr. K'ing said to me, "and try some tea. Miss Winter has been released and sent home in a cab. I was just telling your employer that I have never seen a better fight. It was a treat to see the great *Shi Shi Ji* in the ring, and every man here tonight shall have a story to tell his grandchildren. This fight shall be discussed in ports and river towns around the world."

I took one of the dishes of tea and tossed it off in one gulp. Like all Chinese tea, it tasted like dishwater.

28

BARKER GOT UP THE NEXT MORNING, DETER-mined to go to work. Despite Mac's and my protests at the breakfast table that he needed more rest, he refused on the pretext that he had already dressed and going back to his bed and nightshirt would show a lack of progress. He had his way, of course, but I noticed he was slow getting into the cab. His face bore several sticking plasters and his jaw was swollen, but he paid them scant concern.

At our chambers, Jenkins raised his eyebrows, as if it were my fault the Guv was there. Barker sat down in his big chair with a contented sigh and tented his fingers. He wished Jenkins a good morning and received one in return. Then he picked up *The Times* and began to read the morning news. It reminded me of an anecdote I'd heard once about a Scottish lord who finished his breakfast each morning by going out in front of his castle and announcing that he had broken his fast; the rest of the world was now free to eat. Cyrus Barker wasn't going to let simple matters such as kidney failure or a fight with a Chinese giant stop him from solving a case.

Barker seemed inclined to think that morning, which was a relief. No one was beating down the door searching for the book. No prospective clients arrived on the step to beg the Guv's custom. After reading *The Times* and the *Pall Mall Gazette* front to back, he drew designs on the corner of his desk with his finger, then got up and went to his smoking cabinet. He took down a meerschaum pipe and, stuffing tobacco into the lion-head bowl, sat to smoke. Nothing was heard for the next half hour but the scratch of my nib on the ledger: cab rides, meals, maids and nurses, doctor bills and more doctor bills. I was wondering again where Barker got the money for this office and his house and garden, and, oh, yes, the wages of his employees, as well.

Barker got up, knocked out his pipe, ran a pipe cleaner through it, and put it away. Then he reached for another. The Guv rarely smoked two pipefuls in a row. It was a little Chinese Mandarin's head this time, with a hole in the crown of his pillbox hat. He filled it, lit it, and settled into his chair again. Nothing was happening of any import. Or so I thought.

"Ah," he suddenly said five minutes later. "You little beggar."

I looked up, but he wasn't speaking to me. He got up and began pacing, which is always a good sign. He went to his pitcher and glass behind him. They were empty.

"Thomas, get me some water, would you?"

I would, of course; anything to help with the case. I went out the back door and when I did, I saw something there. I'm not the sort to believe in signs. I like to think of myself as a practical person, but there was a robin on the handle of the pump. It was a little thing, a mere morsel of life, barely worth the Lord's time and effort, but its appearance cheered me immensely. The sun picked up the vibrant red in its breast. I dared not move from the doorway. It cocked its head this way and that, and finally it flew away, up and over the wall. It was a harbinger, I thought, a harbinger that the blasted winter was going away and that spring would eventually come. Death was dead and life would spring anew, and, yes, this case would soon be over and the Guv would finally get to the bottom of it all.

I pumped the water into the jug so quickly it overran and I had to pour some out. I brought it in and hurried back to my desk. Barker was seated again, but he was humming to himself off-key, another good sign. I poured him a glass and he drank it. Ten minutes went by. Fifteen. Then he spoke.

"Lad, run along and fetch Terry Poole. If he balks, tell him I'll solve the case without him."

I was out the door in the time it took the robin to fly over the wall. I sprinted into Whitehall Street and 'round the corner into Great Scotland Yard. Poole was not in his office, but I found him talking to a sergeant in the hall, looking harried and irritable as usual. I gave him the message and watched as he frowned at the ultimatum and heaved a sigh. What else could he do but comply with the Guv's request?

"Tell him I shall be along directly."

I nipped back to the office and dropped into my chair again. Barker was humming "How Can I Sink with Such a Prop as My Eternal Lord" from Spurgeon's *Our Own Hymn*

Book. As usual, he was mangling it, but I wouldn't have stopped him had my life depended on it. I don't know if miracles happen in our day and age, but sometimes it seems as if the Guv occasionally gets a divine message or two.

Poole appeared shortly thereafter, looking like a fellow who'd just come in second in a race.

"What is it, Cyrus?" he asked, pulling up one of the chairs in front of the desk.

"I need to arrange something quickly," Barker said.

"I don't like the sound of that. What exactly do you want to do?"

"I want to set up a meeting and bring all of the suspects together into one room."

"A meeting? You've gone mad," he barked. "What makes you think any of them will come?"

"That's what I need you for, Terry. You could make them come. It is the Yard's case, after all."

"Oh, now you want my help, after being obstinate and impeding our case for days."

"Someone official must take the killer into custody. I thought you should get the credit."

"I would have to get approval," the inspector said doubtfully, but I could see he was imagining the look on Henderson's face when he brought in the murderer.

"Hang approval," Barker said. "You are in charge of the investigation, are you not? What happens if, at the end of it, you have the confessed killer of Inspector Bainbridge shackled to your wrist?"

"I'd be a bloody hero," Poole admitted. "But ordering

some people to come won't mean they'll come. That Foreign Office blighter will stay away just to spite me. How
could I possibly get him there?"

"Tell him he cannot come. Or, better yet, you could let
out that I am ready to surrender the text."

Poole leaned forward. "Now you're talking. So you have
had it all along, then."

"I didn't say that. But I might be able to lay hands on it."

"All right. We'll do it your way. Where shall this meeting
be held?"

"At Ho's."

"Ho's! No, no, never," he protested hotly. "I've seen
enough of that place to suit me for the rest of my life. I
can't have an official meeting there."

"Why not?" Barker countered. "The inquest took place
there."

"Because holding it there would indicate that we had
been wrong to arrest him in the first place."

"But you were wrong to arrest him. He was innocent of
any wrongdoing."

"If that man is innocent of anything, then I'm one of
Her Majesty's ladies-in-waiting. He's the closest thing to a
pirate in the East End, and I suspect half the crimes in London are plotted in his tearoom."

"I concede that point, but many of the people I want at
that meeting reside in Limehouse and it is the only meeting
place in the area."

"Let me think about it. Will you invite Mr. K'ing to this
little party of yours?" the inspector asked.

"I would say he is too canny to step into any such snare,

but he will be certain to send along a representative, if he does not come himself."

"Do you have a theory as to who Bainbridge's killer might be?"

"I do," Barker said.

"Then tell me who it is!"

Barker shook his head. "I shall let you know at the proper time, in order to arrest him."

"I've been working for the Yard almost fifteen years now, and I've never come up against a case like this," Poole complained. "I cannot make heads or tails of it. Everything is incomprehensible."

"If it is any consolation, Terry, I believe no one could have solved it who hadn't spent decades in China."

"It feels like I am turning a pot 'round and 'round, looking for the handle, but there isn't one," Poole said, looking desolate.

Barker gave a cool smile in sympathy. "I'll give you a handle, though I'm not certain it shall help you. The primary question, obviously, is who committed the murder, but it helps to ask a second one, which is, what did the killer plan to do with the text once he had it?"

"Do with it?" Poole repeated, a trifle lost, but then, I was, too.

"Yes. As has been pointed out many times, the book has almost no monetary value."

Terence Poole ran a hand through his long side-whiskers, in danger of plucking them out in frustration. "I wasn't ordered to find the book. My duty is to find Bainbridge's killer. I shan't rest day or night until I find him."

"All shall be revealed in the fullness of time. You

look agitated, Terry. I shall have Jenkins brew some green tea."

Poole snatched his bowler from the edge of Barker's desk. "You can keep your sophisms and your blasted tea. I've got work to do. Have your little meeting if you like, but you'd better be ready to reveal who murdered Bainbridge, and you'd better bloody have proof."

After Poole had gone, Barker turned his swiveling chair my way. "Get out your pad and pencil, lad. We've an invitation to write."

I got out my pad and waited until Barker began to dictate.

With the compliments of Scotland Yard, Mr. Cyrus Barker, private enquiry agent, invites your attendance at the tearoom of Mr. Ho, near the Commercial Road, Limehouse, in order to discuss a text which has aroused the interest of many. Anyone with said interest in the text or who wishes to acquire it may hear Mr. Barker's explanations of events pertaining to the volume and its arrival in this country and its subsequent history. The meeting shall be at seven o'clock on the evening of the seventeenth. Your humble servant, Cyrus Barker.

"That will do," he said. "Type it up and make several copies. Let us see now. Send them to Mr. K'ing, Pollock Forbes, Charlie Han, Miss Petulengro, Mr. Woo, Campbell-Ffinch, and Mr. Hooligan. Am I leaving anyone out?"

"Not that I can see, sir." I got out the Hammond typewriting machine and set to work.

London has several postal deliveries per day, but I feared

that one of the important messages might miscarry. So, instead, I chose one of the excellent messenger services that ply their trade in Whitehall. I gave the fellow an extra half sovereign to see that all were delivered reliably, because I knew that was what Barker wanted. For a Scotsman, he could be surprisingly liberal with his money, but then, he left the ledgers to me.

"Let us go to Limehouse and prepare," he said.

When Barker says the least, one knows that he is planning something. I tried twice to get him to tell me what was happening, but he was as unwilling to show his hand as a whist player. He spent most of the journey to Ho's with his face tilted down toward his feet while I tried to reason through everything, without getting any further than Poole.

At Ho's, he rattled down the steps through the tunnel as nonchalantly as ever, leaving me to hurry along behind him. Once in the tearoom, he conferred with Ho in low tones. The latter was back to ignoring me, I noticed. It wasn't fair. If I took the blame for causing the fight Barker had been in, then I should also get the credit when Ho came away with his winnings.

The two men got up and moved to the back of the room. Ho took a key from his pocket and opened the doors to the private banquet room, where a few days earlier the jurymen at the inquest had gone to deliberate. I thought it fitting that the case might end where it had begun, in Ho's tearoom.

There was nothing remarkable about the room. One wall was stone, the other three made up of vertical planks of wood gray with age. Scattered tables and chairs looked as if they had been left as they were when the jurors returned to the court with their verdict. A thin layer of dust had settled. Ho called to one of the waiters, who came in with a bowl of water and a rag and began to clean.

Ho began moving tables about while he and Barker strategized in Chinese. I couldn't help much with my injured shoulder, but I shuffled chairs around with one good arm and my knee. The tables were set up in a in a T pattern and chairs arranged around the outside to seat ten. This was quite a party Barker was preparing. I hoped at the end of it, he would unmask Quong's killer and we could bid adieu to this godforsaken end of town for a good, long while.

29

THE NEXT MORNING BARKER AND DR. APPLEGATE arrived at our door simultaneously. In Mac's room, the doctor checked my employer's jaw, swabbed iodine onto the scratches on his cheek, and asked him several private questions concerning his kidney function. Apparently, Barker gave satisfactory answers, for the doctor pronounced him on the mend. He also inspected Mac's leg and said our butler would regain full use of it soon and could return to his duties.

"What about me?" I asked. "Could you cut off my cast?"

"You are not my patient, young man," Applegate told me. "I would not presume to interfere."

Quacks they are, and charlatans, I thought, *especially when they collude.*

Coming out into the hall, Barker did something he'd been wanting to do for days. He sacked Madame Dummolard. It would have taken me a half hour of blustering and reassuring to get it done, but Barker is a blunt man. It took him exactly one sentence.

"Thank you for all you have done," he said to her in the

hall, "but Mac is recovering well and we no longer have need of your services."

I was preparing for a tidal wave of vitriolic French as Madame took in a lungful of air. Just when I thought she would burst out, however, she slowly exhaled.

"Very well, monsieur," she replied. "As you wish. Ladies! *Allons!* We must pack our bags."

That was that. Had it been left to me I'm certain there would have been hysteria all up and down the hall, but people think twice before facing down Cyrus Barker. Twenty minutes later, Madame came down with her maids and suitcases. She shot me an annoyed look.

"What is it, Madame?"

"*Cochons,*" she said. "All men are pigs."

She went into the kitchen, perhaps to take out her frustrations on her husband, but for once, he would not rise to the bait. Eventually, a vehicle came to the door, and she and her entourage decamped.

"Peace," Barker pronounced with some satisfaction. "Peace and tranquility. I must send for my suitcases from the office. I shall sleep in my own bed tonight." He went upstairs to his room.

Left alone in the hall, I took a few steps and stood in Mac's doorway. He was staring down at his bandaged leg and wiggling his toes.

"So, it's back to work soon, then?" I asked. "No more reading Mrs. Braddon?"

"Very funny," he said acidly.

"How did the romancing go, by the way? Are you betrothed to any of the nurses?"

"No, drat the luck. She was married."

"What about the maid? She couldn't have been more than eighteen and she was a stunner."

"I'll give you that, but no thank you. Her name is Clothilde, and she is Madame's daughter by a previous marriage."

"Is she, by Jove? I suppose we are well out of it, then." I tried to imagine having Madame Dummolard for a mother-in-law, patting and kissing you one minute and shying bric-a-brac at your head while screaming gutter French at you the next. "I'm sure it will be good to get back on your feet again. I know I can't wait to get this cast off."

Mac sat up on his bed. "Oh, yes. You know the first thing I'm going to do? I'm going to take some soap and hot water to these floors. I won't rest until I get whatever concoction they put on it scrubbed off. I'm going to mop everything and put a wood preserver on it. I have the recipe in one of my books."

I was suddenly in danger of being bored to death. Maccabee's idea of a good time differed dramatically from my own. I nodded absently as he prattled on until Barker came down the stairs. I offered to step out and find a cab.

All that day in our offices in Whitehall, I was aware of the impending confrontation at Ho's later that evening. Would the killer be unmasked, or was he too canny to fall into Barker's trap? Would his staying away be taken as a sign of guilt? I could not say. At one point I was convinced there was something wrong with the clock in our office and it couldn't possibly be only one o'clock in the afternoon, but just then Big Ben chimed once. If there was a conspiracy, it had to be on a much grander scale.

As for Barker, he sat most of the day, smoking or drinking tea, deep in thought. I believe he was formulating questions but I dared not ask.

At five we left the office, bound for Ho's. When we arrived, everything was almost ready. Inspector Poole came in with all the weight of Scotland Yard behind him. Half the clientele of Ho's restaurant hurriedly finished their meals or simply left them unfinished and sidled away toward the tunnel and freedom. I noticed Poole and Ho did not look each other in the eye.

The inspector came over to Barker and they conferred in hushed tones.

"Did you get it?" Barker asked.

"Yes. Your man gave it to me. Where shall we sit?"

"There," the Guv said, pointing to a chair. "Are you prepared?"

Poole nodded and then sat down in the seat Barker indicated. I tried to see if he were nervous about whoever was coming, but he was too deserving of his position to betray any emotion. Whatever this big event, everyone was either keeping their own counsel or looking a trifle bored.

A waiter shuffled in with a tray of tea, followed by Ho, who deposited a large tureen on the table. Perhaps at least we'd have a spot of dinner. Barker nodded to Ho, who tucked his hands into the yoke of his apron and to Poole, who had his arms crossed, sitting in his chair.

"We are ready."

The first to arrive was Pollock Forbes. He shook hands with Poole when Barker introduced them. I could see Poole tried to ascertain just who he was and what part of the proceedings he would have a hand in, but neither Forbes nor Barker was forthcoming.

I heard Trelawney Campbell-Ffinch before I saw him. His leather boots clicked across the restaurant floor. More silently, Jimmy Woo followed him.

"Have you got it?" Campbell-Ffinch demanded eagerly as he swept into the room.

Barker ignored the question. "Please be seated. The owner shall serve tea shortly."

"Tea? I don't have time for tea," the Foreign Office man snapped. "I want to see the book. I demand to interview this fellow you have in custody."

"We have no one in custody yet, sir. All in good time," Barker answered.

"For sheer brass, Barker," Campbell-Ffinch said, "you have no equal. Very well. It's your show for now. You've got just enough rope to hang yourself." He dropped into a vacant chair, a look of disgust on his face.

"Mr. Barker," Woo spoke up. "Surely you could have found a more seemly place for a meeting than this notorious establishment. My reputation suffers frightfully to be seen here. There are far better Chinese restaurants if that is your desire—"

"Thank you, Mr. Woo, for your concern," Barker said. "This case began here and it shall end here. I assure you, sir, the tea is quite adequate. Ho and I share the same merchant. Please take a seat."

Campbell-Ffinch gave a hard look in Ho's direction. "I say, is this chap going to stay here the entire time? This is an important matter for Her Majesty's empire, and this fat fellow is a known provocateur. The Foreign Office has had its eye on this place for some time. It would require but a command to shut it down permanently."

Ho's eyes looked like two slits in his face. "Your agents are as subtle as water buffalo. A child could recognize them."

"Gentlemen," Barker warned.

Just then Campbell-Ffinch's eye caught that of his old university classmate. "Forbes, what in blazes are you doing here?"

"Keeping an eye on you, Lonnie," Forbes drawled. "Seeing that you stay out of trouble."

Hestia Petulengro and her swain arrived next. She looked carefully at the men in the room before coming inside. She was the only woman I had ever seen at Ho's. She towed Charlie Han along and then sat down beside me.

"I need to explain," she said to me in a low voice.

"You don't, actually," I responded. "It was just dinner, after all, not a proposal of marriage. I'm not exactly overjoyed by your personal arrangements, but of course you are free to make your choice."

"No chance for another dinner sometime, then?"

"Well, not while he is living in your house, no. I do prefer no audience when I kiss you."

She smiled, but what it meant exactly I could not tell. I was distracted by the arrival of Mr. K'ing himself. He had not sent an emissary but had actually come in person. The triad leader swept through the door and set his wide-brimmed hat upon the table.

"I cannot be in this room!" Woo announced. "This fellow is a known criminal, and as an official of the Asian Aid Society, I must not be seen to have dealings with such a person!"

I was about to ask why he should be so particular now,

when I had seen him get out of Mr. K'ing's cab the other night, but I stopped myself. Barker might not care to have that information revealed.

"Mr. Woo, I warn you that the text must not be translated for the Foreign Office," K'ing stated. "It is the personal property of the Chinese imperial government and must not be read by the English."

"It is not your part to say what the property of the imperial government is or is not," Woo answered. "You are a common criminal."

"Nonsense," K'ing countered. "I am a businessman."

As they bickered, I heard the last invited guest behind me before I saw him. One could not mistake the sound of hobnails on a wooden floor.

"'Zis a private party?" Patrick Hooligan spoke in his raspy voice. "'Ello, K'ingy, old boy."

Now it was K'ing's turn to be uncomfortable. "You are in triad territory," he snapped.

"Yes, well, I got—what's the word?—I got *dispensation*. An invite from old Push hisself here. Command performance, you might say."

Hooligan took a seat at the table and immediately started cleaning his nails with a knife, as if the proceedings did not interest him at all.

We were all assembled. At the head of the T-shaped table, Barker and Poole sat. I flanked Barker while Ho stood at his elbow. Down the right side sat Hettie Petulengro, Charlie Han, and Trelawney Campbell-Ffinch. Pollock Forbes sat at the foot, and on the left were Patrick Hooligan, Jimmy Woo, and Mr. K'ing.

Barker stood to address the group. "I have called you here today because you are all involved in the investigation of the death of Inspector Bainbridge or my late assistant Quong or one of several other murders that have occurred. I am not implying that anyone in this room is the killer, merely that each of you is involved in some fashion."

The room erupted. Everyone began speaking at once, denying the accusations and blaming each other.

"Silence!" Poole boomed. "You can take your medicine here or you can take it down in A Division. Which'll it be?"

That silenced the group. Barker surveyed them and continued.

"Thank you. Let me begin by saying that one of you is not as he seems. Forbes?"

Pollock Forbes knit his fingers in front of him. "Ah, yes," he began. "At Mr. Barker's request, I did some investigating at Cambridge. It appeared they do have a record of a James Woo, a student from China, but no one there seems to recall him, and if anything, I think Mr. Woo here is rather memorable. I took a closer look at the registry entry. I am afraid it was a forgery."

Barker turned to Woo and said, "Would you care to comment, Mr. Woo, if that is your name?"

Woo looked a little deflated. He removed his monocle and put it in his pocket.

"Very well, Mr. Barker," he said, adopting a more serious tone. "You leave me no choice. I am an agent of the imperial government," he explained. "I was sent to recover the text by the Empress herself. When I arrived here, it became necessary to adopt an identity and search for it street by street. I chose to work as an interpreter at the Asian Aid Society, so I could get to know the Chinese in England. I inserted the record in the files at Cambridge."

"You also worked for the Foreign Office and for Mr. K'ing," Barker pointed out. "That's quite a conflict of interest."

Woo looked uncomfortably at the triad leader. "It became necessary to get to know Mr. K'ing's operations and what the Foreign Office was doing to recover the text. I thought it likely K'ing had the text in his possession."

"If you had acquired the text, what would you have done with it?" Barker asked.

"I would have taken it back to the Forbidden City, old sp—sorry. I would give it to the Dowager Empress."

"And what would she do with it?"

"Whatever she wishes, of course. It would become her property. I assume it would be watched by armed guards with the other treasures in the palace. Not that it is a treasure, mind you."

"It would not be returned to the Xi Jiang Temple?"

"I wouldn't think so," Woo said. "It is best to keep it in the Forbidden City. The area near the Xi Jiang monastery has been unstable since the Heavenly War. The south is still full of revolutionaries, anxious to overthrow the Manchus."

"I can't believe this," Campbell-Ffinch finally spoke up. "This little popinjay, an agent for the Chinese government?"

"Do shut up, Campbell-Ffinch," Woo said. "The hardest part of my assignment has been working with you. If all Foreign Office men are as incompetent as you, I fear for this country of yours."

"Well, I never!" the English agent blustered.

Looking across, I saw a slight smile on Pollock Forbes's face.

Barker turned to Patrick Hooligan. "And you, Mr. Hooligan. If you had the text, what would you do with it?"

"I told yer, Push, I'd sell it. Sell it to the highest bidder. All this talk about it not having worth is codswallop. Start threatening to sell it to someone else and you'd be surprised at how high the biddin' can go."

"What would you do with the money?"

Hooligan looked over at his rival, Mr. K'ing, who was eyeing him as if he were vermin. Barker and I knew he'd use it to gain more power and influence in the East End, but he wasn't about to say it in front of K'ing. "Dunno. P'raps buy a good racehorse. You can make a powerful lot o' money with a good racehorse."

"I see," Barker said. He turned and faced the other side of the table. "Miss Petulengro, let us say for the sake of argument that you owned the manuscript. What would you do with it?"

"I did have the manuscript," she pointed out. "It means naught to me. It's just a book with stick figures in it. I can't read it. It's nothing but trouble as far as I'm concerned. I'd give it to you. You might be a copper, but you seem straight as an arrow to me."

She couldn't help looking at me and I at her. If Barker noticed the fraternization between his assistant and one of the witnesses, he didn't let on. Instead, he turned to Charlie Han.

"And you, Mr. Han. Let us say I were able to put the text into your hands right now. What would you do with it?"

Han shrugged. "I dunno. I cannot read. I sell it, buy more betel nut, if Hettie don't want it."

Barker turned to Mr. K'ing. "Sir," he said. "Shall I repeat the question I have asked everyone else?"

K'ing ran a finger over his thin mustache. "I have no personal interest in the text, Mr. Barker. I realize it is dangerous. I suppose I would see it delivered to China on the Blue Funnel line and into the hands of a responsible person, who would take it back to the Xi Jiang Temple."

Barker nodded. "And you, Mr. Campbell-Ffinch, I suppose you would—"

"I'd give it to the Foreign Office, of course," the man said. "The book would be analyzed, perhaps with the intention of producing a training manual for us, if these techniques are all that they are purported to be. After that, who knows? It might be passed on to Her Majesty's army."

"Mr. Forbes," Barker said, turning to the last person seated at the table, "you've shown some interest in this case. If you had the text, what would you do with it?"

Forbes leaned back in his chair and raised a hand to his lips. I noticed for the first time an insignia on his ring, a cross inside a crown. It was a symbol, I realized, of some secret society.

"I'd take it to a place of safekeeping, where the knowledge would not see the light of day," he replied.

"I see," Barker said. "Thank you, Pollock. This has been very enlightening. Seven individuals have given me as many answers." He paced a circuit around the room and we all watched him. I knew he was about to spring something upon us, I just wished I knew what. Barker looked slowly about the room, from face to face.

"I am now willing to entertain offers for the book," he stated at last.

Everyone began talking at once, apart from Poole and Forbes, who I noted remained silent. Hestia Petulengro began calling Barker names. K'ing conferred with Woo, and Campbell-Ffinch was crowing that my employer had really had the text in his possession the entire time. Hooligan's raspy voice was heard over all.

"That leaves me out, I reckon. I can get yer a good price for it, but I can't bring enough ready to the table to make it worth your while."

"Mr. Woo, if we may still call you that, are you prepared on behalf of your government to make an offer?"

"Provided the authenticity of the text can be verified, I am authorized to go up to a specified amount. We have always thought that at some point we might have to purchase the text in order to get it back."

"And you, Campbell-Ffinch, are you prepared on the part of Her Majesty's government to put forward an offer?"

"I shall have to speak with my superiors, but I believe we may be able to do so. But what's he doing here?" the Foreign Office man said, pointing toward Poole, who had been sitting and watching everything.

"Inspector Poole is here to see that order is maintained. That is all."

I knew it had to be a lie, as was Barker's entire offer. Poole had his eyes glued on Barker, not sure whether to agree or not.

"What about you, Mr. K'ing? Are you prepared to enter into the bidding?"

"I am, but only with the intention of doing with it as I told you."

"Of course. The winning bidder may do with the text whatever he wishes. Excellent. We have three bidders, then. Who shall vouch for its authenticity? I could translate it easily, but it is not for me to judge, being the one who shall produce it."

All three bidders offered their services, including Campbell-Ffinch, whose knowledge of Chinese must have been rudimentary at best. Barker looked about, trying to choose.

Finally, he said, "Mr. Woo, I think your interpreter's skills make you the most informed person to look over the text."

"Thank you, old fellow. Quite decent of you."

"Llewelyn, will you give Mr. Woo your seat?" I stood and moved to the side, offering my chair to Woo, who slid into it ready to see the much-sought-after text. Poole looked at Barker for instructions.

"Show him, Terence," the Guv said.

Reluctantly, Poole reached into his pocket and removed the packet we had picked up from the pawnbroker two weeks before. He set it down on the table, and Woo grabbed it eagerly, sliding the book out of the protective envelope and opening the cover. It wasn't the text. I recognized it immediately as a book from Barker's own library, one of a handful of Chinese texts my employer kept on his shelf.

"No, wait," Woo cried. "This isn't—"

Before he could move, there was a click as Poole's police regulation bracelets locked onto Woo's right wrist. A second click almost simultaneous with the first came as Barker clapped a second about the fellow's left one. The two detectives had carried them tucked in their coat sleeves, locked about their own wrists. With a sudden shove, all three of their chairs were tipped back and hit the floor as Barker and Poole held the struggling Woo. From the far side of the table, Ho pulled a set of manacles from the tureen and stepped forward to lock them on Woo's ankles. In a trice, they had him as immobilized as any man could be while the rest of us leapt to our feet in astonishment.

30

I WASN'T GOING TO RISK ANOTHER BLOW TO MY kidneys, thank you," Barker said as he and Woo lay nose to nose on the floor of Ho's back room with Inspector Poole shackled to his other arm. Barker, Ho, and Poole helped Woo right his chair, where he sat as trussed up as a Christmas goose.

"You must forgive the subterfuge, gentlemen and Miss Petulengro, of course," Barker said to the rest of us. "This was the only way I could lay hands upon this man without getting someone killed. This is the fellow responsible for the deaths of Inspector Bainbridge, Quong, Mr. Petulengro, Jan Hurtz, Luke Chow, and the sailor Chambers, as well as the attack upon my manservant, Jacob Maccabee, and myself. He was also responsible for the break-in at the Xi Jiang Monastery and the deaths of the two monks there."

"You've made some kind of mistake," Woo insisted. "I'm no killer."

"I've always heard you were eccentric, Barker, but this really is beyond anything I've ever seen," Campbell-Ffinch said. "If this prancing little Chinaman is our man, even if he is an agent for his government, I'll swallow my mother's blessed bonnet."

"You call yourself a keen fighter, do you not, Mr. Campbell-Ffinch? Then presumably you'd recognize another of your kind. What is the term? To 'smell the blood'? Take a look at these, then."

With a tug, the Guv pulled off one of Woo's silk gloves. Woo's knuckles were enormous, like a child's set of marbles, and there were hard yellow calluses upon the palm and edge of the hand. It was the hardened hand of a killer.

Woo struggled again and almost reached his hand into his coat pocket, but Poole was three stone heavier and trained in antagonistics by Barker himself. He turned Woo's wrist and dipped into his pocket, tossing a pistol onto the table far enough away that no one could reach it.

"I reckon that's the weapon used to murder my friend Inspector Nevil Bainbridge and young Mr. Quong."

"So, is that the real text or not?" Campbell-Ffinch said, looking at the book on the table.

"I'm afraid not. It is an obscure book called *The Art of War*. I borrowed it from my library because it is roughly the size and color of the text."

"A decoy!" Campbell-Ffinch cried. "Damn and blast! Where is the text?"

"I got rid of it almost the same day I got it," Barker explained. "I gave it to a Chinaman. By now, it should be halfway to Canton, where it will be returned to the Xi Jiang Temple. All of your efforts," Barker said, looking at Woo beside him, "were for naught. The manuscript is where you shall never get to it."

Jimmy Woo sat very stiffly in his chair, still shackled to

Poole and Barker. I thought he might not admit to anything, but finally he unwound and sat back in his chair.

"Oh, very well. I suppose it is gone and there is nothing I can do about that now, but I shall not confess to murder in front of witnesses. I have diplomatic immunity. I am an official of the Forbidden City. You can take me to jail, but it is only a matter of time before I am sent back to Peking. I shall have that manuscript yet, Mr. Barker. I have dedicated over two years of my life to it and I consider it mine."

"How did you first hear about the text, sir?" my employer asked.

"I am a steward of the imperial Prince. When I heard word about the text from Luke Chow, I told the Prince and he agreed it was necessary that he obtain it."

"And should you have obtained it, what sort of reward did you expect to receive?"

"Reward?" Woo said. "Not so much as a tael. I hoped to be given permission to study the book."

Barker looked at Campbell-Ffinch, who himself might have killed in order to lay hands on a new fighting method. "You hoped to be a better fighter?"

"No," Woo answered. "I mean, yes, I hoped to learn the secrets and to become a better fighter, but not for my own gain. I wanted to create an elite corps of boxers chosen from among the imperial troops."

"I see," Barker said. "An elite corps. And just what, Mr. Woo, would the elite corps do with that knowledge?"

Woo put his head down and mumbled something under his breath.

"I did not hear you, Mr. Woo."

He looked up again and his easy manner was gone. I saw fire in his eyes. "I said, we would kill all foreigners within China's borders, every American and Englishman and French and German and Austrian and Japanese that has been infecting our country. We would wipe out foreign business along the Bund in Shanghai and in the European settlements in Peking and Canton. We would execute your missionaries with their poisonous religion as an example to their weak-willed converts, and we would shut our borders again. China for the Chinese. It is the only way, you see."

"You're mad," Campbell-Ffinch insisted. "Her Majesty the Dowager Empress would never countenance the wholesale slaughter of honored guests in China. We have been assured of that fact."

"Campbell-Ffinch, if you believe that, you are naive," Mr. K'ing spoke up. "I've heard she was responsible for the death of her eldest son for being a spineless weakling. She would no more fear the slaughter of non-Chinese than she would the fleas on one of her prized dogs. If the Prince agreed to such an agreement, even in unofficial terms, one can assume he knew he could convince Her Majesty of the necessity of his actions. I have heard her referred to as the Dragon Lady. She has quite a villainous reputation."

"There is but one person in this room who has spoken to the Dowager Empress herself and might best resolve this question," Ho said. Heads began to turn back and forth, until finally, all gazes settled on my employer.

Cyrus Barker cleared his throat, as if postponing an unpleasant task, before he spoke. "I have indeed met the Empress and it is true that she has been ruthless in the past, but at other times, she has been lenient. I believe she has relied

314 — Will Thomas

on one advisor after another over a span of forty years. The Prince is one of those advisors. He is a cold specimen, but she dotes upon him. I believe he could have convinced her of the need of such a course."

"I regret we have not had the opportunity of finishing our fight, Mr. Barker, in the tunnel," Woo said. "I would have enjoyed such a challenge. I suppose there is no chance now?"

"None whatsoever. I have not come here to fight but to avenge the murder of my late assistant."

"Had I known then what I do now, I don't believe I would have shot Quong and risked bringing myself to your attention. To tell the truth, I did not believe such a skilled fighter as you existed in the West. To think, the mighty Stone Lion of Canton, an Englishman."

"Scotsman," Barker corrected. "I am a Scotsman."

There was a silence in the room for a brief moment, and then Ho clapped his hands. "Tea!"

Barker had made good his promise to Poole, and the two of them rose with their prisoner in hand. My employer opened the door, waiters came in to serve us tea, and then there was a sudden commotion in the doorway. Poole, Woo, and Barker all cried out at once. One of the waiters turned toward us and raised his arms. In his hand was a bloody knife, which he dropped onto the floor with a clatter. It was no waiter at all, despite the apron he wore. It was Old Quong.

The next I knew, Dr. Quong had been tackled by Campbell-Ffinch, who had finally reasoned that something had gone wrong. I caught a glimpse of Woo through the tangle of limbs. His face was set in a rictus of pain, and the lower half of his suit was covered in blood and gore. Old Quong had cut him horizontally across the abdomen, and rivulets of blood seeped onto the floor and his patent leather boots. I watched his face slowly relax and his eyes roll up as the killer of so many gave way to death.

"Vengeance!" Old Quong called from the floor as Campbell-Ffinch subdued him. "Vengeance!"

Poole swore and reached for his keys, having no desire to be shackled to a corpse, while another killer rolled about on the floor. Barker, I think, had the oddest reaction of all. He merely stood and shook his head, amazed at the proceedings.

So much happened after that that I could hardly keep track. Poole was upset that a murder had occurred right in front of him. Campbell-Ffinch was angry at losing both the book and the killer. Hooligan clapped his hands as if this had all been staged for his entertainment, while Hettie and Charlie Han took the first opportunity to depart.

As for the inscrutable Mr. K'ing, he spoke not a word but bowed and retrieved his hat, slipping out before Campbell-Ffinch and Inspector Poole noticed he was gone. Forbes was a step behind him.

Dr. Quong's wrists were locked in Woo's blood-spattered restraints and he was led off. We covered the body with a tablecloth as waiters came and went with rags, mops, and buckets and cleaned the blood from the floor. Poole arranged for the body to be removed in one of Ho's laundry carts, which Ho would bill the Yard for later. Hooligan went into the tearoom for a meal, and Campbell-Ffinch stalked off to make his report.

When the room was sufficiently clean, Ho locked up

and we three went to his office. Ho moved to a cabinet in the back of the room near the shrine. He took out a small white porcelain bottle and three cups and poured each of us a drink.

"To memory of Quong," he said and we all downed the fiery liquid, possibly plum brandy. It took the breath out of my lungs and when I got it back, the cups had been refilled.

"To Dr. Quong," Barker stated, and down it went a second time.

Afterward, the Guv smacked his lips and rotated the tiny cup in his hand. "It is convenient that Dr. Quong was here. It is almost as if he were let in."

Ho picked up his water pipe and began running a wire through the mouthpiece. "I don't know what you are talking about."

"It occurs to me," Barker replied, "that Woo may have escaped English justice, but he did not escape Chinese justice."

31

THAT EVENING THINGS WERE ALMOST BACK TO what passes for normal in the Barker household. Mac was on his feet, though still walking with the aid of a cane. My employer was returning to health rapidly and I had hopes of getting my own infernal cast off and sleeping comfortably at last.

We were in Barker's room, on either side of a coal fire with a pot of tea at his elbow and a pot of coffee at mine, both of which he had carried up himself since Mac couldn't manage stairs and I couldn't carry a tray. Barker had a pipe going and the pleasant aroma of his tobacco floated about my head. It was a pleasant scene, even as the firelight glinted on the racks of spears, swords, and other weapons suspended on the low, sloping ceilings. My mind was turning over the case as if it were an object in my hand, holding it this way and that. I had to admit this was the part of private enquiry work I could not do. I could assemble suspects and search for motives and opportunity, but the discounting of persons until one could say without hesitation that this fellow alone was the murderer, well, I couldn't do it yet. I began to fear I lacked some gland in my brain.

"You look dissatisfied this evening, Thomas. What is wrong?"

"I cannot sort this out, sir. How did you know it was Jimmy Woo and not a half dozen others?"

Barker dismissed my remark with a shake of his head. "You give me too much credit. Had my mind not been clouded with grief and guilt over Quong's death, I might have tracked down Jimmy Woo a year ago."

"He was subtle," I said, "and his disguise excellent. Who would have suspected a funny little interpreter would be a black-hearted killer?"

"I should have," Barker insisted. "Now that I look back on everything, I should have realized that being a eunuch put him in the perfect place for receiving word of a secret manuscript. Imperial eunuchs fall into several categories. Some, perhaps the best of them, give up the pleasures of the body and become scholars. Others, devastated by the loss, become exaggeratedly effeminate, simpering like court women and collecting scores of outfits. That, in a way, was what he emulated, but he was actually a member of a third category. Worried that his condition would result in a flaccid body, as it often does, Woo trained and honed himself tirelessly, choosing a martial form of life, obsessing about the ways to overcome an adversary. You will note his ability to shoot. Even at this advanced date, the Chinese prefer sword and spear. To find a Chinaman voluntarily learning to use a firearm is remarkable."

"I'm still lost, I'm afraid. I don't know anything about the Chinese court."

"Let us take it chronologically, then," the Guv said, stirring the fire with a poker. "About a year and a half ago there was a eunuch who lived and worked in the Forbidden City. We do not know his true name, but he was a steward of the Prince, and was interested in Chinese boxing. He was in a position with a great deal of pressure, as all the court constantly jockeys for position around the young Prince or the Dowager Empress, making alliances and ingratiating themselves. Often eunuchs are well connected throughout China in order to bring exotic foods, objets d'art, or information to the city. In order to win favor, a great deal of money is made and frequently changes hands. A monk whom we now know as Luke Chow came across a text that had almost been forgotten in the library of his temple. He sent a fragment to this eunuch who agreed to pay him for the text. Woo knew this was his only opportunity to lay hands on something he'd wanted for years. There are over a dozen such texts in China, but they are closely guarded by the monks to whom they are entrusted. Something happened between them, although we may never know what. Perhaps after letting him into the monastery, Chow realized how dangerous Woo was. In any case, after two of his brother monks were murdered, Chow took the text himself and made his way to Shanghai, signing on aboard the Blue Funnel liner the *Ajax*. Discovering where Chow had gone, Woo took a faster ship, or perhaps several, and arrived here ahead of him. He waited until the *Ajax* arrived and followed Chow and the crew to Coffin's penny hang, where Woo killed him in the middle of the night but was unable to find the text. As a safeguard, Chow had given the text to the only European in the crew, probably with a warning to get rid of it if anything happened to him. Chambers complied with those instructions once Chow was dead, selling the text to the chandler with Chow's other effects.

"The text came into Petulengro's chandlery and might be there still if Quong had not happened along and realized what it was. Then he and Woo must have seen each other, and Quong realized he was in danger. Somehow, he managed to elude him but in order to get rid of the text temporarily, he pawned it to Hurtz, hoping a Chinaman would not look there. Woo shot Quong, searched the body, and threw it into the river, but he never found the pawn ticket tucked in the sleeve of the jacket."

"Lucky for us," I said, taking the poker from Barker's hand and banking the coals and ash properly. Scotsmen only understand peat fires.

"You know I don't believe in luck," Barker went on. "I bungled it. I got the message that Quong was dead, and all I wanted was to find the killer and avenge his death. Had I been less grief stricken, I would have noted the unusual number of deaths around that New Year's Eve, as you did, and realized they were all connected.

"Petulengro and Chambers died next, a day apart, one supposedly during a robbery and the other as the result of an accident. I still believe Petulengro was helped into the Great Beyond by Inspector Bainbridge, for reasons we've discussed earlier."

"But at Ho's you said Woo killed Petulengro, not Bainbridge."

Barker smiled. "You caught me out, lad. I lied. I'm not proud of it. I'm very certain that Bainbridge killed Petulengro. He was besotted with the man's niece. I thought it best to put the blame on Woo, rather than the inspector. The man has a widow and men who look up to him. He was at a rough time in his life when age was overtaking him. I thought it best. When one is a private agent, one can make such choices. Where were we? Oh, yes, Chambers. Woo must have asked around the docks about which sailor was Chow's closest friend, and when Chambers was mentioned, he tracked him down and killed him, using the skills he learned from the fragment of the book. Unfortunately, all these deaths didn't help Woo find the text. It was lost somewhere in Hurtz's pawnshop." He paused. "Good fire."

"Thank you, sir," I said. I added a scoop of new coals to the fire and sat back in my chair.

"He was stymied," Barker went on, "but he knew the manuscript must be somewhere in Limehouse. He settled in to wait for it to surface. He created a role, the eccentric Jimmy Woo, and got a position working for the Asiatic Aid Society. His skills were so good he was hired as an interpreter for the Foreign Office as well, whose people, he must have known, would be hunting for the text themselves after a formal request by the Chinese government. He created a false history for himself as a student at Cambridge, much as K'ing has created his own legend. Woo even inserted a false record of his attendance, should he ever be investigated by Scotland Yard."

"How did he come to follow us once we had the ticket?" I asked.

"He wasn't following us at all, but Bainbridge. The inspector had been visiting all the old sites, sifting for information. It was easier for Woo to let him do the work and to eventually lay hands upon his notes. Bainbridge came to me, however, which was a factor Woo hadn't anticipated. It then became necessary to kill him before he passed on too much information, but by then it was too late. I had the text and, as he found out in the tunnel, it wasn't going to be easy for him to make me give it up."

"I still can hardly believe it," I said. "Woo, with his old school speech and eccentric manner, could kill all those people."

"You recall me using the phrase 'smell the blood.' It's a term fighters use to describe another of their kind. One learns to look for swollen knuckles and strong wrists, but Woo chose the perfect disguise. The silk gloves covered his boxer's hands quite well and we had other suspects who were fighters such as Campbell-Ffinch and Hooligan. He was an excellent actor. It would not surprise me if he had been trained as a youth in the Peking Opera schools."

My mind tried grasping what went on in the Chinese court, but it quickly shifted back to our own little plot of China, Limehouse. "But you had so many other suspects. I would have thought K'ing was our man."

"Aside from the mythical elements that surround him, I believe he is what he claims to be, a businessman. He was probably a sailor or porter who came here several years ago on short leave and saw the potential. While his brothers, figuratively speaking, were saving their money to return as wealthy men, he was buying up land along the docks. With the money he made, he exported English goods to China and created a monopoly there. When he had created his base of operations down in those neglected sewer pipes, he acquired toughs like Manchu Jack and began to extort businesses, but only in a small way. It is the Chinese manner and expected of him. With the money he received, he consolidated his organization and began giving back to the community with funds to the Asian Aid Society and the

Strangers' Home. He might allow certain men he was ex-
torting to skip payments if they passed along the fictional
legend of a long-lived criminal leader named Mr. K'ing. It
would stick in the imagination of the Asians along the
docks and from there, turn into the general legend of the
community. From a humble sailor, he became the unofficial
head of the Limehouse community or, in Chinese terms, a
warlord."

"How do you know that?" I demanded.

Barker gave me one of his wintry smiles. "Because that
is exactly what I would have done in his circumstances."

"I'll accept that," I said, "but that doesn't preclude the
possibility that he killed all these people."

"K'ing oversaw the fight in the arena and he is in charge
of the lion and dragon dancers which employ some small
amount of boxing in their dances, but one look at Mr.
K'ing's hands proved to me he is no fighter. They were as
soft as any London businessman's."

"But as a businessman, if he got hold of the text, couldn't
he sell it?"

"No, it only had worth to someone who planned to
study the forbidden knowledge. K'ing has no personal or fi-
nancial interest in it. He was more concerned when you
began using Chinese fighting arts to attack his people that
day you paid a visit to Bok Fu Ying in Limehouse."

"I was not attacking," I stated. "I was defending."

"Aye, but they thought they were the ones defending;
defending Bok Fu Ying's honor."

"But I wasn't using Chinese arts at all. They were the
Japanese ones you taught me. I can't believe they didn't
know the difference," I insisted.

"You assume all Chinese men know Chinese boxing. Do all Englishmen box?" he asked.

"No, not hardly."

"The fellows you fought had very little training. They were sailors, stevedores, and shipping clerks. As far as they knew, you were attacking them with something that looked Chinese rather than English."

"And what of Campbell-Ffinch?"

"I shall admit, lad, that Campbell-Ffinch was my chief suspect through much of this case. He is both ruthless and desperate enough to have committed all those murders. He is also accustomed to following clues and knows the Chinese way of doing things. I thought it just possible he knew some *dim mak*. Ultimately, however, there are two reasons I discounted him. The first was the break-in. It wasn't his style to rifle through things secretly in thief's clothing. He would have knocked on the door, put a bullet in each of our heads, and looked for the book at his leisure. Besides, he'd already gone through everything once, using proper channels. It had to be someone else."

"And the second reason?"

"An Englishman never would have shot an inspector outright. He'd have known how seriously Scotland Yard would take such an action. Only a foreigner with little regard for English law would have killed Bainbridge so cavalierly."

"What about Charlie Han? He was a possible suspect."

"He was, but only until I finally saw him. The boy is no criminal. Oh, he has broken some minor laws and been arrested, but they were not laws in China. The poor fellow's a victim of Bainbridge's jealousy and his own lack of knowledge of how things work here. I feel sorry for him."

"I don't," I said. "He's got the Belle o' Pennyfields looking after him. Heaven knows what she sees in him."

"There must be something. Miss Petulengro seems very canny and she doesn't seem the type to suffer fools easily. Perhaps she'll rub the corners off and make a better man out of him."

"I'll take your word for it," I said, unable to keep the bitterness out of my voice.

"She seems to inspire jealousy wherever she goes," Barker judged. "But then, attractive and unmarried young women often sow seeds of destruction in their wake, even among old married men like Nevil Bainbridge."

"I suppose it is possible," I muttered to myself.

"Another girl who has escaped from your matrimonial clutches, Thomas? I am glad to hear it. She was quite the cheekiest thing in a dress I have ever met. I don't believe I could have stood the pair of you together. Also, though I am not saying she wouldn't make someone a fine wife, wouldn't you have preferred a girl with tastes similar to your own?"

"Surely you're not suggesting we are not of the same class—"

"Oh, stop that, lad. You know I feel the class system is artificial. But the two of you are so different. It is the very same reason that I would not find you a proper suitor for Bok Fu Ying."

I began to feel positively wretched. First I discover Hettie is having a relationship with another man and then I am warned off Bok Fu Ying. My mind conjured up her China doll face and earnest eyes, the smell of jasmine in her hair. "What is to happen to Miss Winter then?"

I saw Barker frown a little. He was her guardian, after all, and these were weighty matters. "I shall find a worthy suitor for her eventually, or she shall find one for herself without my help. Really, lad, I've never seen a fellow so eager to get himself betrothed. You're but a pup, but you're as bad as Robbie Burns, falling in love at the drop of a hat. Ours is not a profession for taking wives, and especially not at your age."

"What of Pollock Forbes?" I asked, in order to change the subject.

"Pollock? What makes you think we should include him as a suspect?"

"He knows a great deal about what was going on, and he was in K'ing's opium den. Also, he has a ring, sir, with an insignia on it. I believe he belongs to a secret society of some sort."

Barker gave me one of his wintry smiles. "He smokes opium because of his tuberculosis. As to secret societies, if we arrest a fellow for being a member of one, I would be the first on the list. Don't forget, lad, that we called *him* into the investigation."

I got up and nodded good night. I was on the stairs when I suddenly turned. "The text, sir. The Limehouse text. Is it really on its way to China?"

"No, lad, it is still here. In such a case as this it has been necessary to keep all my cards to myself. You understand now how vital it was that the book be kept safe, and so I gave it to the man I most trusted in London."

"Old Quong?"

"Dr. Quong was indeed the Chinaman I gave it to, but he

immediately passed it on. It was you, lad. He gave it to you."

"Me?" I demanded, confused.

"Yes. The text is plastered against your left shoulder blade at the moment."

All power of speech left me. I'd had it the entire time, while the killer was searching half of London for it? I was Barker's most trusted man?

"But my injury, sir . . ." I began.

"Oh, there was nothing really wrong with your shoulder, lad. Once Quong set it back in place, it was right as rain. The tendons there are quite elastic. I hope you'll forgive the minor inconvenience."

I thought of the many sleepless nights I had with that hard cast biting into my shoulder, the discomfort as I drove the cab, the taking notes with one hand, the preparation of Barker's dinner. It all began boiling up.

"I believe I'll just take a walk, sir. I need some fresh air."

Barker reached into a drawer of his desk and removed a pair of stout scissors with short curved blades. "Certainly, but I shall need the book. Take off your jacket."

He proceeded to cut me out of the cast. Plaster rained onto the floor as he wrenched the small package from my back. It had been wrapped in cloth and looked the same as always, a dull yellow, perhaps a trifle wrinkled.

"None the worse for wear, the both of you."

It was easy for him to say. My limp, pale arm looked ready for one of Vandeleur's postmortems. I tried to move it, but it hung there at my side uselessly.

"Raise it up over your head and down behind you in a circle, lad. That's the best thing for it."

I tried, but halfway up, the atrophied muscles seized up and cramped. I cried out, then used a few choice words I'd learned in prison.

"Really, lad," Barker said dryly. "You must learn to control your temper."

"Thank you sir," I said tightly. "I believe I shall put on a fresh shirt and take that walk now."

"You do that, Thomas. You realize there is still one thing I haven't worked out."

"And what is that?"

"I still must decide what to do with the text."

I passed the Elephant and Castle, decided not to stop for a pint, and walked down the Old Kent Road. It was cool that evening, but I believe winter's hold on London had finally been broken. I walked, and as I walked, I thought. The book, that bloody, bloody book, had been in my cast from the beginning. Jimmy Woo, Mr. K'ing, Campbell-Ffinch, and Inspector Poole might have reached out at any time and laid hands on it. Barker had fooled them, had fooled us all. It was brilliant, though I hated to admit it.

When I came back in the front door, I noticed a smell and when I reached the staircase I realized it was burning paper. *He's done it,* I thought. *He's burnt the manuscript.* I took the staircase two steps at a time.

Barker looked over his shoulder from the fender where he knelt poking the fire. There was ash and black shreds of curling paper rising up the chimney.

"You burnt it!" I murmured.

"No, but I sat here for the last half hour considering it. It would be a wise decision, but ultimately I do not believe it is mine to make. The text belongs to the monks of the Xi Jiang Monastery."

"So what did you burn?"

"I made a copy that first night, in the basement, a personal copy. It is not a long book, not more than seventy-five pages."

"But if Woo had laid hands on it, he wouldn't have needed the original."

"I know. I translated it into Yiddish. I assumed the killer would search for the book here and be able to read English and possibly Chinese."

"But why burn it now?"

"It is knowledge no one should have, not even I. I already know too much about *dim mak* and wish to learn no more. I do not desire to become a personal engine of destruction. Do you recall making nitroglycerine in the Irish case last year? Do you remember what you told me afterward?"

"Yes, sir. 'Never again.'"

"Exactly. I feel the same about *dim mak*. Never again."

"So what shall you do with the real text, sir?"

"I wish I knew, lad. I shall spend a long night praying over it. Perhaps I shall have an answer in the morning."

32

I LEFT BARKER WITH THE TEXT AND TOOK MY-
self off to bed. I was still dissatisfied and felt that justice had
been thwarted somehow, but at least I had my cast off and
could finally get a good night's rest.

The next morning, Poole arrived at our chambers. One
would think that after the successful capture of a murderer,
an inspector would be jubilant, but apparently, such was not
the case.

"How did Chief Inspector Henderson receive the
news?" Barker asked his friend.

The inspector sighed. "Let us say he was less than enthusiastic. Don't forget, Cyrus, a murder suspect died under
my supervision."

"But you caught him, nonetheless, and his murderer at
the same time. That is two in one."

"That's not how Henderson sees it."

"You are not under report or suspended from duty, are
you?" Barker asked.

"No, but he gave me an earful I shall not soon forget."

"That is not so bad," the Guv pronounced. "Earfuls,

one can live through. I thought you might be in disgrace, but it turns out you are merely in trouble. You successfully arrested the killer. Why should your superiors be so particular?"

"They know it was you who uncovered Jimmy Woo and they were not impressed by my cooperating with your plan to bring all the suspects together at Ho's. Henderson had some choice words about that."

"And yet he is acting smug enough in *The Times* this morning. 'Inspector's Killer Meets Fate.' It has only been two weeks since Bainbridge's death. I wouldn't have your position for anything, Terry. If you ever decide to become a private enquiry agent, you might consider putting up your brass plate outside and taking one of the vacant offices upstairs."

"Don't tempt me," he said, putting his bowler back on his head. "Next time you decide to bring all the suspects together in one room like that, let me know so that I may get safely out of the country. Good day, gentlemen."

We watched him leave the room. I moved to the bow window and gazed out as he marched along Whitehall to his offices, swinging his stick so aggressively I thought he might strike a pedestrian.

"Ungrateful, I call it," I said.

"When one works for Scotland Yard, one must always deal with superiors and their quest for power. That is one reason I prefer private enquiry work."

Not long after that, Campbell-Ffinch made an appearance in our chambers. He looked somewhat diminished and tired and fell into a chair at Barker's invitation. I would not have been quite so charitable as my employer.

"For the last time, Barker," he said wearily, "where is the text?"

"I made that perfectly clear yesterday," Barker stated. He sat immobile in his chair, and the situation was rather reversed from how things had been when we'd first met Campbell-Ffinch at the Oriental Club.

"I do not believe you, sir, but I cannot compel you to hand it over to me, though I believe you should for the good of the country."

Barker offered the fellow a cigar from the box on his desk. As Campbell-Ffinch took a vesta to it, I wondered if my employer was seriously considering the request or merely stalling.

"I am not the sort of person who believes every weapon should be given to the army or the Foreign Office, for that matter. Some knowledge is best forgotten."

"Perhaps," Campbell-Ffinch conceded. "Perhaps not. I am not certain anymore. It doesn't really matter anyway. I'm being sent to Mongolia."

"Mongolia? When?" Barker asked.

"Almost immediately. As far as the Foreign Office is concerned, I've been doing nothing this entire year and getting paid for it. My superiors are not pleased."

"Yes, but confess it. You were making even more money on clandestine matches in the middle of the night."

Our visitor actually chuckled. "I did, at that, I suppose, but that is all at an end. The Hammersmith Hammer is done for, I'm afraid."

"Not necessarily," Barker said, holding up a finger. "The Mongolians appreciate a good fight and a good wager, and they are certain to have some talented lads."

"Will they, by Jove? I hadn't realized," Campbell-Ffinch said, eyeing his cigar speculatively. "I shall work my way back to London yet. I have done it before and I'll do it again. When I do, I challenge you to a match."

Barker ran a finger along his jaw, which was still slightly swollen. "Rules?"

"Five rounds, no holds barred. Anything goes, but no tricks before the fight. I don't want to end up like Woo."

"I thought you didn't care for Mr. Woo."

"I hated the little blighter. He got what he deserved. But I am an Englishman. I expect better treatment than that."

"Very well," Barker stated. "I accept your challenge. Until we meet again."

They stood and shook hands.

After a morning of such arguments, we ate a lunch of sausages and mash at the Rising Sun. The meal and the memory were not worth mentioning save for one thing. Soho Vic, a boy Barker and other enquiry agents in the area employ, appeared and the Guv scribbled a message. He folded it and passed it into Vic's filthy hands, along with enough money for the boy to take a cab. Somehow during the brief conversation, the urchin managed to nick my last sausage. I added it to a growing list of grievances I have against him. Someday, he would turn eighteen and I would sock him in the eye.

An hour or so later, Vic came breezing through our office, helping himself to one of Barker's cigars for his trouble. He leaned on my rolltop desk causing the lid to crash down on my fingers as he looked all innocence. It was another notation for the list. What really annoyed me, of course, was that Soho Vic had just been on an errand and

Barker had not told me what it was about. He was one up on me, and I hated nothing more. My employer read the message he brought and handed Vic another shilling. The last I saw of the street arab, he was outside, passing by our bow window, puffing on the cigar and flipping the coin in the air as carefree as a lark in spring.

Barker read for the next hour at his desk. It was one of the Scotsman George Macdonald's pastorals, *Donal Grant*, I think the title was. It could not be related to the case at all, but something was brewing, I knew. The Guv only read at the office when he was marking time for an appointment.

At three o'clock, Big Ben chimed in our ears and Barker put a thin strip of tartan in his book and set it down before rising.

"You coming, lad?"

"Yes, sir," I said, reaching for my coat. Half of my job is to be intuitive and the other half to just look like I know what is going on. This was definitely the latter.

Our destination was the Reading Room of the British Museum, one of the places in London I love best. It was here that I had whiled away my hours before I found employment and it was here also that I first spied Barker's advertisement offering "some danger involved in performance of duties." The Reading Room is the British equivalent of the fabled library at Alexandria, containing the sum of all modern wisdom and the accumulated knowledge of the ages. It is the repository for all of the important books in the world, and in a way, I thought of it as home.

The Guv pulled the repeater from his pocket and opened it. It was an old watch, grime having worked its way into the crevices of the filigree, but apparently it had sentimental value to him, for he rarely kept anything that was not in pristine condition.

"Three o'clock to the minute," he stated. "I hope our appointment shall not keep us waiting. Look, I believe that is the man there."

Barker pointed to someone standing between two rows of books in a suit of brown check. He was turned away from us, and all I could see was that he had black hair and spectacles with thick tortoiseshell rims. I recognized the bent shoulders of the inveterate scholar. We crossed the room to where he was standing, and when we were a dozen yards away he turned toward us. The fellow was Mr. K'ing.

"Thank you for coming," Barker said to him, as if actually grateful to this man who had come so close to ordering our deaths.

"Of course. I must say, Mr. Llewelyn looks rather stunned."

"I'll admit to being curious myself. Is this your normal attire or is the other?"

"I am inclined to say both. I feel more comfortable in silk when I am in Limehouse, but I prefer normal English attire when I am conducting business in the West End."

K'ing looked about the room at the readers and shelves and the thousands of books.

"I thank you for suggesting this place. I used to come here often, but lately I have been too occupied. I am afraid I have another appointment at the Bank of England in half an hour."

"I believe," Barker said, "that should give us enough time. May we sit?"

We found two desks together between a stout man with

a beard and an anemic aesthete with a drooping mustache. I was obliged to pull a chair over from nearby.

"Thank you for responding to my request," Barker said.

"Are you sure you have come to the right man?" K'ing asked.

"Of all the people whom I questioned concerning the manuscript yesterday, you gave the only satisfactory answer. I believe you are the man I can trust to see that it gets safely back to China."

"Ah," K'ing said, nodding. "Who is the recipient?"

"Huang Feihong of Canton."

"Was it he that taught you? I should have recognized the Tiger Crane style. Might I be permitted to know what Feihong will do with this . . . package?"

"He shall see that it is delivered to the Xi Jiang Monastery. I shall send a telegram by steamer today so that he can expect its arrival. He shall wire me when the mission is complete."

"China is far, far away, Mr. Barker. How do you know that I can guarantee its safe delivery?"

"You will do so by placing it in Blue Dragon Triad hands, aboard a direct Blue Funnel liner. That, along with suitable threats and inducements, should secure its safety. I assume your power extends to Canton, at least aboard ship."

"I shall see that it is safely delivered."

My employer then reached into his pocket and held out the book. "Be careful," he said. "It bites."

"So I understand," K'ing replied, tucking it into his coat pocket. "The courier I assign will be careful and discreet."

"Thank you."

We all rose. Barker bowed, little more than an incline of his head. K'ing gave him one in return.

"I must apologize, Mr. Barker, for underestimating you. To think that Manchu Jack, by his very size, could best you. I had counted upon the fact that you had been long away from China and might be out of condition. Obviously, such was not the case."

"Until we meet again, sir," Barker said, and we went our separate ways.

Outside, Barker stopped, raised both arms over his head and stretched. The men and women streaming in and out avoided him like the other eccentrics that sometimes inhabit the museum.

"Ahh!" he exhaled. "I was never so glad to rid myself of anything in my life. May all hidden texts remain well and truly hidden and never cross my path again."

"If all goes according to plan," Barker said, "in a little over a month and a half, the Xi Jiang Monastery shall send word to the Forbidden City that the manuscript has been found misfiled. It never officially left the grounds."

"And Jimmy Woo?"

"A former imperial eunuch who died in an accident. London's dockyards can be a most dangerous place for Chinamen, as most of them know."

"That all sounds very convenient," I couldn't help saying.

"Do you know what one does with a mystery in China, lad? One buries it in a foot of rubble, then two feet of soil, and one plants a public garden over it so that no one shall ever dig it up again. I think we've done enough for one day. Let us go home and have some tea."

"I think I'll have Darjeeling, sir," I said, as Barker raised his stick for a cab. "I'm rather off the Chinese at the moment."

ACKNOWLEDGMENTS

I would like to thank my martial arts instructor, Don Morrison, not only for his aid with technique but in the study of *dim mak* and Asian medicine. Thanks also go to the employees at the Tulsa City-County Library, who have supported me and helped track down key information. As always, it was a pleasure to work with my agent, Maria Carvainis, and my editor, Amanda Patten.

And, as always, thanks to my wife and muse, Julia.